SA
D0361764

"Reed pollinates t_____
story, characters who lea_____
interesting material about beekeeping. It will keep you busy."
— *Richmond Times-Dispatch*

"The characters are as colorful as the rainbow . . . [This] has the perfect blend of humor and drama and a gutsy heroine . . . Readers will be thoroughly entertained by this madcap mystery." — *Romantic Times*

"Story Fischer is one of the spunkiest heroines of a cozy mystery that I have had the pleasure of reading! I love the character's strength, her fearlessness, and her smarts! With the Queen Bee Mysteries, Hannah Reed has created a delicious series that is a sweet treat for cozy mystery fans! . . . Yummy honey-related recipes make a great addition to an already great story!"
— *Sharon's Garden of Book Reviews*

"The prose is witty, charming, and peppered with beautiful imagery, the plot is rich and complex, and the mystery is cleverly constructed and skillfully written, tying past events to the present in a way that adds import and intrigue to both. Story makes for a fabulous heroine and an engaging narrator. Strong, smart, snarky, and positively bullheaded in her independence, she's a character for whom readers can't help but root . . . The book's supporting cast is marvelous as well . . . Run out and buy yourself a copy; it's a great way to pass an afternoon." — *The Season*

continued . . .

Buzz Off

"If you're wondering how beekeeping and mysteries go together, then pick up Hannah Reed's *Buzz Off* and see what all the excitement is about. Reed has come up with a great setting, rich characters, and such a genuine protagonist in Story Fischer that you'll be sorry the book is over when you turn the last page. Start reading and you won't want to put it down. Trust me, you'll be saying 'buzz off' to anybody who dares interrupt!"

—Julie Hyzy, award-winning author of *Affairs of Steak*

"Action, adventure, a touch of romance, and a cast of delightful characters fill Hannah Reed's debut novel. *Buzz Off* is one honey of a tale."

—Lorna Barrett, *New York Times* bestselling author of the Booktown Mysteries

"The death of a beekeeper makes for an absolute honey of a read in this engaging and well-written mystery. Story Fischer is a sharp and resilient amateur sleuth, and Hannah Reed sweeps us into her world with skillful and loving detail."

—Cleo Coyle, national bestselling author of the Coffeehouse Mysteries

"A sparkling debut . . . Delicious."

—*Genre Go Round Reviews*

"You'll get a buzz from this one, guaranteed."

—*Mystery Scene*

"Reed's story is first-rate, her characters appealing—Story's imperfections make her particularly authentic—and the beekeeping and small-town angles are refreshingly different."

—*Richmond Times-Dispatch*

"Will appeal to readers who like Joanne Fluke and other cozy writers for recipes, the small-town setting, and a sense of community." —*Library Journal*

"A rollicking good time. The colorful family members and townspeople provide plenty of relationship drama and entertainment. The mystery is well plotted, and this series promises to keep readers buzzing." —*Romantic Times* (4 stars)

"Everyone is simply going to go buzz-erk over the marvelously quirky cast of characters in this fabulously funny new series . . . Hannah Reed has a deliciously spicy, adorable sense of humor that had me howling with unabashed glee. You couldn't get as many colorful characters if you poured them from a box of Froot Loops. *Buzz Off* has just the right blend of mystery, romance, and humor that will charm anyone's socks off. If this fantastic whodunit doesn't buzz to the top of your list, I'm simply gonna have to sic Grams on you . . . and she doesn't mess around! Quill says: If you are in need of a quirky, light, incredibly humorous cozy, look no more. Hannah Reed has whopped 'n chopped and stirred up a formula for a mystery that will line up an audience who will beg for more!" —*Feathered Quill Book Reviews*

"In her debut book, Hannah Reed combines an intriguing whodunit with a lively, action-filled story to create one sweet cozy mystery! . . . *Buzz Off* is a charming beginning to what promises to be a fun series! . . . A yummy treat for fans of cozy mysteries." —*Fresh Fiction*

"Highly entertaining." —Associated Content

"A honey of a series debut . . . [A] honey of a book filled with lots of interesting bee information as well as some yummy recipes." —*Cozy Corner*

Berkley Prime Crime titles by Hannah Reed

BUZZ OFF
MIND YOUR OWN BEESWAX
PLAN BEE

Plan
Bee

Hannah Reed

BERKLEY PRIME CRIME, NEW YORK

THE BERKLEY PUBLISHING GROUP
Published by the Penguin Group
Penguin Group (USA) Inc.
375 Hudson Street, New York, New York 10014, USA
Penguin Group (Canada), 90 Eglinton Avenue East, Suite 700, Toronto, Ontario M4P 2Y3, Canada
(a division of Pearson Penguin Canada Inc.)
Penguin Books Ltd., 80 Strand, London WC2R 0RL, England
Penguin Group Ireland, 25 St. Stephen's Green, Dublin 2, Ireland (a division of Penguin Books Ltd.)
Penguin Group (Australia), 250 Camberwell Road, Camberwell, Victoria 3124, Australia
(a division of Pearson Australia Group Pty. Ltd.)
Penguin Books India Pvt. Ltd., 11 Community Centre, Panchsheel Park, New Delhi—110 017, India
Penguin Group (NZ), 67 Apollo Drive, Rosedale, Auckland 0632, New Zealand
(a division of Pearson New Zealand Ltd.)
Penguin Books (South Africa) (Pty.) Ltd., 24 Sturdee Avenue, Rosebank, Johannesburg 2196,
South Africa

Penguin Books Ltd., Registered Offices: 80 Strand, London WC2R 0RL, England

This is a work of fiction. Names, characters, places, and incidents either are the product of the author's imagination or are used fictitiously, and any resemblance to actual persons, living or dead, business establishments, events, or locales is entirely coincidental. The publisher does not have any control over and does not assume any responsibility for author or third-party websites or their content.

PUBLISHER'S NOTE: The recipes contained in this book are to be followed exactly as written. The publisher is not responsible for your specific health or allergy needs that may require medical supervision. The publisher is not responsible for any adverse reactions to the recipes contained in this book.

PLAN BEE

A Berkley Prime Crime Book / published by arrangement with the author

PRINTING HISTORY
Berkley Prime Crime mass-market edition / January 2012

Copyright © 2012 by Deb Baker.
Cover illustration by Trish Cramblet.
Cover design by Judith Lagerman.
Interior text design by Kristin del Rosario.

All rights reserved.
No part of this book may be reproduced, scanned, or distributed in any printed or electronic form without permission. Please do not participate in or encourage piracy of copyrighted materials in violation of the author's rights. Purchase only authorized editions.
For information, address: The Berkley Publishing Group,
a division of Penguin Group (USA) Inc.,
375 Hudson Street, New York, New York 10014.

ISBN: 978-0-425-24621-4

BERKLEY® PRIME CRIME
Berkley Prime Crime Books are published by The Berkley Publishing Group,
a division of Penguin Group (USA) Inc.,
375 Hudson Street, New York, New York 10014.
BERKLEY® PRIME CRIME and the PRIME CRIME logo are trademarks of Penguin Group
(USA) Inc.

PRINTED IN THE UNITED STATES OF AMERICA

10 9 8 7 6 5 4 3 2 1

If you purchased this book without a cover, you should be aware that this book is stolen property. It was reported as "unsold and destroyed" to the publisher, and neither the author nor the publisher has received any payment for this "stripped book."

Acknowledgments

This book is dedicated to those among us who support the delicate life of our honeybees by:

- planting bee-friendly flowers
- buying honey from local producers
- choosing to coexist with weeds rather than apply deadly chemicals

And most of all, to the keepers of the bees.

Special thanks to Judy and Lee Maltenfort, who introduced me to the most delicious honey coffee, and to Heidi Cox for her killer recipes.

MORAINE

Creamery Rd.

Rustic Road

N
W E
S

Oconomowoc River

Clay Story Patti

Willow Street

Moraine Gardens

Koon's Custard

MAIN St.

Stu's Bar + Grill

Library

Post Office

Antique Shop

Corn Stand

Wild Clover

Church Cemetery

One

🐝

My mother came at me like the bulldog she is—jaw set and thrust forward, steady thunderous gait, slight tilt to her head, intense eyes. I stood my ground at the entryway to my grocery store, The Wild Clover, thinking she was about to ruin a perfectly good Saturday morning.

I put on my smiley face to go along with the August sun shining above, an expression that meant I was pretending to be positively happy, even if it killed me.

"Story Fischer," Mom said, "I thought we had agreed." She halted, almost nose to nose with me. "No live bee displays."

For the record, we hadn't been on that same communication wavelength at all. I simply hadn't responded when she'd come up with yet another rule for me to follow.

Believe it or not, somebody had gone and made my mother head of the steering committee for this weekend's Harmony Festival, an annual event in my hometown of Moraine, Wisconsin. Two months of intense planning, and "harmony" had flown right out the door, flapping madly for cover. Mom and I were barely speaking to each other. Or at least, one of us was barely speaking. The other one was yakking plenty.

"So it's true," she said, hands on hips now. "Emily Nolan over at the library told me you went ahead with it anyway. Behind my back, I might add. Oh my gawd. Is that it?"

She glared at a table I'd tucked under the store's awning to protect my honeybees from direct sunlight. The movable hive was framed in with cedar. Double-thick glass on both sides gave spectators a great view of the magical world of bees. Once the festival began at nine o'clock, my table would be a popular destination. I was sure of it. Especially with kids. Good thing the portable hive was screwed into the table to prevent it from tipping over. A brilliant idea, even if it wasn't mine.

Stanley Peck had designed the observation hive, and he planned to stick around to explain the inside workings of a hive to those who stopped by. If they were lucky, folks might even get a view of the queen laying eggs.

Stanley is a sixtyish widower and a newbie beekeeper. He looks up to me regarding anything bee related even though I've only been at this about a year longer than he has, and I've sure had (and continue to have) my share of problems and mistakes. But Stanley's smart. He's letting me learn everything the hard way, while he takes copious notes on how to avoid the same close encounters and difficult issues. The learning curve in the bee business is challenging at times.

"It's just an observation hive," I said, determined to stay upbeat in the face of my mother's gloom and doom. "And it's perfectly safe. The bees are behind glass and can't get out. Not that they would hurt anybody if they got loose. They're honeybees, not wasps. Don't worry."

"Where's Grant Spandle?" Mom said, clearly intent on

shutting me down. Her head swiveled, searching for the big boss to back her up.

How had this happened? I'd specifically told the so-called advisory group that my mother and I don't work well together. As if anybody in this small town didn't know that fact already. Lori Spandle, the town's only real estate agent and my longtime nemesis, must have plotted behind the scenes, messing with me as usual. Her husband Grant is town chair. He's the one who made the decision to appoint my mother. And Lori must've instigated it. I'd bet the store on it.

That woman has been a thorn in my side since the first day of kindergarten when she pushed me down the slide, then went crying to the teacher, claiming I was the one who'd pushed her. Lori hasn't changed one bit in the twenty-nine years in between. I take that back—she's even worse now.

Usually, I enjoy the closeness of our community— knowing everybody's name and most of their personal affairs, sharing life's little ups and downs with them while they shop at my store, walking down Main Street exchanging greetings and gardening tips. Sure, I have to put up with a few unpleasant people, but doesn't everybody have neighbor problems? And family issues? And thorns from their past embedded in their flesh? It's the cost of small-town living, a price I'm willing to pay for all the perks.

Although at the moment, while squaring off with my mother, the price was skyrocketing.

Before Mom could expound further on the future of the unwelcome hive, something exploded down the street. Since this was only the latest in a series of recent *kaboom*s, we knew exactly what it was and who was responsible: Stanley's twelve-year-old grandson, Noel, who dreamed of a future in large-structure demolition. Every time he visits Moraine with his garage chemistry experiments, mixing hardware-store and under-the-kitchen-sink-type combos, he rocks the town. Literally. The kid is a menace, but he's brilliant in a crazy-eyed sort of way.

And even though flames have been shooting and the air resonates with explosions, he hasn't actually damaged anything. Yet.

"For cripes' sake!" my mother yelled, about-facing and bulldogging away from my store to give somebody else a piece of her overactive mind.

I couldn't help feeling grateful to Stanley and his grenade-lobbing grandson.

"I can't believe Stanley won't control that kid," Carrie Ann Retzlaff said, coming out of the store where she worked for me part-time. "He's going to blow up somebody."

Carrie Ann's not only my employee, she's my cousin—and the last person who should talk about control, since she barely has any at all. Carrie Ann is attracted to addictions like honeybees are to clumps of blooming sunflowers. I'm pretty sure she currently has a social-networking problem, judging by how many times I've found her in the back room, checking in with her online friends or playing games involving farm animals, poker, and treasure hunts.

In my opinion though, her latest obsession is a giant step up from the bottom of the beer barrel, where she's been plenty. And she has an ongoing battle with every bottle of vodka she comes across, though she did manage to permanently quit smoking. So I've looked the other way about the online stuff. Besides, in addition to being a relative, Carrie Ann is one of my oldest and dearest friends. Not letting our employer-employee relationship interfere with that can be dicey at times.

"I'm surprised he still has ten toes and fingers," I said, spotting my mother down the street, where she was doing a pretty good pyro job herself, roasting the future physicist over the flames shooting from her mouth.

Noel is just a skinny, pimply, geeky sort of kid. And he

has good manners when he needs to show them. They were on display as he took his medicine from Mom with his head hanging. He would walk away exuding contrite acceptance. Until the next blast.

"Your mother put me on a committee," Carrie Ann said, running her fingers through her short, spiked, yellow-as-corn hair. Since my cousin quit smoking, she's gained a few pounds. They look good on her. "She didn't even ask me if I wanted to volunteer," she continued. "I'm on the crime wave committee."

"Is this some kind of joke?" I wanted to know.

Carrie Ann shook her head. "She was serious."

"What kind of crime wave problem is she worried about?"

"She said—and these are her words, not mine—that after the last fiasco, when you embarrassed the entire family by going head-to-head with the police chief and making the lead story on all of southeastern Wisconsin's evening news channels, she's sure your behavior will attract criminal elements and rabble-rousers to the festival."

I rolled my eyeballs heavenward, catching the glint of morning sunlight as it struck the stained-glass etchings on the upper part of my store. It had been a church before the congregation outgrew it and built a larger space on the outskirts of town. I'd converted the building into a grocery store, specializing in local produces and products—cheeses, wines, bakery items, flowers, fresh fruits and vegetables, and a long list of seasonal items.

The exterior was exactly as it had been back then, except for the addition of a blue awning with The Wild Clover name imprinted on it and some colorful Adirondack chairs out front that I'd painted myself. It even had the old bell tower—not that we rang it these days—and a cemetery on the far side, where a whole lot of Lutherans rested in peace.

As to the confrontation with our police chief, Mom was sort of right. The physical fight with Johnny Jay had been captured on film, and she wasn't about to let me forget it. Ever. Not that the altercation was my fault in any way. Johnny Jay really dislikes me, and he doesn't try to hide how he's always gunning for me.

Believe me, the feeling is mutual. He was a big bully as a boy. Now he's a big bully adult.

"There isn't any crime wave committee," I informed Carrie Ann. "Mom just made that up so you would tell me exactly what you just told me. Another shot across my bow."

"I really believed her," Carrie Ann said, heading toward our outdoor booth where she would sell honey products and other items from the store for the duration of the festival. "Don't tell me your mother's starting to make up stories, too?"

I grimaced at the reference to the history behind my nickname. Melissa is my real name, but somewhere way back I became Story due to an innate ability to reshape the truth. Those days of tall tales are behind me, and most of my friends, family, and acquaintances have forgotten the "story" behind the nickname. Except one or two. Like Carrie Ann. And my mother.

Sometimes when I'm the most frustrated, I feel like my mother doesn't have a single redeeming quality. But Mom has a lot of friends, so I have to imagine that she has a kind and generous side. Just one she hasn't revealed to me. My younger sister Holly must see it, because she and Mom get along just fine. Though that might be because Holly doesn't have a spine when it comes to dealing with Mom; she just lets Mom take control of whatever she wants.

One thing I will say about our mother—she isn't into gossiping. She doesn't start rumors, and she doesn't spread them. And believe me, there's plenty of muck going around in a town this small and intimate. But on the other hand, she believes most of the gossip she hears, no matter how salacious, especially when it pertains to me.

Just as I was about to duck inside the store, my grandmother pulled up in her Cadillac Fleetwood, with Holly, looking terrified, in the passenger seat. Even though Grams is a hazard on the road, nobody is going to pry her out of the driver's seat until she decides to leave this earth, which isn't likely to happen anytime soon. At her last physical, the doctor said she'd be good until at least a hundred.

I moved closer to the building in case Grams jumped the curb.

She didn't. But I heard the Caddy's front bumper kiss the parked car in front of it.

"Back up a few inches," I called out, and she did. Good thing there wasn't a car behind her or that one would have been an innocent victim, too.

Holly slid out looking all sleek, with a new hairstyle that wrapped around her face à la Marilyn Monroe. My sister may dress just like the rest of us—in shorts, sandals, sleeveless summer tops—but she carries an air of wealth around with her that is only achievable with real bucks. That's because she's filthy rich, having married Max the Money Machine, and her clothes cost five times as much as mine or anybody else's in Moraine.

But a hefty price came with her financial freedom—for me, that is. Holly's husband is on the road all the time, so Holly compensates by involving herself in my store's business, of which she is now co-owner after lending me the cold cash I needed to keep it running through some tough times. Holly also developed a serious text-speak problem and is seeing a therapist to correct it, thanks to Mom stepping in and declaring enough was enough—just when I'd finally learned how to text-speak back with a decent range of acronyms.

"How'd it go?" I asked, since Holly had just had a counseling session. I saw her glance nervously over at the bee table.

"Great, Ms. Passive Aggressive." She hurried past, bolting for the store.

"What?" I sort of shouted in disbelief.

"You heard me," she called from the interior.

"Aren't you supposed to be working on yourself?" I shouted back.

"I am. But you're part of my problem."

With that shocking disclosure, she vanished inside. I couldn't believe it. My own sister, the one I cherished as my best bud and the only person whom I thought understood me inside and out, upside and down, was dissing me?

What was this? Dump on Story day?

"Hi, sweetie." My grandmother stepped onto the curb.

I bent down to give her a cheek kiss. "Hi, Grams."

"You look bright-eyed and bushy-tailed today. Give me a great big smile."

Grams, always camera-ready, snapped a picture of me with her point-and-shoot, then asked, "Where's Helen?"

"Mom's off patrolling the town," I said, gazing at my grandmother with loving appreciation. Grams is the sweetest woman in the world, which makes me wonder what Mom would be capable of if only she'd lighten up some.

Grams wears her gray hair in a tight little bun, and likes to weave in whatever flower is blooming in her garden. Daisies are her favorite, but today she sported a silver tiara with sparkling rhinestones and crystals, since she's this year's Grand Marshal in the Harmony Festival parade.

"We're supposed to be having a meeting about tomorrow's parade," Grams said. "Everybody's at the library waiting on Helen."

"Well, here she comes," I said, seeing Mom spot us, my cue to duck and run for cover inside.

TWO

I slunk away from my mother and into the back room of The Wild Clover, which doubled as a storage room and my office. Carrie Ann and I both jumped about two feet when I opened the door. I hadn't expected to find anyone back there, and apparently she hadn't either, probably assuming I'd be busy outside with festival preparations. My cousin had a dog on her lap and her fingers poised over the keyboard of my computer.

"Uh, just checking for messages," she said, quickly closing the browser window before I could see the screen. Then she passed the little mutt over to me on her way out.

Somehow I'd become a permanent dog-sitter for Norm Cross, one of my old neighbors, who had had a family crisis a while back, and had dumped his dog Dinky on me, claiming he'd return soon. Then he decided not to come back at all, which I suspect had been part of his original secret plan from the very beginning. Plus, he informed me that his new digs didn't allow dogs. Which was just great.

Dinky is a Chihuahua mix with hair in all the wrong places and a major-league small-dog complex. She'd been the runt of the litter so, according to Norm, had had to fight harder for her share of food and attention. At least that was his excuse for her bad behavior.

Dinky licked my face and snuggled closer. She *was* affectionate; I'd give her that. She regally adjusted herself on my lap when I sat down, as though she was Honey Queen and I was her throne. Well, she could think that way for now, but I was looking for a new home for her and her wayward attitude.

Did I mention Dinky prefers doing her business indoors rather than outside? Or that if she likes a person, she pees on them? Or that I didn't have a single pair of panties without chew holes? She's even turned some of them crotchless, which never fails to amuse my boyfriend, Hunter, whenever she drags a pair out to share with him.

I spent basically my whole life until now in total fear of dogs, ever since a nasty dog attack when I was a kid. But I did a 180 recently, and I have Hunter and his awesome K-9 partner Ben to thank for my conversion from a trembling mess to an avid admirer. Although Dinky works my nerves hard.

Hunter Wallace, my main man, is a county cop and head of the K-9 unit. His hours are varied and long, but so are mine. The long absences and brief moments together work for us.

Hunter and I have a history as long as I've had my nickname. We were friends before high school and had a serious relationship during. Then I got wanderlust and moved away to Milwaukee, where I married the wrong man. While I was gone, Hunter had made his own share of mistakes, too, including apparently going through just about every bottle of booze he stumbled across. But by the time I came back and got my divorce, he'd long since turned himself around, even sponsoring Carrie Ann to help her the same way his sponsor helped him.

Hunter doesn't mind wearing the label of recovering alcoholic, but I have a serious issue when someone labels me. Like a few minutes ago when my sister called me passive aggressive.

Once I was settled in my office chair, I went online and looked up the definition of *passive aggressive* just in case the term had evolved into a hip, new, positive meaning. Holly was always ahead of me on the latest fads, fashions, and definitions.

All I found was the same old bad stuff, some of which I already knew. My sister had not been paying me a compliment. No big surprise, since her tone hadn't been exactly bursting with friendliness. According to the definition, a person with this condition has a deep seated resistance to following through with another individual's expectations. Now who would think that of me?

But there was more. Symptoms included:

- stubbornness
- procrastination
- intentionally failing at tasks

Causes might involve:

- repressed feelings
- vindictive intent

None of those things matched my personality. Not one thing. Although ignoring Mom's no-bee-zone demand might be considered borderline by some people. But I never put off things until the last minute. With a successful store to run, how could I? And intentionally failing at tasks? Like what? I worked hard, and it showed in The Wild Clover.

And stubborn? Well, okay, maybe a little.

But wasn't practically everybody?

After shutting down the computer screen, last-minute festival details got in the way, and it wasn't until a little later that I had time to focus on Holly and her annoying, outrageous statement. As if she knew I was thinking about her, the next time I went into the back room to get Dinky and take her for a walk, Holly trotted in and plopped down in a metal chair next to my desk.

"How can I possibly be your problem?" I blurted out, a trait I'm trying to control, with limited success.

"I'm in therapy because of your honeybees," Holly said, starting the Fischer family blame game, which I liked to call "the lame game." Somehow, some way, it was always somebody else's fault. I worked hard to suppress that particular gene, but sometimes it raised its ugly head in spite of my efforts.

Holly is scared silly every time she ventures near the Queen Bee Honey hives. I've been helping her (okay *helping* might not be the right word, since this isn't mutually agreed on) overcome her completely unwarranted fear by trying to get her more involved. After all, she owns half of everything. "You have to stop making me go near them," she announced.

"Let me get this straight. Your therapist said that I should quit asking you to help in the beeyard?"

Holly nodded. "She thinks the exposure and the anxiety it produces is the reason I text-speak."

"You did that text thing long before I started raising bees." Which was absolutely true. "You didn't tell her that part, though, did you?"

Holly squirmed. I pressed on, "And I thought counselors were supposed to help patients get over fears, not run away from them. Did she really say I was passive aggressive?"

"Not exactly in those words, but she would have if I'd

discussed it with her. Since I've been in therapy, I've been studying personality disorders at the library. You have all the symptoms." Well, that was a big fat relief. The last thing I needed was my sister and her therapist raking me over hot coals behind my back.

"So *she* didn't say that. *You* did."

"If the shoe fits . . ."

We stared at each other. Then Holly giggled and I knew things were back to okay between us.

"Sorry," she said. "I get super stressed every time I have a session."

"It's working, though. You didn't break into text-speak. Not once."

"TX," Holly said, grinning. Then, "JK."

"You better be," I said, easily recognizing *thanks* and *just kidding*.

"Trust me, I'm practically cured," she said.

"So, you don't want to help outside today near the observation hive?"

"I'd rather have my toenails ripped out."

I glanced down at her perfectly pedicured feet. That was a profound declaration, considering the source happened to be a serious primping queen.

"Okay," I said. "Stay inside the store and help the twins."

That got a big happy smile from her. "Any luck finding a good home for Dinky?" she asked.

"Not yet."

"You'll make sure it really is a good home, right? Not just the first person who comes along?"

"Of course." And I meant it.

"And make sure you have visiting rights so we can still see her."

"Sure." Dinky twisted in my lap and worked her way up to my face, where I barely had time to dodge an open-mouthed lick.

By the time I walked back outside with Dinky on a

leash, Main Street's sidewalks were starting to see some decent action. Stanley and Carrie Ann seemed to be handling things just fine at our booth. If past years were any indication, sales would be brisk. I glanced at our eye-catching displays, created with a little help from my friends and coworkers.

We were showcasing delicious honey products from my side business, Queen Bee Honey: processed honey along with raw and creamed varieties, plus honey sticks in a number of flavors—not just pure wildflower honey, but also lemon, cherry, sour apple, orange, caramel, and root beer—a new flavor this year. My honey sticks are biodegradable straws filled with nectar of the gods. I like to carry a few with me for those times my energy crashes. When that happens, I open one of them, suck out every last drop of honey, and I'm back on top of my game.

Lately, too, raw honey has been flying off the shelves since customers have begun to realize all the benefits of unprocessed honey, especially as an antiallergen. Local honey contains sources of pollen, dust, and mold, which sounds disgusting, but a few teaspoons every day boosts immunity against 90 percent of allergies. I'm living proof. It worked for my hay fever.

I saw Stanley's grandson Noel next to the observation table, watching the enclosed honeybees and sucking on one of the honey sticks from my store. He spotted me approaching and grinned. "These root beer honey sticks are awesome. I could live on them. I almost bought all of them."

I smiled. Kids of all ages love my honey sticks. "I have more in stock."

"Did you like the way I rescued you?" he said.

I must have looked totally blank, which I was. "Come again?"

"I set off the last explosion to help you out of that bad situation with your mom."

"Gosh, thanks so much," I said, slow to catch on that

he'd intentionally distracted my mother so I could escape her clutches. I always *did* like the kid, whose particular nut hadn't fallen far from the tree. Noel is the spitting image of his grandfather when it comes to firepower. Stanley loves weapons, and the rumor is he's got a buried stash of them just in case our federal government decides to outlaw certain makes and models. He's also been known to carry, but that's inside information. It's a miracle our police chief hasn't busted him yet.

"Really, thanks," I said to Noel with heartfelt gratitude.

"Anytime," he muttered, and I could tell by his eyes that he was back inside his skull, mixing and matching potions. He slipped a notebook out of his back pocket and began scribbling away as he walked off.

I looked around. Everything looked to be going as planned. Helen Fischer (aka Mom) might have a brisk, tactless, no-nonsense approach to life, but she sure knew how to organize an event. This one promised to be the best yet.

My job during the two-day festival, as assigned by my mother, was to make sure nothing "upset the applecart." I was pretty sure that was meant to be another personal zinger, but I intended to follow through by making sure the cart stayed upright. None of us wanted trouble or bad press.

Besides, how hard could it be? After all, this was Harmony Fest. The whole point of it was fostering goodwill.

Aurora Tyler's flower booth was right next to my store. It was crammed with bouquets from her business, Moraine Gardens. Besides the bouquets, some of which were bunches of colorful dried flowers, she had potted native plants like swamp milkweed, catmint, and coneflowers. A few honeybees had discovered them and were working the pollen. A cheery sight.

Although not everyone agrees with me.

Moraine's residents are divided on the benefits of honeybees, even after all the efforts I've made to educate the locals. Preconceived ideas die hard. I really hoped our beehive display helped dispel lingering doubts. We need more people on our side, supporting our efforts to save the honeybee's diminishing population.

Dinky growled from down below. Following her glare, I spotted Grant Spandle marching my way. In addition to being my archenemy, Lori's husband, and the town board chairperson, he's also a land developer. Which should have been a huge conflict of interest regarding a position on the board, but small-town politics are unbelievably lax, mostly from lack of any education in the fine art of legality.

Lori has played around on Grant at least once, a solid indisputable fact, since I had caught her red-handed cheating with my ex-husband before the sleazebag left town.

"Your mother is extremely upset," Grant stopped to tell me. "And I'm sure our liability insurance doesn't cover bee attacks if we knowingly and irresponsibly put our residents in harm's way."

"Harm's way? Oh come on. Do you see bees attacking anybody?"

"Let me rephrase that, then: *potential* bee attacks— *potentially* in harm's way."

"No way would that happen," I said, while Dinky continued to quietly growl. She knew the difference between steak and roadkill, and she sensed exactly where Grant fit into the food pyramid.

"Only one sting," Grant said, holding his index finger up in case I didn't know what *one* was. "Just one allergic reaction, and we'd have all kinds of trouble. The consequences could be devastating for the town's finances."

"Look over there." I pointed to Aurora's potted flowers where honeybees buzzed from petal to petal. "Honeybees. They aren't inside an observation hive. They're free to fly wherever. We can't control nature's creatures; they have free will. Besides, these aren't yellow jackets. In another month, wasps will be all over the place, landing on our food and stinging plenty of us. But honeybees, as I've said over and over, don't attack unless they're defending their hive from intruders."

How many times have I had to remind people? Hundreds? Thousands?

"Nevertheless, they have to go," Grant said, crossing his arms and putting as much authority into his voice as he could muster.

I hate when my bees are messed with, so I took him to the mat with the only weapon I had at my disposal. "Then I say DeeDee has to go, too."

DeeDee Becker is his wife's (much) younger sister, and Grant, in an unbelievable show of blatant nepotism, had crowned DeeDee the First Annual Honey Queen of the Harmony Festival. But DeeDee has been caught shoplifting in my store repeatedly, and eventually I'd have to permanently ban her from The Wild Clover. I couldn't bring myself to press charges against her though, even if she was Lori's sister. But no way did she deserve that title, the klepto.

Okay, I have to admit I'm a bit jealous, a tish disgruntled. As the town's only actual beekeeper (not counting Stanley, but he's a guy), that Honey Queen crown should've rightfully gone to me! Not DeeDee! Anybody but her! "DeeDee goes, too," I repeated.

"What is that supposed to mean?" Grant said, eyes narrowing. "Are you threatening me?"

"No," I said. "I'm threatening the Honey Queen. How will that look in *The Reporter*?" The local paper, *The Reporter*—or *The Distorter*, as I call it—would eat up the shoplifting charge, chew it up as big-time news, and spit it right out on the front page. "I can see the headlines now. 'DeeDee Becker, Sister-in-law of Town Chair, Caught Stealing.'"

"You wouldn't."

"Yup. I really would." Was I bluffing? Probably. "We have several of her sticky finger episodes on our hidden camera," I lied. The Wild Clover didn't really have hidden cameras.

But Grant believed me. His face did a few amazing twitches before he got it under control. "Fine!" he said, then turned and retreated.

I assumed that meant my bees stayed.

As Grant stalked away, I noticed that over on the cemetery side of The Wild Clover, Aggie Petrie was setting up to sell her junkyard wares. Even though Aggie doesn't even live in Moraine, for the last two years she and her husband, Eugene (who serves as her gopher and is majorly henpecked in spite of his years as a big tough marine), and their son, Bob, and his wife, Alicia, have shown up at the Harmony Festival, claiming Aggie's trashy items are priceless treasures. But it was common knowledge that she found them mostly in Dumpsters and on Milwaukee city curbsides on trash pickup days.

We can thank our town chair Grant Spandle for breaking the tied board vote two years ago. We—meaning the vendors who live, breathe, and work in Moraine—have all complained plenty at the monthly meetings, knowing if we don't nip this in the bud, more of us will be challenged by outsiders. How could he let non-residents show up at our annual festival and compete directly with us? What if he let another honey producer set up on the other side of Main? Moraine isn't nearly big enough for two of us.

But shake a few dollar bills in Grant's face and he's all yours.

I strolled over to greet the Petries anyway, reserving my hard feelings for Grant. I scooted around a broken tricycle and a rusty push mower.

"Come right in," Aggie said, shaking a cane at me, which we all knew she only used for effect. "Get first dibs before the crowds come and haul it all off," she said, hawking like a seasoned carny. Since she never bought anything from me, I didn't have any problem reciprocating by ignoring her sales pitch. The last thing I wanted to do was support a business that took customers away from us local shop owners.

"Hi, Aggie," I said. "I just came over to say hello. How have you been? You look good." Aggie hadn't changed much in the last year. The crow's-feet in the outer corners of her eyes had deepened and she'd shrunk another inch or two thanks to a bad case of brittle bones and spine compression, but her personality hadn't changed one bit.

"If you aren't going to buy anything, beat it," Aggie said. "I have work to do, can't be jawing with other vendors. What's in it for me?"

Better than a poke in the eye with a sharp stick, I could have said, since that image was going through my mind. Instead I asked, "Where's Eugene?"

"Making water," she said, eyes rolling toward a line of Porta Pottis down the street.

Um, okay, then. "Well, tell him I say hi," I said.

"If I remember," Aggie said.

After that, the applecart my mother had been concerned about almost overturned.

Because Tom Stocke was barreling toward us. And he didn't look one bit happy.

Three

What can I say about Tom?

He isn't homespun like many of us. In fact if he has a past, he didn't bring it with him. In the five years he's lived in Moraine and operated his antique shop, uninspiredly called "Antiques," we haven't even found out where he originally came from. Presumably he was married once, since he wears a plain gold wedding ring, which sort of implies that he's a widower. Or divorced and unwilling to face the truth. Or . . . anyway, we just don't know.

The most exciting thing about Tom was that right after he moved here, he won the Wisconsin lottery and walked away with a chunk of change amounting to three million dollars (although I'm sure taxes sucked off a good part of it). That made for some awfully good gossip, but nothing really seemed to change with him personally. He still runs his antique business by himself, still lives in a small apartment attached to the back of his store, drives a used car with a lot of miles on it like the rest of us, and pretty much blends into the woodwork, which is where he seems to feel most comfortable.

Tom never answers a personal question directly, preferring to weave around sensitive subjects with unrelated anecdotes until people tend to forget what they asked him in the first place. Makes me think he'd be a really good politician and a potential candidate for next spring's election. Grant Spandle has got to go.

Anyway, Tom minds his own business, and we used to try to mind his, too. Until we realized it was useless, and since we didn't have a choice, we decided to take him at face value.

Which isn't saying much on the physical side. Tom looks like a post office wanted poster. He has a big broad face with a flat crooked nose that looks as though it's been rearranged a time or two. Nobody is born with a nose like that. But he doesn't cause trouble in the community, didn't even shown up to defend himself when we went to bat for him at the town meetings regarding competition from Aggie Petrie.

Gruff, quiet, polite in a sort of reserved yet friendly way. Usually.

Except now he looked mad as a hornet (not to be confused with a honeybee).

"Aggie Petrie." He rolled to a stop. "Rumor has it you are bad-mouthing me to some of my regular customers."

"Not you personally, Tom. It's that junk you're pawning off as antiques."

I couldn't believe my ears. Had Aggie really just said that? She had to be kidding, right?

Tom's eyes darted across one of Aggie's tables. "Junk? Who's calling whose wares junk?"

Aggie came up to about Tom's armpits, but she wielded that cane like a club and had a hyena's cackling nerve. "Your stuff is pure garbage!" she said.

Tom's face turned bright red from internal heat getting ready to combust.

Suddenly, I remembered that according to my mother, my job was to make sure the festival ran smoothly, keep that applecart from tipping over. Darn. Today was my day for wading into conflicts, and I really, really hate conflicts.

"Please, you two," I reluctantly joined in. "There's room here for everybody." That wasn't a bit true, but what else could I say?

"No, there isn't," Aggie said, agreeing with my unspoken opinion about how much room we really had. "And get your patronizing mug out of our business."

"Me?" I said. "Are you talking to me?"

Tom had a finger in Aggie's face. "I'm warning you . . ."

"What's going on here?" Eugene Petrie arrived on the scene with his son and daughter-in-law.

"This man is threatening me," Aggie said to Eugene. Seeing that we had observers, she hid her cane behind her back and said to Tom, "You bully!"

By now, we had enough spectators to draw even more unwanted attention our way. Get the right amount of people clumped together, and everybody else within range would hone in on the ruckus, too.

Aggie noticed them, and decided to turn the attention into an opportunity. I swear I saw dollar signs ring up in her eyes. "I have business to attend to," she said, turning her attention to the bystanders, and completely ignoring Tom's accusation and my attempt to smooth things over.

"Come on, Tom," I said, giving him a gentle nudge to get him moving.

We'd just turned our backs on Aggie's theatrics when I heard a blast.

"Cherry bomb," Tom said, turning and grinning like a big kid when he saw Noel take off from behind Aggie's booth.

Eugene, after a stunned moment, recovered and chased after Noel but soon realized that he'd never catch up.

"Scared the bejesus out of me," Aggie said. "And scared off customers."

Coming back, Eugene said, "Wait till I get my hands on that kid."

"Never going to happen," Tom muttered, suddenly in a much better mood. Then he chuckled and said to me, "My brother and I used to do the same thing when we were kids, sneak up on unsuspecting adults and try to cause trouble. In fact, my brother actually made his own bombs."

"So does Noel," I said.

"If you two would re-create your altercation with Aggie," I heard from behind me, "I'll get it on video."

I turned to see my nosy neighbor Patti Dwyre, aka Pity-Party Patti, aka P.P. Patti, with her homemade press pass dangling from her neck.

"Count me out," Tom said, walking off.

Patti earned the Pity-Party part of her name by whining incessantly about the condition of her life, which is exactly the same as the rest of ours. It's all perception, how we view the challenges in our lives. Patti isn't very good at taking life in stride, though she's been slightly less whiny since snagging her job as a local reporter, an occupation right up her alley.

My house is one long block from Main Street on Willow. Patti is my neighbor on the east side. Not to be confused with my ex-husband's, Clay's, vacant house on the west. His property is up for sale, listed with Lori Spandle, who isn't doing a very good job of selling it. And he's been threatening to move back here from Milwaukee if it doesn't sell soon. (Oh no—now that I thought about it, what if Lori was intentionally stalling the sale to get Clay back into Moraine and into her cheating arms? That would *not* be good.)

Anyway, Patti has a telescope in her window, electronic gadgets up the kazoo, and an overly inquiring mind, making her the closest thing to a P.I. we have in Moraine. Her reporter gig with *The Distorter* is new, so she's eager to make a lasting impression. Sometimes she goes overboard.

Patti also dresses like the rest of us—jeans, tees, hoodies—but unlike my rich sister, who comes across like a catwalk model, my neighbor prefers dark, brooding colors. "In my line of work, I need to blend in," she once explained. That means all in shades of black, with lots of pockets, gadgets on a belt, and a ball cap pulled down to either shade her eyes or hide her features, depending on the situation.

If Tom reminds me of a most-wanted poster, Patti looks like the bounty hunter chasing him down for the reward money.

Patti flipped on her pocket-sized video recorder and tried to make a pass over Aggie's table with it, but Aggie caught on and snagged Patti's arm with her cane. "No photographs," she said, almost causing Patti to drop the recorder.

"I don't know what's wrong with everybody today," I said to Patti while we walked back to my booth. "Everybody's so snappy."

"Full moon," Patti said. "Brings out the beast in all of us."

"Doesn't that apply only to nighttime? It's a gorgeous sunny day. Everybody should be happy."

"Full moons bring out the worst in people no matter what time it is," Patti went on. "Violence, suicides, accidents, everybody's more aggressive than usual, but more so after dark."

"Mom's ripping into me," I said, ticking off my complaints, sounding suspiciously like the woman I was talking with. "Aggie and Tom are arguing, even Holly is more snarly than usual."

"You're lucky," Patti said, putting some whine into her voice, the Pity-Party part of her personality floating to the surface like this was some kind of contest between us to see who had it rougher. Because if it was a competition, Patti intended to win. "You have family and friends and a boyfriend," she said. "Look at me; I'm all alone."

This was my cue. We'd been through this same scene before. "I'm your friend, Patti."

"You keep saying that, but we don't hang out like friends."

That was certainly true. Patti was weird, impulsive, and whenever we did get together, got me into more trouble than I really needed. I managed to make enough of my own problems without any outside interference.

"What's Hunter up to tonight?" Patti asked.

"I'm not sure," I made the mistake of saying, instantly wanting to take the words back. Hunter and I had spent time together the night before and didn't have any plans for later tonight since I was immersed in the festival *and* managing the store, my booth, and the educational honeybee hive. But if I had to choose someone else to spend time with, it wouldn't be Patti.

"How about hanging out tonight then?" Patti said, brightening. "We could check out all the full-moon mental cases together. I might even dig up a story."

"Gee, that sounds like fun," I said, thinking exactly the opposite, "but I have so much work with the festival. I have to move everything inside, including the bee observation hive, and . . ."

"See? We aren't real friends."

"Of course we are. Okay, all right, I'll go wherever you want, at least for a little while." Was I easy, or what? But I just couldn't stand the pathetic expression on her face for one minute longer.

Patti's face transformed instantly into a big, wide, excited grin. "Good. And just because you're my best friend, I'm going to share some news with you that I think you'll appreciate knowing, even though it isn't exactly the best news."

I'd begun to turn away, my mind more on Stanley's observation beehive and the three-deep group of interested spectators surrounding it. I wanted to be over there with them, telling honeybee stories. The first thing I would talk about was the way my bees sounded when they were busy and happy, which for bees went hand in hand. I can tell by the low frequency when I walk among my hives. They actually sound happy as they fly over to inspect me. And if their collective mood changes because of some perceived or real threat, they warn me with a loud, shrill, high-pitched sound.

What Patti said next stopped me in my tracks, and if I were a honeybee, I'd be piercing the air with the same hostility they reserved for their worst enemies.

Because Patti said, "Something's going on over at your ex-husband's house. I think Clay is back."

Please, say it ain't so! Please!

I instantly experienced all the physical symptoms of a woman suffering a major heart attack. Since I'd experienced these same feelings many times during our marriage, I wasn't too worried about my actual health. But I felt clammy, sweaty, and light-headed just thinking about the jerk.

An anxiety attack threatened. To describe my immediate future as "impending doom" was Patti-like overkill, but imagine something two degrees milder. And I was sick to my stomach remembering some of the stunts he'd pulled. I should have burned down his house as soon as Lori Spandle mentioned that he might come back.

Not that Clay was some kind of monster. He didn't drink excessively or blow through our money during our marriage. He wasn't abusive, either physically or mentally—unless you want to count the long list of embarrassing affairs. Sadly, the man had an uncontrollable sexual addiction. Or so he said. And I was supposed to be understanding and supportive, even when he propositioned every one of my female relatives. My guess is that his so-called sexual addiction didn't really exist as a certifiable medical condition. Certain people just don't have any self-control, so they try to shift responsibility away from themselves. Clay fit that bill.

Having my ex-husband living next door had sucked big time, and I was *not* going back to that bad situation even if it meant extreme measures. Like, as I said before, torching his place.

After all, I have Patti for a friend. She'd jump at the chance.

And I had the effects of a full moon to blame if I was caught.

Four

"Are you absolutely sure he's back?" I asked P. P. Patti, collapsing into one of the Adirondack chairs in front of The Wild Clover.

"Someone's over there. That's all I know. Who else could it be?"

"Didn't you use your telescope to get an ID?"

She shook her head.

Leave it to her to miss an opportunity to use the thing when it counted the most. Patti swung that thing in every direction, which was the main reason I had solid, thick shades on all my windows.

"It's daylight," she informed me. "I can't see inside windows until night."

"You don't have infrared?"

"Don't I wish." Patti looked wistful, then she perked up. "Should we check out the house? Do a little investigating?"

Part of me wanted to race right over there, but the other

part of me put on the brakes. "Maybe later," I said, not willing to deal with my ex yet. "I have work to do."

And with that, I made a sweep through the inside of the store to be sure everything was running smoothly. Then I joined Stanley and Carrie Ann at our booth and observation table. For a few hours I didn't want to think about anything troubling, so this was the perfect place to perch, next to the familiar routine of honeybees and the wonderful byproducts of all their hard work.

Stanley Peck might have a lot to learn about beekeeping, but he really had a gift for entertaining a crowd of spectators.

"I have a big batch of mead ready to bottle," he told them, referring to the honey wine most of us beekeepers like to make. Mead is the oldest alcoholic beverage known to humans. Ancient cultures planned weddings around full moons and served lots of mead, which is where *honeymoon* came from.

That little trivia popped into my head, reminding me of our own full moon and Patti's pessimistic (but textbook) view of its effects on human behavior.

"You should have brought some of your mead to the festival," someone said to Stanley. "We'd buy it."

"Yeah," someone else said. "Go get a case or two."

Stanley shot me a questioning look. I shook my head to remind him that that was a really bad idea. We'd discussed his mead earlier. Before putting some products up for sale, they have to get a seal of approval by passing government inspection. Mead was one of them.

And Stanley, a bachelor since his wife died (and you sure could tell by his habits), made mead in his bathtub. No way was it ever going to pass. Not that he really planned on trying. An outspoken group of locals, of which Stanley happens to be the ringleader, avoid government interference like bird flu.

But, come on? The bathtub? Who'd want to drink anything that came out of Stanley's tub?

The rest of the morning flew by. I didn't see much of the people who had given me grief earlier. Occasionally I'd glance over at Aggie's booth, where surprisingly she appeared to be steadily selling her junk and making a nice profit. Aggie, I noticed, made serious eye contact with people as they wandered past, stunning them with something similar to hypnosis and drawing them in like snagged fish dangling on hooks.

How did she do that?

I tried to copy her but only got strange looks for my efforts. Besides, we were doing well without it, so I put away the hypnotic stare and went back to being my normal self.

Aggie's son, Bob, wandered over and joined the beehive enthusiasts. He's a big guy and a hothead, I've heard. We didn't see much of the Petries around Moraine; they live in a small community called Colgate, like the toothpaste, about twenty minutes away. Most reports of Bob's wrongdoing come through snippets in the local paper or unconfirmed tongue-wagging in the store. Bob's wife, Alicia, is okay. Last year she came to a class I gave on making honey lip balm, and I got to know her a little.

All the vendors were doing well, judging by the crowds and all the shopping bags I spotted.

My hometown is located in southeastern Wisconsin, nestled between ridges and valleys that occurred naturally during the ice age, and it's right on one of Wisconsin's most scenic drives. So we draw a lot of tourists who come our way sightseeing, fishing, camping, all the outdoor activities that make a place special. Water lovers can even put their canoes and kayaks in the Oconomowoc River at a launch near my house.

Good old Moraine was coming through for us again. Maybe this wasn't exactly a Harmony Festival for me, but it was living up to its name for our visitors and sellers.

I spent at least two blissful hours having fun, meeting

new people, and chatting up friends from other communities who turned out for the festival. But eventually, after meeting and greeting, the ex-husband situation was back in my mind and I couldn't shake it off.

Throughout the lunchtime hours I couldn't find any time to get away, but mid-afternoon, after my staff took turns getting something to eat, I dropped Dinky in the back room for a much-needed nap and walked over to my house.

My family home now belongs to me. I'd been raised here, so it really *is* home. After my father had a fatal heart attack, Mom relinquished it willingly when I expressed interest. Mom likes to have a lot of say in other peoples' business, so she moved in with my grandmother where she has the control she craves. And since Grams is a carefree soul, she doesn't seem to mind at all. A win-win situation for all of us.

I'd repainted the pretty Victorian house bright yellow with white trim and planted bee-friendly flowers and bushes all around it. Someday I hoped it would have another family living in it. My own. Although with my "man luck," which until recently has been zilch, children and a faithful husband might turn out to be a pipe dream.

Of course, I *do* have Hunter, a really appealing prospect. The guy is hot and well worth pursuing. But I suspect a serious commitment issue. Carrie Ann claims he never married before because he was waiting for me to get my act together. That might be true. Or not.

Whatever the case, our relationship is moving as slow as the proverbial molasses, and at thirty-four and counting, I can't help feeling like my days are numbered. Everything has a shelf life, and mine will expire eventually, like a loaf of moldy bread. Lately, it's all I can do not to look at Hunter like he's a piece of prime steak I want to wrap up and take home.

Desperation does not look good on me. How come that

little ticking clock is so darn loud and intrusive and hard to ignore?

As I crossed the street, I wondered if Patti's self-pitying attitude was contagious, because I was starting to feel sorry for myself big time. Especially if jerk-face was really back next door. I couldn't stand the possibility.

The truck parked in his driveway didn't look familiar. And Clay's modus operandi didn't include driving a truck, anyway. He liked to own chick magnets like red sports cars with convertible tops. So this was encouraging.

I knocked on the door. As it opened, I saw a red and yellow Hawaiian shirtsleeve. This was so un-Clay I wanted to break out in song.

I looked up at the rest. Fiftyish, scruffy, beer belly, bulbous nose, and missing a tooth, which became obvious as soon as he smiled. Definitely not my ex-husband, who prided himself on keeping trim and fit for all his extracurricular activities.

"Is Clay here?" I asked just to be on the safe side.

"Clay who?"

Those two words were music to my ears. What a relief! My ex wasn't back. I'd been worried for nothing.

"Never mind," I said. "I thought you were somebody else. I live next door."

He looked up from my chest and over at my house. "Is that right?" he said, with kind of a leering look back at me. "I'm Ford. Why don't you come in and stay awhile, keep me company. Just how friendly a neighbor are you, Tootsie?"

I had a pretty good idea what that question was supposed to mean. Nobody had ever called me "Tootsie" before, and I decided I didn't like his attitude.

"You didn't buy this house, did you?" The for-sale sign was still out by the curb, but I felt those heart-attack symptoms coming back, imagining this guy living next door for an extended period of time. I wasn't a snob, but Ford had *trouble* stamped all over his Neanderthal forehead.

"I rented it," he said. "A nice real estate lady had an ad in the Milwaukee newspaper to lease it on a month-by-month basis, but I talked her into short-term."

I felt all the blood drain out of my head. Lori Spandle and my ex-husband had rented the house to this character? "But it isn't even furnished. What are you doing? Sleeping on the floor?"

"I brought my camping gear. And it's just for the weekend. By then we'll be done."

I should have asked what he meant by that. Looking back, much later, I wish I had, especially the "we" part. But at the time, I was so grateful that he wasn't going to be my permanent neighbor that I just wished him a good stay then backed away and trotted off.

The rest of the afternoon's activities went as smooth as silk, as American as apple pie, as rosy as an heirloom tomato. Mom stayed out of my hair, too busy to bug the bees. Or else Grant had actually taken my threat against DeeDee seriously enough to tell her to leave the beehive exactly where it was. In that case, Mom would be mad and I'd hear about it eventually. But for now, life proceeded without a glitch.

At five o'clock the vendors began to shut down their booths and organize for tomorrow, which should be another big day. Sunday would feature the noon parade with Grams as Grand Marshal and DeeDee as Honey Queen. I could just imagine that little thief, sitting on the backseat of a convertible waving her sticky fingers at the crowd as she lapped up the moment.

I refocused before that particular topic carried me back into a funk. I firmly believe we can control our minds and attitudes, and that we get what we create. My mom's negativity is a case in point. I banned her from my mind, right along with all other pessimistic thoughts. Gone.

I raised my eyes to the sky, taking in lazy cotton-ball clouds, lit orange from the setting sun. A flock of Canadian geese flew overhead in their familiar V-formation. Here in Wisconsin in August the days are getting shorter. That's a clue for the monarch butterflies, bats, and migratory birds to fill up their tanks for the trip south.

Trent and Brent Craig, the twin brothers who'd been working for me since they were sophomores in high school, offered to close up. They were both thoughtful college students now, and helped out as much as they could. School wouldn't start for several weeks, so I had them both on the schedule for the entire weekend. It didn't take me long to accept their offer.

The rest of us dispersed. Some of our local diehards headed for Stu's Bar and Grill to imbibe. Others went home.

Carrie Ann shot off to Stu's. Maybe not the best or smartest place to hang out considering her drinking problem, but she'd been behaving herself lately, even the times she spends at the bar, thanks to several watchful eyes. The first set belongs to Hunter, who's been her sponsor through all her ups and downs. Then there's her ex-husband, Gunnar. He often reminds her of certain responsibilities, like their two children who live with him and need a sober mom. And, of course, all her friends keep tabs on her, too.

Holly walked home with Dinky and me, since she'd parked her pricey Jag at my house to avoid crowding and the possibility of damage to its perfect paint job.

"What's going on over at Clay's?" she said, noticing the truck parked in the driveway next door. Lights were on inside the house, and through the window I could see several cans of beer on a metal camping table in the kitchen.

I told her how Lori had rented Clay's house to Ford for the weekend.

"He doesn't sound like our typical tourist," Holly muttered as she got into her car. "Is he somebody's relative?"

I shrugged. "He didn't mention anything like that."

"That was a smart move on Lori's part, earning some income for Clay."

"Ugh. Wait till you meet this guy. He's a real winner. Want me to introduce you right now?"

"No thanks."

And with that, my sister blew off in her Jag, leaving me alone and without the time or energy to kayak on the river like I usually enjoyed doing after work. Instead, I headed back toward town with Dinky, and ended up on the street outside my store, where the sidewalk action had wound down for the evening. I let Dinky lead the way.

That was my first big mistake.

Five

❦

In my opinion, dusk is a creepy time of day.

That brief but hauntingly eerie bit of time right between light and dark, when my eyes play tricks on me and inanimate shadows stretch out long and take on life of their own.

It's the end of one thing, the beginning of another.

And with a full moon rising.

I remembered Patti and her theories about the madness of tonight's lunar event.

If the moon affected my actions, made me do bizarre things, would I recognize the change in myself?

Those were the random thoughts bouncing around in my mind as I stood outside of my store. That's when Dinky started tugging on her leash. Granted, she was a little pip-squeak, so her efforts to pull me around hardly counted. But Dinky, stubborn as she could be, kept at it, racing the full length of the leash to the very end, tipping up on her back legs, and yapping, then doing it all over again.

Talk about shrill. And annoying.

"What is it?" I said to her. "What's wrong with you?"
She didn't answer.
Not that I expected her to.
I wasn't in a big rush to get anywhere. Patti would find me when she was ready to howl at the moon, so I let Dinky take the lead. Anything to shut her up. Dinky promptly headed in the direction of the cemetery.
Some of the headstones had inscriptions dating back as far as the early 1900s. None of the grave markings inside this graveyard were uniform and neat like more modern cemeteries. Stones leaned this way and that way.
I'd walked past, or near, or through the cemetery almost every day. I'd been there plenty of times before, several times recently with Dinky. But with night falling, the moon rising, and Patti's prediction that we all would basically turn into uncontrollable werewolves, every little hair on my arms was standing at attention.
Dinky, still in the lead, stopped at one headstone after another, and at every single one she sniffed around as though she were hunting for something. After a few more pauses, she found something on the ground and started chewing.
"Oh no you don't." I quickly bent down and tried to wrestle whatever it was out of her mouth. But she wolfed it down, gulped, and it was gone. I sensed a vomiting episode in our near future. We'd been there, done that, more times than I cared to remember.
Next, Dinky ran behind one of the headstones and wound the leash around a crabapple tree's trunk enough times that she could barely move. Before I could reach down to untangle her, I tripped over something, lost my balance, and hit the ground hard, face-first, barely having time to break my fall with my hands.
Dinky barked only once when I went down, and then hushed up, becoming perfectly quiet. I felt her breath on my face and her tongue in my ear, licking away. When I

rose up on an elbow to brush her back, I spotted the outline of the thing I'd fallen over.

After sitting up and more carefully considering the object, I realized what had really tripped me up.

A human leg!

Attached to a body!

(Thank God. Because an unattached leg would have totally flipped me out on the spot. Not that I was holding it together all that well anyway, because the body wasn't moving. Not a good sign.)

I was pretty sure the person on the ground was a male, judging by the manly shoes on his feet. I couldn't tell for sure, though, because the face and shoulders were covered with an extra-large black plastic garbage bag.

I'd like to think I'm braver than I really am, that I have the courage to face the unexpected with calm and resolve. In hindsight (that twenty-twenty kind), what I should have done was rip that plastic away and reveal the person underneath. If I'd done that, it would have saved me a lot of grief later on.

But the last thing on my mind at the time was checking to find out who was under the plastic.

Instead of displaying bravery beyond the call of duty, I grabbed Dinky, unclipped the tangled leash to free her, leaving it wound around the tree, and dashed for the bright lights of the store.

"What happened to you?" Brent called as I blew by him, racing for the back room. "You look like you saw a ghost."

I had a lump in my throat the size of a grapefruit. "Be all right," was all that came out before I slammed the door and slumped down in my office chair.

I tried to calm myself with deep-breathing exercises. It didn't work.

Somebody was out in the cemetery, maybe dead—okay, probably dead based on the lack of motion and that black plastic bag. The chicken part of me had the shakes bad, but the businesswoman part was thinking of how the discovery of a body would affect tomorrow's festival.

I weighed my options. I had choices here. One was that I could contain the damage by dragging the body into hiding and pull it back out tomorrow night after the Harmony Festival ended. Then I could fake the same trip over it again.

After not much thought, I threw out that choice as a really, really bad idea for a lot of reasons.

Another option, I could call Patti and collaborate with her on the next move.

She always had plenty of never-thought-of-before-by-humankind ideas. But the reporter in her wouldn't go along with a cover up. She'd want to make it sensational. No, I couldn't tell Patti.

Then I thought, what if the person isn't dead? What if I held a life in the palm of my hand this very moment, and it was expiring because I was sitting here doing nothing?

So I went with the last and final option, the most logical one, though it was the one I liked the least. I called Johnny Jay, our police chief. Or rather, I called 9-1-1, which was almost the same thing as calling him directly since he would know about my call about two seconds after I finished making it. I gave the required information to the dispatcher, pointedly requesting discretion on the part of the responders.

"Please, no lights or sirens," I said. "This might be nothing." That wasn't true. Something, rather than nothing, was out there, but the less the other residents knew, the better.

The first vehicle to arrive at the scene was Johnny Jay's police SUV, running full out with lights and siren. "Fischer," he said when he got out and spotted Dinky and me waiting outside under the awning. "Figures you're involved."

I caught his typical boring, superior attitude. We exchanged a glare.

Johnny has the clean and polished lines of a Boy Scout, which proves you can't go by looks. He also has a linebacker's build that he uses to intimidate the weak and the helpless. His bully tactics have never worked on me though. That's a good chunk of the reason behind our animosity. I don't like how he tries to bully me; he hates that it never works.

"Johnny Jay," I hissed. "I specifically requested a quiet arrival. Why ruin the rest of a perfectly wonderful festival by scaring people away? What's the matter with you?"

"Cut the crap and show me what you claim you found." Tough talk, but at least he reached into his SUV through the open window and turned off the bells and whistles.

"Where's the ambulance?" I asked.

"Here it comes. And it better be needed."

The ambulance made lots of noise as it raced up Main Street from south of town with a fire truck right behind it. And I heard more emergency sirens in the distance, all running every noisemaker they had. How could I have forgotten how gung-ho our emergency workers really are?

By now, customers were pouring out of Stu's Bar and Grill down the street to check out the situation. So much for discretion and a low profile.

"I tripped over a body in the cemetery," I told Johnny, keeping my voice low.

"Dead?" he asked.

"I don't know. I think so. He was covered in plastic."

Johnny eyed me carefully. "How do you know it's a man?"

"I don't. I'm just assuming."

"Okay, let's go."

Brent came out of the store. Johnny addressed him next. "Tell the ambulance crew to stay put at the curb until I say otherwise."

"And please take care of Dinky for a few minutes," I said to Brent, passing the small dog over to him.

"What's going on?" somebody from Stu's called out.

"Stay where you are," Johnny called back to them.

"Better do as he says," somebody else said. "He's armed and dangerous." I recognized the voice as belonging to Stanley Peck, who probably was more armed and dangerous than the police chief.

Johnny had a flashlight in one hand and kept his other hand on his gun belt as we walked slowly and cautiously into the cemetery.

"Over there," I said, heading for the crabapple tree, staying to the side of Johnny instead of in front, just in case he opened fire. Our police chief wasn't impulsive or rash, but walking in front of a man who doesn't like you and who's carrying a weapon is just plain stupid.

It wasn't completely dark yet and with the moon beaming down like its own sort of pale sun, I didn't need a flashlight to see that I had a slight problem.

Or maybe a major one.

Because the body was gone.

Six

❦

"Fischer," Johnny Jay ranted, "you'd better have an explanation for calling out *my* police officers, *my* ambulance, *and* the town's firefighters on a wild-goose chase." Johnny Jay was hopping mad. He jerked Dinky's leash from around the tree trunk and gave me an exasperated glare. "I could arrest you for pulling a stunt like this."

"That belongs to me," I said, reaching for the leash. "I'm dog-sitting."

"I know that, Fischer. Only I hear Norm isn't coming back to town. That makes you a dog owner, not a sitter. Too bad the dog can't speak up and take your phony-baloney side. That's the thing with you. You never have any real witnesses to back up your outrageous claims."

"When I called, I specifically told your dispatcher to keep a low profile. It's not my fault you sent all the big guns."

"Start explaining. *NOW!*"

"Just shine your flashlight on the ground," I advised

him. If we didn't find an enormous puddle of blood or a smoking gun lying on the grass, I was in such big trouble. "Maybe we'll find a clue."

Johnny Jay snorted and made all kinds of threatening noises. "You and your cock-and-bull stories. You want a clue? I'll give you a clue." He held up a pair of handcuffs. I was familiar with them from certain past events. "What does it mean when I get these out?"

I heard murmurs across the street where the contingency from Stu's was watching and waiting to see what entertainment might unfold between the two of us. By now, the ambulance and fire trucks had pretty much blocked off Main Street to vehicles, rerouting traffic, but the bar had been busy and all of Stu's customers were congregating as close as possible on foot.

"The grass right here is compressed," I said. "See? Somebody was lying here, just like I told you." Actually, the grass had been cut recently and looked short and perky, but I had to at least try.

A paramedic from the ambulance walked over. "Do we have an emergency or not?"

"Not!" Johnny yelled. "Clear out." Then he looked over at Stu's customers. "And, all of you, get off my street, or I'll Breathalyzer every last one of you. Public drunkenness is a crime in my town."

That's our police chief, unhampered by any normal human longings for things like honor and respect. Give him power and control and he's perfectly happy. Johnny might not know how to make friends, but he sure knew how to disperse a crowd. Everybody vanished.

"So Fischer," he said next. "I suggest you file a report. I'll get the paperwork out of my vehicle."

That surprised me. Johnny Jay had put away his handcuffs, wasn't going to arrest me, and was actually cooperating for once. Something was up. I followed him out of the cemetery against my better judgment and waited while he took his sweet time getting a clipboard, pen, and form for me to fill out.

"Once you complete this," he said, clicking open the pen and handing it to me, "I'll be able to officially investigate."

"About time," I said, poised to fill out the form. "Only this pen isn't working."

"I'll get another one."

"Stop!" I heard right behind me. "Don't do it!"

I'd recognize that grating voice anywhere. Patti Dwyre! My neighbor has an unhealthy fascination with stealth, sneaking around on tiptoes and blending into the woodwork, always coming up behind her target. She's managed to scare the daylights out of me more than once.

This time was no exception.

The useless pen went flying out of my hand.

Johnny Jay attempted to give me a new one.

Patti grabbed it instead. "She isn't interested in filing a report."

"What are you talking about?" I said, attempting to take the pen away from her. "Of course I'm filing a report."

"If you do," she said, "the police chief will nail you for filing a false report."

I glanced at Johnny Jay and caught the smirk on his face just before he hid it.

"Is that true?" I said, getting really ticked off. Uncontrollable rage bubbled to the surface before I could stop it. Everybody has a breaking point. He'd found mine.

"I stumble over someone on the ground in the cemetery," I said, getting right in his face. "A body. Foul play could be involved, for all we know. And you can't even shine your damn flashlight around the area. You're way too busy messing with me. Two can play this game, you know. I ought to file harassment charges against you! And entrapment charges! And incompetency charges!" Although I wasn't sure he could be charged for that.

"You better lower your voice, Story Fischer," he said, grabbing the clipboard. "And just so you know, filing a report for a crime that didn't occur and wasting taxpayer's valuable dollars by fraudulently calling for emergency services is a misdemeanor."

Patti was right. He had been setting me up!

I realized that I was wasting my time and energy trying to be cordial to Johnny Jay. He didn't deserve respect or consideration from me in the future ever again. Not that he'd had any from me in the first place, come to think of it. Well, the gloves were coming off. And round one was going to be mine.

"Johnny Jay," I said. "Remember that day in high school when you asked me to prom?" That day, when I turned him down flat, was what many residents think started the war between the two of us. They don't realize that Johnny Jay and I have been enemies since the playground years. "I am so glad I said no. Hunter had then, and still has, more sex appeal in his big toe than you'll ever have in your entire body."

And just in case that wasn't the event that made him so mean toward me, if he was gunning for me because I went out of my way in the past to protect little kids from his big bully tactics, I said, "And I was the one who turned you in to the principal and got you suspended for bullying Eddy Arts."

"Fischer," Johnny Jay said after a moment of silence while he absorbed my claim, "you're nuts."

And he got in his SUV and drove off.

"Wow," Patti said. "I didn't know you had it in you. A full moon suits your personality."

"I've had a really bad day."

"Kind of juvenile behavior though, digging up stuff from way back when."

"Johnny Jay brings out the worst in me."

Brent came out of the store with Dinky. "I'll lock up," he offered.

"Thanks," I said, taking Dinky from him. "That would be great."

"Come on." Patti took my arm. "Let's end this day on a better note."

"What are we going to do?" I asked. All I really wanted to do was go home, take a shower, and read a good book.

"We're going to find that body."

"You believe me?" At least someone did. Even if it was only a dirty-laundry digger.

"Of course I do! How could I doubt my best friend?"

I really wished Patti would stop with the best-friend routine. Did real friends need constant affirmation? Not that I was aware of, although I'm certainly no expert. With the store and my bee business, I rarely had the extra time for regular girlfriends. When I have a spare moment, I usually take a long, hot bath or spend a few hours with Hunter if he's available.

"Besides," Patti continued. "I've got a story either way. If we don't find a body, I still have you and the police chief going nose to nose."

"I'll deny it."

Patti held up a pocket-sized camera. "Pictures," she said.

Darn it. Maybe we should try to chase down the missing body instead. My family wouldn't be too happy if I made the local *Distorter* in a negative way.

"Where are we going to look?" I asked, suspecting this was a bigger problem than Patti realized. "The body could be anywhere."

Patti scowled in thought. "You think it was a guy, right?"

I nodded. "Guy shoes."

"What kind?"

"Um . . . brown ones."

"Gee, that's helpful," Patti said. "And you're sure he didn't get up and walk off?"

"Not exactly, no, I'm not sure. But why else would he be

covered up with a garbage bag like that and not even react when I tripped over him?"

"Tell me the whole thing, front, middle, and back."

So I did as we walked back to my house. Patti waited while I took care of making sure that Dinky was fed and watered and comfortably tucked in for the night.

"One thing's for sure," Patti said once we were back outside. "We have a missing unconscious person."

"Yup."

"Maybe dead, maybe not. Either way, let's assume he needed help moving from the spot where you found him. Based on the evidence we have, that is."

"Right," I said, opening the driver's door of my trusty blue pickup truck. "Somebody strong, probably another man."

As we drove off something strange happened to me.

I started doubting myself. What if I hadn't seen what I thought I saw? What if it was only a figment of my imagination? What if the full moon had cast a spell on me and I'd invented the whole thing? The only proof I had, and it was really, really weak, was Dinky's incessant barking and determination to get into the cemetery. She'd known something was there. Although, usually she was such a scaredy-cat around trouble, she should have been running away from, not toward, the source.

Did that imply something? Did she know the guy wasn't a threat? Could she smell death?

Since it wasn't like the little troublemaker was ever going to answer my questions, I gave up. My sister was the one studying human behavior; I'd have to ask her opinion on my sudden vacillation.

After driving around aimlessly in the dark without a plan of any sort, I had a brainstorm.

"I know!" I said to Patti. "What we need is Hunter Wallace and his dog." Ben, Hunter's K-9 partner, had helped me out of a jam once when I lost Dinky. Not that I'd shared that particular fact with Hunter, since losing her had been irresponsible on my part and I'd exposed enough flaws in front of him without adding any of the hidden ones.

"What a brilliant idea!" Patti shouted. "Ben can guide us to the body."

"I need you," I said when Hunter answered his cell phone, deciding on the spot to wait until he arrived to go into more detail.

"I love it when you need me. Where are you?"

"In the cemetery."

"Okay, that's a little kinky."

"Just hurry."

And that's how we ended up back in the cemetery, waiting for my boyfriend and his dog to arrive. I really hoped they would find some answers.

Seven

Hunter Wallace carries a badge, but although he lives on the outskirts of Moraine, he doesn't have a whole lot of jurisdiction in my town, especially concerning local issues. Hunter works for the county, which is larger and more organized, but he's dealt with Johnny Jay before and has his number just like everybody else.

Johnny Jay controls our small community with tight reins and loose ties to other law-enforcement agencies. Cops from surrounding towns know our police chief is difficult to work with, and they give him a wide berth, which is exactly what Johnny wants. His motto regarding his crime-fighting peers is basically "What they don't know can't hurt me."

At the same time as my main man arrived, Holly's Jag roared up and my sister jumped out.

"What are you doing here?" I asked her, afraid that I already knew the answer.

"Damage control," she said. "Mom knows."

Those were the words that always sent chills up and down my body. Here's what would have happened, as it always does: Somebody from Stu's Bar and Grill, most likely a local with a big mouth, called up one or two of his family members to tell them how Story Fischer and Johnny Jay were going at it again and did they want to bet on the outcome. One of those newly informed individuals would've then punched in my grandmother's phone number and blabbed to Grams. Mom, having hearing more acute than any known species on the planet, would have overhead part of the conversation and forced the rest of the facts out of Grams.

Mom would then have called up Holly and read her the riot act about family responsibilities and how everybody knows Story's a loose cannon and this was on Holly's watch, blah blah blah, thereby transferring blame to Holly and making her feel crappy.

Anyway, Holly, Hunter, and Ben converged at the exact spot where I thought I'd found a body but now seriously doubted myself.

"Hey, sweet thing," Hunter said, giving me a smile as he said it. Our relationship had just advanced to the "honey, babe, sweet thing" level, and it felt good. "What's going on?" he asked, looking at the unlikely assembly in the cemetery.

Patti had already combed the area with a high-powered flashlight from her "I Spy" tool kit. We hadn't found a single thing out of place, nothing to support my claim. I shared that disappointing information with my sister and Hunter, along with the story about tripping over a leg, the tarp-covered body that turned up missing, and how Johnny Jay didn't believe me and tried to nail me with criminal charges. All the while I was explaining, Hunter had his eyes on the ground, flashing a beam of light from his own flashlight among the grave markers.

He looked cool and hot at the same time, something I never failed to notice no matter what the situation. Rugged, confident, lots of leather (I love leather—the smell, the look) when he rode his Harley—though tonight he wore jeans, a black T-shirt, and biker's boots, having pulled up in his SUV instead since Ben, his four-legged companion, hadn't perfected the art of riding on the back of a motorcycle. Although he *was* smart enough to learn.

The dog gazed at me with total self-confidence, just like his sexy partner.

Ben is a Belgian Malinois and is fully trained in everything he needs to perform police work—obedience, endurance, and agility. He's a mean, lean fighting machine when he's on the job. And a big cuddly teddy bear when he's not. Ben is sensitive and devoted to his partner. Hunter and Ben can read each other's reactions like any other cop partners who've been working side by side for a very long time.

Me? I never have a clue what passes between them.

Speaking of clues that might save my credibility, I had an important question. "Ben can track a missing person, right?" I asked. "Even if that person is dead?"

Hunter's eyes cut from the ground to me. "If he has the tools to work with."

"Like what kind of tools?" Patti said from the shadows. I'd almost forgotten she was with us, she blended so well into the background and had been totally quiet until now.

"A scent to go by, I bet," Holly said, on the ball. "Something that belongs to that person."

Hunter nodded.

Nuts, we were back to square one. I didn't have a starting scent for Ben to work from.

"Are you sure of what you saw?" Holly said to me, and all my doubts about my sanity came rushing back.

"Absolutely," I said. "I'm absolutely, positively sure." A person has to appear firm on the outside, even if the inside is going to mush. Besides, if I wishy-washed, I'd look foolish and Hunter might not even try to help.

"We might be in luck," Hunter said. "But only if this alleged person bled."

I really didn't like that "alleged" part. Hunter must have sensed my distress, because he looked at me and said, "I just mean that it's only alleged until it's confirmed. Cop talk."

Did that make me feel better? Not really. The possibility of a permanent stain on my credibility record wasn't pretty. "There goes crazy Story," they'd say. "Making up stuff just like she used to."

"No blood," Patti announced. "I looked. Nothing dark resembling blood in the grass."

"Let's hear what Ben has to say," Hunter said. His canine partner perked up his ears.

I'd gleaned from my association with Hunter and Ben that a tracking dog uses all its senses. I've watched them train together, so I know a thing or two. Ben's eyes are at least as sharp as any human's and his ears are way better. If Ben's ears are erect and forward when he's on a case, that means he heard something. If one ear is forward and one back, he's heard things from more than one direction, which then alerts Hunter that he has more than one possible threat to deal with.

And because police work involves stealth, Ben has been trained not to bark or yelp or growl like a lot of dogs do when they sense danger or are afraid. He remains quiet unless Hunter gives him the okay to bark.

"Go ahead," Hunter said quietly, and the big dog sitting next to him rose and went to work, starting next to the crabapple tree where I'd found the prone body.

A little while later, Hunter called him back. "Nothing," he said. "There are too many other scents. It doesn't help that the chief and ambulance attendants walked all over around here."

Holly glanced at me. "Are you absolutely sure you saw a body on the ground?" she asked again.

"Of course she is!" Patti answered for me. "I believe her."

"What's the next step?" I asked Hunter.

He shook his head and since I was feeling extra sensitive at the moment, I took that as a sign that he didn't have the same faith in me that Patti did. "Without evidence of a body, a struggle, or a weapon," he said, "we wait and see what happens next."

"Let's drive around some more," Patti suggested.

"Do I have to?" I said. "I'm exhausted."

"You promised, you know. The night's young. Want to come with us, Holly?"

"Sure," Holly said. "Where are we going?"

I glanced at Hunter. He gave me a wide grin and told Holly exactly where we were going without even being informed. "You're going looking for trouble," he said.

Patti pulled down the visor of her ball cap, getting into sleuthing mode.

"Where are you going to start?" Hunter asked, amusement playing across his face.

"Stu's Bar and Grill, where else?" I answered, looking down the street and seeing that the bar was still packed. "Want to come along?"

"No men," Patti said. "This is a female mission all the way. Sorry, Hunter."

Hunter laughed. "But I could be useful. I have weapons."

"But you have to pay attention to a lot more rules than we have to," Patti said. "Besides, we have our own means and methods."

"What does that mean?" he asked her.

"Never mind," I said, shushing her.

"Call me if you need me," Hunter said to me in a low voice, giving me a few hot and sexy thoughts regarding his offer.

I smiled and kept them to myself.

Eight

After Hunter and Ben took off, Holly, Patti, and I made a beeline for the bar. A fact or two about beelines, which, believe it or not, really *do* exist:

- A foraging honeybee leaves the hive first thing in the morning as soon as the air temperature is just right.

- She (the boys don't work at all) does little circles to warm up, just like we do before exercising.

- While she's warming up, she's also getting her bearings.

- Once her muscles are nice and loose, she flies up in the air, gaining altitude like any good pilot.

- Then she takes off, fast and straight, on a direct flight.

- Other foraging bees will follow her path.

• After flitting from flower to flower, loading up with pollen and nectar, she and her fellow workers make a beeline home.

Which is what I should have done.

Made a beeline home.

Straight as an arrow—straight as the crow flies, Grams likes to say—to my warm, cozy home.

Because I'd temporarily forgotten about my close encounter with our police chief.

But not only did Stu's nosy customers remember the exchange with crystal clarity, they were deeper into their pitchers of Wisconsin microbrewskis and had a few good jokes at my expense.

"Story danced like nobody was watching," one wiseacre said. "Court date pending."

"Was she naked?" another one wanted to know.

"'Course she was."

That's how stupid rumors get started in this town—drunks in bars, making stuff up. By the next morning all that nonsense could be on the streets and nobody would remember who started it.

They weren't done yet, either. Stanley Peck was sitting with a bunch of old guys and joined in. "Johnny Jay caught her drinking battery acid and he *charged* her. Get it? Battery. Charged."

"Good one," I said, laughing along since I knew everybody at his table, and most of them were just out to have fun.

But there's always one bad apple in the bunch. Or in this case, two rotten ones.

"Story Fischer has a real problem with authority," I heard from a corner. Lori Spandle and her sister DeeDee Becker sat behind beer glasses and some sort of hip-spreading cheesy appetizer that I hoped was working its fat magic on them both at this very moment. DeeDee still wore the Honey Queen crown on top of her head. "And she has an attention issue," Lori said good and loud. "That's why she makes up all those stupid lies. Now she's trying to ruin our festival by making all kinds of noise to get attention! A body in the cemetery? How lame is that?"

I should probably point out that most of Moraine's residents really like me. And I like them. But it's impossible to live in a small town, especially one you've grown up in, without having a few enemies. Lori Spandle and Johnny Jay are downright blatant in their dislike for me. And the feeling is mutual. Of course, there are some other people I barely tolerate and who barely tolerate me, but for the most part, we have some really special people in our community.

I'm long past the stage, though, where I try to please everybody and want everyone to like me. It just isn't going to happen. But I had to wonder why Lori was baiting me, trying to start something in front of everybody.

"Ignore Lori," Holly said to the roomful of people, coming to my aid like a sister should. "She's had too much to drink. Again."

"Why, you . . ." Lori started.

Stu, over behind the bar, cranked up the bar's piped music and that was the end of the public face-off between Lori and me. I was pretty sure I'd lost.

God, that woman irritates me! I marched over for a private showdown. "Since when do you have the authority to rent out Clay's house?" I demanded.

"Since he gave it to me." Lori grinned. "Why, don't you like Ford?"

"Did you check his references?"

"He checked out."

"Of which mental health facility?" I wanted to know.

DeeDee didn't say a word, hardly making any eye contact at all. She sipped her beer and kept her head down, as well she should after stealing the Honey Queen title. First she raids my store's shelves, then she runs off with the crown that should have been mine.

Not that I'm bitter or anything.

Holly and Patti came rushing over before I could get any farther. They each grabbed one of my arms and carted me away to a table in the opposite corner.

"What we have to concentrate on," Patti said firmly, digging a notepad out of one of her pockets, "is the missing person. I'm going to write down the names of every man in this bar. That's a starting point. At least then we can eliminate those guys from our search."

Since Patti was a relatively recent newcomer to Moraine, moving here just before I came back almost three years ago, she didn't know as many people as Holly and I did, so we helped her out with names.

"What if the missing person is from out of town?" Holly asked.

"It's possible," Patti said, still making notes. "But I'm an investigative reporter and that means I cover all the bases, starting with what I know. And right now what I know is that a whole lot of people in this bar aren't dead or unconscious."

"Lori Spandle's unconscious," I offered, doing a little wishful thinking.

"She's the walking dead," Holly agreed.

"Lori doesn't count," Patti said.

Stu called out for our orders and we all asked for beer and brats (short for bratwursts, Wisconsin's special soul food). I hadn't realized how hungry I was until now. Our three foaming beers arrived along with our brats, loaded up with onions, sauerkraut, and mustard, and nestled in brat buns, not to be confused with hot dog buns, which are a completely different thing and not at all qualified as an acceptable substitute. We dug in.

"Don't let Lori engage you anymore," Holly said, while

we ate. "I've been reading up, and people like that want you to get mad. You played right into her hands."

"Since when did you become Doctor Freud?" I asked.

"Mock me all you want," my sister said. "But the human mind is interesting stuff. I like learning about it."

Just then, Mom walked in the door. I almost choked on my brat, because she wasn't the type to hang out at Stu's. Yet here she was, on a Saturday night, out on the town. She was wearing a blue dress, a necklace so awesome I'd wear it, and a warm expression on her face, like she was actually enjoying a slice of her life. What was wrong with this picture?

Not only that, but I saw Tom Stocke, the antique-store owner, walk in right behind her. And he was cleaned up like he was on a date, wearing a blue button-down shirt, khakis, and (the dead giveaway) a tie. Mom spotted a small table open near the front window, and Tom stayed right behind her.

"Why's he following Mom around?" I asked.

"Boy, are you dense," Patti said. "They're on a date."

"HS! (*Holy Sh**!*)" Holly said.

My sister broke into text-speak for the very first time all day, but she had a legitimate reason to do so. Our mother had *never* been out on a date with anyone other than our father. I mean *never*. Mom and Dad had met in high school and stuck together like two pieces of Velcro until he died five years ago. Since then, she hadn't even looked at a man.

Or so I'd thought.

"Look at them, sitting close together," I pointed out.

"This isn't their first date," Patti said. "I can tell by their body language. Better put Tom's name on our list."

"Unbelievable," Holly said, staring at Mom.

"You two go say hi," Patti said. "I'll stay here and double-check my list."

"Okay. I'm going over," Holly agreed.

"Me, too." I trailed behind, letting her pave the way in

case Mom didn't appreciate being interrupted. What was going on? As her daughter, I should know these things. After getting past the initial shock, a little part of me wasn't comfortable seeing my mother with a man other than my father.

By the time it was too late to retreat, I remembered that Mom knew about me making that emergency call to report a body in the cemetery. I bet she thought it was some prank I came up with.

But as it turned out, she was on her best behavior, par for the course in the world of dating. Everybody's at their very best in the early stages of romance, behaving better in those first few weeks than they ever will again. Men and women both do it. That's why there are books and articles devoted to how to act on dates. "Be yourself" is definitely not one of the rules, because nobody would be foolish enough to follow that one, not if they wanted things to progress in the right direction.

At least Hunter and I have known each other long enough to let it all hang out. Mostly.

"Hi, girls," Mom said, flashing a brilliant smile, one I didn't recall ever seeing before. "Say hi to Tom."

Tom, Holly, and I murmured at each other, and I could tell we all felt a bit awkward. Mom acted like she was holding court, suddenly the queen of small talk, chatting about the festival and not once mentioning my altercation with Johnny Jay. A few minutes later, while Mom and my sister were huddled in a discussion about Holly's amazing progress in returning to human-speak, I spotted a rust-colored stain on Tom's shirtsleeve.

He saw me notice and looked down. "Where did that come from?" he said, after studying the stain, sounding as surprised as I was. "I must have cut myself and didn't even notice."

Mom tuned in and dunked a napkin in a glass of ice water, saying, "We better get to that right away or it'll never come out. Here, let me." She went to town rubbing. "It would be easier if you took your shirt off."

"Now, Helen," Tom teased. "What would people think?"

Mom blushed. Holly and I took that as a cue to leave and vamoosed.

"I can't help thinking," Patti said after we ordered another round of beer, "that we need to establish a premise and conclusion."

"Okay," I said.

"Huh?" my clueless sister said.

"Let me guess," Patti said to Holly. "Not so good in the sciences, right?"

Holly just looked more confused.

"Here's our premise." Patti glanced at her notes. She's determined to be a stereotypical journalist. They love pads of paper, particularly spiral ones that they can flip. Patti flipped hers. "People don't usually lie still on the ground under black plastic unless they're dead. Conclusion then is, therefore, the person is dead."

I'd pretty much figured out that one a long time ago, but didn't say that.

"We're looking for a body, a dead one," Holly agreed. "And a killer, since most dead people don't cover themselves in plastic, right?"

"So everybody in this bar is a suspect," Patti said. "This is a big job. I hope you two are going to continue to assist me in breaking in to journalism. This could be important to my career."

"Help you?" I said. "This isn't only about you. It's about my believability." Okay, that sounded just as selfish as Patti's comment. So I corrected myself. "But mostly it's about somebody else. About finding out what happened and exactly who it happened to."

My sister gave me a long, studied look. "And you're positive of what you saw?" she asked me for what felt like the zillionth time.

"Absolutely," I said again. "I'm heading home. Tomorrow's going to be a long day."

I left Holly and Patti at the bar and walked the short distance home.

Dinky greeted me at the door, where she'd been lying on a soft blanket I'd placed there just for her. Only it wasn't looking so soft and fluffy anymore. She had barfed on the blanket, regurgitating a clot of who-knows-what that wasn't meant to pass through her digestive system—grass, stringy digestive goo, lumpy this and that. Ewww.

I knew this moment was part of my future the minute she gobbled up whatever was on the ground in the cemetery. Sure enough, I'd been right again. I hate it when I'm right, especially when it has to do with Dinky.

I swiped it up with a wad of paper towel, dumped it into the garbage, and put the blanket in the laundry bin.

Yuck, that dog was trouble.

Nine

Marauding hive robbers.

That's what I found early the next morning at one of the beehives in my backyard apiary. Dinky was on the sidelines watching, after having done her business on the kitchen floor right before I opened the door to take her out. Not the best start to the day, and now this.

One characteristic humans share with honeybees is a penchant for war, with the winner taking all the spoils. Sad, but true. And just like us when we are threatened, each hive posts guard bees at the entrance, ready to defend the colony. Their job is to identify invaders.

Robber bees will fly around a hive looking for opportunities to steal honey by getting past the guards and in through the entryway. An experienced beekeeper pays close attention.

If bees are going into the hive with honey, that's as it should be.

But in this case, bees were leaving with honey. Not

good. Not good at all. The entrance to the hive was frantic with activity.

I grabbed protective gloves and quickly ripped up some grass, digging my fingers in deep to get a grip on some dirt, too. Then I stuffed the wad around the hive entrance to make the opening smaller and hopefully easier for my bees to guard. Since they were fighting for their lives, embroiled in combat, some of my bees mistook me for the other side, so I sustained a few war wounds despite the gloves.

Ouch, they hurt.

But I felt I deserved it. This was all my fault; in the bee-yard I'm supposed to protect my wards from harm. I was supposed to be paying attention, on guard all the time. But right now I didn't have time to wallow in guilt. I had to help the bees fight back.

I grabbed a sprinkler, jammed it on top of the hive, ran to the faucet, and turned it on. Bees really hate getting wet, so a downpour of water that simulated rain was guaranteed to deter another looter attack. The rotating sprinkler gave me time to get a spray bottle filled with a mix of liquid bee smoker and water. I sprayed the heck out of the entrance.

Then I surveyed the damage. Not too bad. My bees were groggy from the bee smoke I'd sprayed. The only wet ones were those closest to the entrance and they would dry off just fine. I must have caught the invasion in time. As for my condition, not only did I have stingers stuck in me, I was also dripping wet.

Just then Hunter showed up in my driveway on his Harley.

Figures. Timing has never been kind to me.

"Am I interrupting something?" he said, swinging off the bike and strolling over, staying dry on the fringe of the sprinkler's range while I stayed in its spray, making absolutely sure that my mission had been accomplished. At least I'd scraped the stingers out of my hand.

"I know you like your bees," he continued, "but showering with them? Don't you think that's a little over the top?"

I glanced at the beehive entrance. Hopefully, everything would return to normal now. "We're bonding," I said.

"I can see that. Would you like a bar of soap? You could wash their wings and I could wash your . . ." He paused and grinned.

That did it. Before Hunter could finish, I rushed him, catching him off guard and pulling him into the sprinkler shower. He deserved a dunking for his cocky attitude. But I promptly tripped and fell. He tried to stop my fall but ended up on the ground on top of me, the sprinkler blasting on us, and Dinky, thinking it was playtime, dove in and jumped on top of us.

Hunter's face was inches from mine when he said, "I was thinking of something a little more romantic, you know, something involving a walk along the river, a soft blanket."

"You don't think this is romantic?"

"Actually, I do." Water dripped from his face as he bent the rest of the way and gave me a long, sweet kiss.

Then I remembered my creepy new next-door neighbor on one side and nosy P.P. Patti on the other with all her surveillance equipment, and I no longer felt like Hunter and I were alone in my backyard.

Rats.

I gave him a reluctant shove, rolled away, and stood up. "I'll go turn off the sprinkler and get towels," I said.

A few minutes later we were sitting out at my patio table. I'd changed into new clothes and Hunter wore my yellow bathrobe while his clothes were in my dryer.

I truly *did* try to keep him inside the house while we waited, but he insisted on coffee outside. I was afraid to tell him about Patti's telescope in case the way she used it was illegal. I didn't really want to get her in trouble, though I had questions about her voyeuristic tendencies. Like, was it actually lawful for her to watch me through binoculars or a telescope as long as she stayed on her own property? What about Peeping Tom laws? Did Patti's actions qualify?

So anyway, there we sat, sipping coffee. I'm pretty sure I saw motion in Patti's upstairs window, like a gleam of sunlight hitting a metal reflector.

"You look cute in my robe," I mentioned. "A little tight, but that's what makes it special."

"Thank you. I'll have to get one of my own. Yellow's my color."

"It really is." My eyes swept over the too-short sleeves, man-hair poking out of the cuffs. Our eyes locked. "You look good in yellow."

"Is that a pass?" Hunter asked. "Are you making sexual overtures?"

"Maybe. But not for right now. I have work to do. We'll have to take a rain check."

"No more water, please."

We both laughed and sipped coffee, content as I imagined we would be if Hunter and I had been living together for a long time. I snuck a few peeks at his feet, because he has the sexiest ones around and I'm a big fan of feet. Hunter's are manly, just the right width, a little hairy like they should be, and tanned a golden brown.

I was jarred out of my fantasy world when Hunter said, "How did last night go? Any bodies crop up?"

"Only live ones. We opted for a process of elimination at the bar."

"I checked around—police dispatch, hospitals, emergency clinics. No John Does. Nothing out of the ordinary."

"Is Johnny Jay still foaming at the mouth?"

"He passed a 'Girl Who Cries Wolf' law against you. No more responding if Story Fischer calls in an emergency."

At first I thought Hunter was still joking around, but his eyes didn't look so funny. "You're kidding, right?"

"Wish I was. You're an immediate non-emergency."

"He can't do that! What if I have a real emergency? The nerve of the guy! Wait a minute, what's a non-emergency?"

"A slow, leisurely response. They probably won't show up at all."

"I haven't abused the system, not once, ever. How often have I called in an emergency?"

Hunter rolled his eyes up in his head, which reminded me that as a matter of fact, I'd used 9-1-1 more often than most residents in our town. But legitimately! It just so happened that I'd gotten myself involved in a few sticky situations. It wasn't my fault I was a trouble magnet.

It was mostly P.P. Patti's fault. She tended to get me into hot spots.

Hunter reached over to take my hand. "I don't know what you saw last night, but whatever happened let's move past it and get on with some semblance of normalcy. Are you free later?"

"You're absolutely right," I said, not meaning a single word that was coming out of my mouth. This was too big to move past. "I'm going to forget all about it."

"Good."

"Want to watch the parade from the store's booth? Grams is riding in it as Grand Marshal."

"I have a few work-related stops that can't wait. How about meeting me at Stu's after the parade?"

"Sure. You can buy me lunch."

"Deal."

The mention of Stu's reminded me to tell Hunter the story of running into Mom on her date with Tom Stocke.

"Do you know anything about Tom?" I asked. "He's pretty closemouthed. If he's interested in my mother, I need to know his history."

Hunter chuckled. "Look at you, sticking your nose into their business. It's about time your mother had some fun."

Hunter was being kind to my mom, considering he knew what she thought of him. Like I'd mentioned, Hunter had a drinking problem way back but hasn't touched a drop for years and years. Mom doesn't trust him to stay sober, and she complains about my involvement with him every chance she gets. But, honestly, would she approve of anybody I liked? Probably not.

I glanced at my ex-husband's house and the truck sitting in the driveway. "This guy named Ford is renting out Clay's house for the weekend," I said. "Kind of a slimebag."

"Maybe your ex is having you watched," Hunter suggested.

"Hiring somebody to spy on me?" I said, shaking my head. "That's not Clay's style." Or was it? The idea certainly had possibilities. The creep I'd been dumb enough to marry had stuck around for a while after the divorce (like lingering skunk smell), claiming he hoped to reconcile, but all the time sleazing around with any female who looked his way. Like that would get me back. Finally, he'd given up and left town.

Had he sent Ford to spy on me, to see if I was living alone, still available and vulnerable?

"Want me to run the license plates?" Hunter asked.

I gave him a big grin. "You'd do that for me?"

"You know I would."

I sighed. "Thanks, but that's okay. He'll be gone soon. No big deal."

"Well, if he's scouting for Clay, let's give him something to report back. Come here."

And so I did. And we did. Nothing too racy, but enough to get the message across that I wasn't available, now or ever.

Ten

Since today was Sunday, the festival opened later than it had yesterday, to accommodate both churchgoing families and Saturday-night partiers sleeping in. Moraine's business owners recognized the fact that nobody was going to be moving too quickly today. The Harmony Festival wouldn't officially begin until eleven, with the parade at noon, and the rest of the afternoon to wander, people-watch, eat, drink, and shop.

That left plenty of time for me to get organized and ready for another busy day. I headed over to The Wild Clover to open up, and found Milly Hopticourt waiting when I arrived with Dinky on her leash. Milly had a kid's wheeled cart brimming with wildflower bouquets—some fresh flowers, others dried, which she sold every day right inside the store's entryway. She also published our monthly newsletter, filling it with recipes she created from scratch, along with gardening tips and bee-friendly suggestions I'd asked her to include.

"How about doing a smoothie in this issue?" my favorite recipe tester suggested while we arranged the bouquets. "Door County peaches are plump and juicy right now. What if I whipped up a peach smoothie with a hint of ginger?"

"I like it," I said. Milly never seemed to run out of ideas to create special recipes with whatever was in season at the time. "What else?"

"Well, corn on the cob is ripe in the fields. How about grilled corn with some kind of honey butter?"

"I can almost taste it."

"And something sweet to finish it off. I'll put on my thinking cap."

While Milly sat down behind the counter to sketch out the next newsletter, I busied myself with honey supplies to restock the outside booth. This was the last of my honey until later this month when I started harvesting, processing, and bottling this year's batch. Honey from our area of Wisconsin consists of a blend—wildflower, alfalfa, and clover nectar. We don't have large monofloral fields like they do up north with their cranberry bogs. Cranberry honey is wonderful stuff, but it isn't in my future unless I move north, something that isn't going to happen.

Today, I'd sell raw and processed honey in bear-shaped jars and regular jars and creamed honey, which is whipped so it spreads like butter. I'd created five different flavors:

- wildflower
- cherry
- cinnamon
- apple
- raspberry

Plus, I had beeswax candles in a variety of fragrances, and cranberry lip gloss (my first effort to make a gloss, and it actually turned out!). I also replenished the flavored honey sticks.

Patti came in wearing her press pass and a knowing leer. "Hunter looks good in yellow," she said, referring to my bathrobe.

"Quit spying on me, Patti."

"Just keeping tabs on my best friend, making sure you're in good hands. Which apparently you are." That comment, along with her smirk, implied that she'd been watching the whole thing, but I let it go. Not that I had much of a choice.

Patti leaned in confidentially. "Aggie Petrie is setting up outside. Same spot as yesterday. Her husband isn't with her, though. She said he's home sick."

"So?"

"So, we have our first missing person."

I thought about that for a minute. Aggie was one nasty woman. And her booth was on the sidewalk right in front of the spot where I'd had my mysterious encounter. What if she'd killed Eugene and stashed him in the cemetery, then when I wasn't looking hauled him off to bury him in her backyard? Who would be the wiser?

Patti and I looked at each other.

"What should we do?" I asked.

"Do you know where they live?"

I shook my head. "Not really, no. Colgate area, that's all I know."

"Let's work on finding out." And with that, Patti disappeared out the door.

Grams came into the store right after that looking sweet and chipper.

"I heard about your trouble last night," she said, "with a body giving you the slip like that."

"Johnny Jay couldn't have been madder."

"That boy always had a temper. Too bad he never

learned to control it. Who do you think that body belonged to? Didn't you get a good look?"

So I told Grams about how the black plastic hid the body's identity and how I'd been afraid to unmask it.

"I had no idea it would disappear," I said. Of course, if I'd known, I would have handled it differently. I still wouldn't have looked, but I would have stuck to it like glue instead of leaving it alone.

"Nobody's perfect," Grams said reassuringly. "But you're as close as they come. I'm going to get some pictures of that beehive you've got outside. It's a real winner." Her pocket camera dangled from her wrist.

I had a question for her. "Do you know where Aggie Petrie lives?"

"She's right outside the store. Why don't you ask her?"

Grams had a point, if my intentions had been a little different. But I couldn't exactly tell Aggie that I wanted her address so we could check to see if she'd offed her husband. So I punted. "I'm sending her a thank-you gift for her contribution to the festival. It's a surprise."

"Oh aren't you the sweet one," Grams gushed. "But you shouldn't tell fibs to your grandmother."

"How did you catch on so fast?"

"That's the meanest woman I've ever met. You wouldn't give her a present other than a swift kick in the pants, which is exactly what she deserves. Besides, I know that you and the other business owners tried to keep her from competing with our locals. You wouldn't encourage her."

"You're one smart cookie." Actually, I was surprised that Grams said anything negative about Aggie. Usually she has only good things to say about everybody whether they're nice people or not. She's extremely tolerant. "So, do you know where she lives?" I asked again.

"You bet I do."

By now my cousin Carrie Ann had arrived. Stanley finished setting up the observation beehive and Holly was due to help out today along with the twins, the same as yesterday. After I wrote down the Petries' address I went outside, called Patti on my cell, and gave her the information.

"Go check it out," I said to her from my end of the phone.

"You have to come along," Patti said from right behind me, scaring me into almost dropping my cell on the sidewalk.

"Patti, you have to stop sneaking up on me. I can't take much more!"

"Thank you. You don't know how much that means to me." She beamed. "That's the best compliment you could give me. Okay, let's go."

"I have work to do. The festival, remember? But here's the address."

"You have a full staff working. And Aggie's house is only twenty minutes away. How long can it take to make sure Eugene's alive and kicking? You'll be back in an hour, maybe less. Meet me at your truck."

I glanced down the street and saw Mom making her way along past the vendors. I decided that I really didn't want to be around when she arrived at our booth. Two seconds later we blew out of the back parking lot for a quick spin down the road.

The tiny burg of Colgate was on the shore of a clear, small lake that had been named Lake Five. Growing up in a fishing family, we caught a few trout on the Oconomowoc River, which runs behind my house. But if we wanted variety, we rented a boat on Lake Five. I'd caught my share of crappies, large-mouthed bass, and bluegills in that neck of the woods.

The Petries lived in a nondescript brick ranch house surrounded by mixed hardwood trees, only a stone's throw from the lake. At one time land here had been cheap, which must've been back when Aggie and Eugene bought in.

Now no one could touch those lakefront properties unless they had big bucks. Some of the locals even had to sell out due to escalating property taxes. Which made me realize that Aggie's junk business must be doing pretty decent for them to still live there. Or maybe Eugene had something going that I didn't know about.

Patti knocked on the door while I waited in the truck. My job was to act as backup, according to Patti. Whatever that meant. I saw her knock again, wait, turn back to me, shrug. Then she made hand motions to indicate I should join her.

"He's not answering," she said, which was perfectly obvious to me.

"Let's look around back." I got out of the truck and headed around to the backyard where the lake shimmered under the morning sun. I saw a dock, a tiny fishing boat tied to it, a small shed off to the side of the yard, and a good-sized garden.

Patti knocked on the back door with the same results.

"Maybe Eugene went to church," I suggested.

"Maybe she buried him in the garden," Patti said, after she walked over and studied the garden plot. "Look there." She pointed. "Fresh digging."

Now that she pointed it out, I could tell that someone had turned the soil along one edge. The dirt there was darker, wetter, and clumpier.

"A shallow grave," Patti said in a stage whisper.

"A row of vegetables recently harvested," I suggested.

Patti crouched down. "Too wide," she said.

"Fine, let's call Hunter."

Which was the wrong thing to say.

Patti gave me a scowl. She thought I relied on Hunter too much, invoking his name whenever things went wrong, which might have a teeny tiny bit of truth to it. Call me a coward, but I like to stay out of Johnny Jay's riflescope. Besides, in my last few escapades with Patti, I'd been the one taken in for questioning and threatened with charges. Not her. Even though she's the one who deserved it.

"Well," I said, "we can't call Johnny Jay. He wouldn't show up after last night's episode. In fact, he has some kind of standing order for dispatch to ignore me. Hunter's our only choice." Which wasn't exactly true. Our other choice was that we could forget this whole thing. I'd only been humoring Patti anyway. I didn't expect to actually find Eugene's body six-feet under.

"We'll take care of this without the help of any man," Patti said, slurring the word *man* like it was the latest dirty word. She went to the shed, opened its unlocked door, disappeared inside, and reappeared with a shovel.

She dug into the garden soil, but hadn't taken more than a few shovelfuls before her cell phone rang. She stopped. "Here," she said, handing me the shovel so she could answer her phone. "Hang on to this a minute."

While she moved off, talking low on the phone while I tried to listen in, I slid my hand across the handle of the shovel and felt a rough spot.

Jeez! A splinter. Right over the stinger wound from this morning. That really hurt. I pulled the sliver out, my hand throbbing with pain.

I turned over the wooden handle and noticed that the wood had a gouged spot, like an animal had chewed on it. That's one of the reasons why most of us keep our shed doors closed up tight at night, to keep out gnawing creatures.

So there I stood, knee-deep in garden dirt, holding that shovel, and who should I see round the corner but Eugene Petrie!

He certainly wasn't dead—far from it—but we were seconds away from that non-breathing state ourselves. Because Eugene had a shotgun clutched across his chest in an I-mean-business sort of way, and he was coming fast. "Freeze!" he yelled at us, planting his feet and aiming the gun.

I froze like an ice statue. Over on the edge of the garden, so did Patti.

"Hands up in the air where I can see them."

"It's me, Eugene—Story Fischer."

"My eyesight is just fine." He still had the shotgun on his shoulder, taking aim. "I said hands up in the air." We obliged.

A woman called out from the house next door. Once I pried my eyes away from Eugene, I saw it was his daughter-in-law, Alicia, heading our way. "What happened?" she asked him.

Eugene eyed us. "I don't know yet, but I'm about to find out what they're up to." I remembered that Eugene had been in the marines when he said, "A little waterboarding ought to open them up like clams."

Waterboarding! I knew what that was. Torture, that's what. Forcing a person (in this case, me) to inhale water and making them feel like they're drowning. Not my idea of a good time. Plus, I was pretty sure waterboarding was totally illegal.

I glanced at Patti, hoping she had an idea, one that would get us out of this mess. But all she did was stare back at me, her eyes wide. Next time we dig for dead bodies, we really need to have a backup plan in place in case we get caught. If there is a next time.

"We heard you were sick," I said to Eugene, "so we stopped by to check on you. Patti noticed you were starting a new row, a second crop of something, so we decided to help you out by getting it ready for your next planting. Weren't we Patti?"

Patti nodded and gulped. "I have press protection," she squeaked, holding up her homemade press pass like that was going to help. If anything, playing the reporter card might have the opposite effect.

"It doesn't sound like much of a crime to me," Alicia said. "Almost neighborly."

Eugene didn't look so sure, but swung the gun clear of us. "Get out of here," he said. "Next time, I'll fill you with buckshot."

And that's how we got out of that one.

Eleven

"Don't ever ask me to help you again," I warned Patti on the return trip. "I understand you wanting to ingratiate yourself with *The Distorter . . .*"

"*Reporter,*" Patti corrected me.

". . . but leave me out of your next harebrained scheme."

"You did a nice job with backup," Patti offered, sounding contrite.

"As far as I'm concerned, from this moment forward, I never saw a body in the cemetery. I made up the whole thing to get attention, just like Lori Spandle said. I'm done."

Once I made that declaration, I felt an enormous weight lift from my shoulders, one I hadn't even been aware of until now. Nobody had believed me anyway. Except Patti, and because of her I'd been threatened with a weapon and waterboarding. I needed some semblance of normalcy— the festival, the store, time with my man—not all this intrigue.

I pulled into my parking spot behind The Wild Clover. The streets were bumper to bumper with cars searching for parking spaces as close as possible. People were staking out parade-viewing spots with lawn chairs and coolers.

Patti went off nosing for news, and I joined my staff at the booth, where the sound of sales ringing up had my spirit doing Zumba. I snagged a honey stick and sucked on it as I people-watched, stepping in to help whenever I was needed.

Carrie Ann's ex and her two kids came by, and they picked out honey sticks before settling near the curb.

Milly wandered over and showed me a scarf she'd purchased.

"It's lovely," I said, thinking I'd like one, too. Scarves are fun accessories. "Where did you get it?"

"Right next to you, at Aggie's booth."

What? From the junk lady? "Really?" I said.

"Her daughter-in-law makes them," Milly said, sliding into a lawn chair she'd used to mark her territory first thing this morning.

Holly showed up just then and admired the scarf. "Cool," she said. "I love the crystal beads woven into the fringe."

"Me, too," Milly said. "Especially these emerald beads. Emerald is one of my favorite colors."

People started milling around, still buying, although that would taper off once the parade came by.

As in the past, the parade participants lined up south of town close to the police station. The bands, vehicles, floats, and the rest would march up Main Street past all the businesses, then cross the bridge over the Oconomowoc River and disband where Creamery Road and Rustic Road forked. Right before the parade began, the police contingency would shut down Main on both ends, and cars trying to pass through would have to wait or find an alternate route.

Lori Spandle and her sister walked past. DeeDee was decked out in a purple pantsuit, a yellow sash announcing her Honey Queen title, and a sparkling crown. DeeDee usually went more for the grunge look. Today she was faking respectable really well.

Lori stopped in front of Holly, Milly, and me. "Doesn't DeeDee look great?" she said.

"She actually looks halfway decent for a change. Who dressed her?" Holly asked, putting some snotty in her tone.

"It certainly wasn't one of you two." Lori glared, but before she could come up with a retort, Holly continued.

"You know, that guy Ford who's staying in the house next to Story is pretty hot. Thanks to you renting to him, Lori, my sister has a new blossoming relationship."

I swung my head her way, astonished by that comment.

"Very funny," Lori said with narrowing eyes. "Story's with Hunter."

"Not since last night," Holly said, suggesting something pretty intimate had transpired.

I opened my mouth to correct her big-time, but stopped when she gave me a slight warning head-shake.

"We'll see about that," Lori said, hustling DeeDee away.

As we watched them go, I finally realized what my sister had been up to and laughed. Lori has had a one-sided competition going on in regards to my men ever since high school. She always wanted them and would do anything she could to steal them away from me. She'd made a play for Hunter when she found out we were seeing each other, but he'd put her down hard, knowing what she was like and what it took to get a message through to her. I felt a momentary sympathy pang for Grant and all he'd put up with from his wife.

If he even knew, that is. Our town chair wasn't the sharpest knife.

Holly giggled. "She'll be after Ford before the parade starts," she said. "He doesn't stand a chance."

"From what I've seen of him, he won't run fast or far," I agreed.

A few minutes later, I was munching on a roasted cob of corn when I heard something explode, making loud machine-gun-like popping sounds, rat-a-tat-tatting. Immediately after that, the band started up.

Stanley beamed proudly and said, "That was Noel's contribution."

"The opening kabooms?"

Stanley nodded. "Your mother decided to put my grandson's special talents to good use."

"That kid better major in chemistry."

The parade came into view with Grand Marshal Grams leading it from her seat of honor in a red Mustang convertible. She gave me her special parade wave as she passed. She had "elbow, elbow, wrist, wrist, touch your pearls, and blow a kiss" down pat. In between, she snapped pictures of the crowd.

Next came every single fire engine in the entire community. Halfway through the line of engines, I turned to Holly and said, "I'm going home. Dinky's in my office. Will you give her a little walk after the parade?"

"Sure, but don't you want to see the rest of the parade?"

"I just wanted to see Grams. But I can't bear the thought of DeeDee Becker representing the local honey industry, even if it's only for one day. She must be due along soon and I just can't stand to watch."

"I hear you," my sister said. "I should have brought some overripe tomatoes."

With that imagery in my mind, I slid through between two fire engines and turned down my block.

Just in time to see Lori Spandle sneaking up the driveway where Ford's truck was still parked.

Unbelievable! She sure didn't waste any time!

I decided to sneak right along behind her. With luck, I'd get a damaging picture on my cell phone for future blackmail. I *did* have a moment where I felt totally juvenile. But I rarely got the best of Lori, mainly because I had better things to do with my life. She's the one who spent all her time and limited brainpower trying to ruin me.

But knowing the enemy was important.

So sneaking after Lori was a given.

I scooted behind Ford's truck and peeked over the hood. I saw Lori knock, and when Ford didn't answer, she tried to open the door.

Locked.

Maybe Ford was at the festival, taking in the parade. Lori dug around in her purse and came up with a set of keys. Of course she'd have keys. Lori was a real estate agent and this was one of her listings. But still, should she let herself in while the house was rented out? I thought not.

She wiggled a key into the lock and popped the door open. What was she going to do—wait for him in her panties?

I slithered over to a window and hugged the wall, peering in. I saw Lori walk past. I plastered myself against the side of the house, facing my yard. Patti's house was quiet, not a bit of motion in the upstairs window, not a single gleam from her telescope lens. Good. The last thing I needed was Patti butting in. Or videotaping me.

Before I could decide what to do next, I heard Lori scream from inside the house, even over all the noise from the parade down the block. The bands and vehicles and clapping and shouting didn't mask it. Every hair on my body went on high alert.

Seconds later, Lori blew past me, slamming out of the house and hurrying down the street with one hand clutching her chest and the other one over her mouth like she had a terrible case of acid reflux.

She hadn't seen me.

Now what?

What could she possibly have discovered to cause that kind of reaction?

And more important, did I have the courage to go inside and find out?

I forced myself through the door Lori had left unlocked and wide open.

The kitchen didn't hold any secrets except for evidence of Ford's occupancy—empty beer cans and beef jerky wrappers, a camping table and chair. Same with the bedroom—a sleeping bag and the stink of B.O. and unwashed clothes.

But when I got to the front of the house, I discovered what had Lori running scared.

Ford's body was stuffed into the fireplace like an enormous log.

Twelve

This wasn't my first dead body. I've been to my share of funerals just like everybody else. And I've even seen death right after it happened, before the funeral home's mortician had a chance to put things back in place. The older I get, the more I'm confronted with death and dying. But it never gets easier.

This wasn't even the first time I'd seen *this* particular dead body, since I was pretty sure that I'd just found my missing corpse from the cemetery.

But this *was* the first time I'd been around a body that was obviously, unquestionably the victim of foul play. People don't crawl into fireplaces to die from natural causes. Even if it wasn't for that, Ford's contorted face, which was turned my way—wouldn't you know it—wasn't pretty. Not that it had been good-looking to begin with, but now it was positively gruesome.

I was seriously flipped out, but refused to handle the situation by running away like Lori had. I moved back a few steps, stopping at the doorway where I concentrated on avoiding looking directly at what was left of Ford while considering my next move. I'd have to alert the authorities. That is, if Lori hadn't done so already. The festival applecart—the one my mother demanded that I watch—was seriously tipped over, contents rolling all over the place and there wasn't a thing I could do about it.

In the distance, I heard the marching band strike up "Ain't No Mountain High Enough," which was going to become my mother's theme song as soon as she found out. There really wouldn't be a mountain high enough to keep her from getting to me.

The parade meant Moraine's cops would be providing security close by. A good thing, considering the circumstances. Better yet, Johnny Jay would be decked out in his finest, pompously driving the chief's special vehicle in the parade. That meant I might be able to circumvent him, at least initially.

First I tried calling Hunter. We'd planned to meet at Stu's Bar and Grill in a little while, but that wasn't going to happen. He didn't answer.

Next I tried to punch in the emergency number. Nine. One. One. Three little numbers. Why was it so hard? Partly because my hands were shaking, but mainly because I suddenly realized that the killer might still be close by. He could be in a closet or around a corner, getting impatient to escape, me standing between him and freedom.

Probably not, I said to myself edging out the door. Ford didn't look like he'd gone to home sweet home in the last little while. But, really, what did I know? I decided to boogie out of there at that point, joining the Lori Spandle scaredy-cat club.

Finally my numb fingers hit the right three digits. "We have an emergency," I said into the phone as I hurried toward Main Street, concentrating on keeping my voice calm and collect. *We* sounded good. I wasn't alone with this situation.

The dispatcher said, "Your name, please."

"Story Fischer," I said too late to take it back. "I mean, Patti Dwyre."

"Sorry, Story, but we've been warned about you."

"I re-found the dead body. You know, the one I lost last night. I mean, I didn't lose it, it . . . uh, never mind. Has anybody called in a dead body in the last few minutes? Because I wasn't the only witness."

"You're the only caller."

Darn Lori! All she cared about was herself and her stupid image, which in my opinion wasn't in very good shape to begin with, so why should she bother? I was talking fast now, telling the dispatcher location details. I finished with, "And this time when you come, you can use your lights and sirens."

Maybe if I said that, they wouldn't use them. You never knew with our local law enforcement. I still didn't want to destroy the last few hours of the Harmony Festival if I could help it, but we had a genuine emergency on our hands and maybe even a killer in the crowd. "Yes, lights and sirens would be good."

"Okay, then," the dispatcher said, and I swear I heard a patronizing tone. "I'll pass this information on to the chief just as soon as the parade is over."

"What?"

But the dispatcher had disconnected.

Dang. Didn't anyone believe me?

I burst onto Main Street to see the tail end of the parade heading north past Stu's and over the bridge. People were already folding up their chairs and moving away from the curb, packing up their cars, oblivious to a dead man stuffed in a fireplace a short block away.

Then I had another frightening thought. My reputation couldn't afford another missing body. I was absolutely sure that I'd tripped over Ford the night before. Someone had hauled him to the house and stuffed him in the fireplace.

What if that same person moved him again before I got back? Before anyone from the police department could confirm my story?

In a state of total confusion, I did a 180 and ran back to the house.

Ford was still there, same place, same position, wearing the same Hawaiian shirt as last time I'd seen him. My stomach did a flip. I talked it out of doing anything more than that.

For the first time ever, I thought: Why did it have to be me? Why couldn't this have happened to somebody else? Why couldn't someone else report a major crime for a change?

I muttered bad thoughts about Lori, who should have been in the hot seat, not me.

By some miracle, my head cleared momentarily, and I remembered my sister. She was fused to her cell phone like a robot to its control panel. She'd answer for sure. I called Holly.

"Get over to Clay's house as quick as you can," I said, so glad to hear her voice on the other end. "And bring backup. Stanley! Bring Stanley. I found the body. It's Ford. And he's dead. Oh, and have Stanley call the police. And just in case Noel's with him, tell Stanley not to bring him along."

What seemed like ten years later, Holly and Stanley arrived. We met in the driveway next to Ford's truck.

"Stanley," I said, "will you go in and take a look at the body in case it disappears again? I want a reliable witness just to be on the safe side."

"I can do that," he said.

"It's not pretty."

"I've seen it all," Stanley assured me, walking toward the door.

"He's in the fireplace."

"You're kidding, right?" Stanley said, skidding to a stop. "Never mind. I can tell you aren't. Be right back."

And he disappeared inside.

Holly, who has been known to wrestle a shoplifter to the ground and use some amazing pinning techniques and brute force against said perpetrator, leaned heavily on Ford's truck and said, "I feel faint."

I ignored her, since obviously I was the one who should pass out, not her. "Did Stanley call the cops like I asked?"

She nodded.

"Well, where are they?" I didn't hear a single siren. "You'd think they would respond pronto. They're right down the street."

"It's gridlock. All the parade vehicles and floats are jammed up and cars are trying to get out. Nothing's moving."

Figures. In our small town we joke among ourselves that none of us better have an emergency during certain times. Like opening day of hunting season. Or St. Patrick's day, which we consider a national holiday worth closing our businesses for. Now, we'll have to add the Harmony Festival to the list of do-not-bother-calling-cuz-nobody's-going-to-respond days.

About the same time, Tom Stocke, Mom's new "friend," showed up. "What's going on?" he asked. "Stanley lit out like his pants were on fire. One minute, we're talking about bees, the next he's gone."

"Dead body," Holly said, muffled since by now she was sitting on the ground with her head between her legs. I knew what she was saying, but it sounded like *debitty*." Tom looked confused.

"Stanley's checking something out inside. We're waiting for the police," I said. "I don't know what's taking them so long."

"I saw a squad car with its lights on trying to get through traffic," Tom said. "They'll be here soon."

"Maybe they should get smart and leave their vehicles behind. Walking a few blocks wouldn't kill them. They could have been here a long time ago," I groused.

Tom glanced at Holly before saying to me, "Is your sister okay?"

"Nothing to worry about."

"I'll go in and help Stanley," Tom offered, and went inside the house before I could warn him.

Then Holly had a text-speak setback, starting with an easy one, OMG! (*Oh My God!*), and ending with some acronyms I've never heard before, which surprised me since I'd really studied up when Holly was flinging them around left and right.

"Take it easy," I said, which she probably interpreted as EZ. "You don't want to have a relapse."

"Why? Why? Why?" my melodramatic sister said, lifting her head long enough to give me grief. "Do you have to get involved in every single crime in this town?"

God, she sounded just like Mom! Like I could help it that I tripped over a body in the cemetery and discovered it later in a fireplace! Sometimes my family wasn't one bit supportive. I expected it from Mom, but Holly?

"The only thing I'm guilty of is finding the body," I said defensively. "I didn't kill him."

"Is it really that Ford guy?"

"It's him."

"Gad!"

Patti appeared on the scene. I was surprised it took her so long. This time she didn't sneak up. She barreled into our group. I brought her up to speed on events. Patti didn't ask a single question, which was good because I only had abbreviated sentences left in me.

"Has anybody seen Lori?" I asked.

"I did," Patti said. "She came through the crowd like a rocket launching. Highly suspicious behavior, so I got a picture of her, see?" Patti held up a small camera and showed me a photograph of Lori looking wigged out—big round eyes to go with her pumpkin head.

"That's exactly how she looked when she left the scene," I said. "Fleeing the scene of a crime is illegal, isn't it?"

"Only if you're the one who committed the crime," Patti said authoritatively, like she knew everything regarding a citizen's legal responsibilities. I was pretty sure nobody could walk away from a crime scene without getting into some kind of trouble.

"Hang on to that picture anyway," I advised. "You never know." Then I added, "Maybe she did something bad."

I ought to let Lori hang out to dry instead of offering the truth. Her fingerprints were sure to show up. Unfortunately, she didn't have time to kill Ford and stuff him in the fireplace. I'd been spying on her and knew that.

A picture of Lori certainly wasn't hard evidence that she'd committed any kind of crime, but I'd love to see her explain why she hadn't reported finding the dead body, like any responsible citizen would.

Finally, the first squad car arrived. I saw Hunter striding down the street toward us. This was Johnny Jay's turf, so Hunter wouldn't interfere with the investigation unless he was asked to, which wasn't going to happen. That was fine with me, because then he'd be available to support me, watch my back, keep the sharks at bay.

He must have sensed I needed a hug, because that's the first thing he did after searching my eyes. Looking over his shoulder during the hug, I saw Johnny Jay running down the street. That man, in spite of his bulky size, could really travel.

I bucked up to go a few rounds with him.

But then Stanley and Tom came out of the house. Apparently Tom didn't have the same steely stomach and strong nervous system that Stanley did, because he wasn't too steady on his feet. In fact, Stanley seemed to be holding him up.

The first thing Stanley said to the gathering crowd was, "Holy moly, you know who that is in there? That's Tom's brother!"

Thirteen

❧

Somebody got a lawn chair for Tom and he collapsed into it. Johnny Jay's police force went into action, some going into the house, some separating us witnesses from the gawkers and herding the latter group down the street where he'd instructed his men to close off Willow Street and make sure nobody crossed to that side unless they belonged there.

"We're going to use your house as a base of operation, Fischer," Johnny Jay said to me. "We need to take statements and try to figure out this mess while the team finishes up here. After that, we'll all walk around and reenact everybody's movements."

"I'm part of the press," Patti said. "You better let me come along. I have a pass." She held out her homemade press pass.

"Beat it, Dwyre," the chief said.

As we filed along the sidewalk, I saw Mom and Grams at the end of the street having a discussion with one of the cops responsible for keeping people away. I could hear Mom arguing with him.

"I'm one of the *town officials* for the festival," she said, putting extra emphasis on titles. "And this is the *Grand Marshal*. We have every right to go through."

The cop shook his head.

"Go home, Mrs. Fischer," Johnny Jay called out. "You, too, Wallace," he said to Hunter.

"I'm staying," Hunter said.

"And what makes you think I'm going to let you?"

"Professional courtesy." Hunter winked at me as if to say he was giving it a good try, but I shouldn't hold my breath.

"This is my jurisdiction and my rules. You want courtesy, go to church."

And with that, the chief slammed my front door right in Hunter's face. Johnny Jay had Stanley, Tom, Holly, and me in his spiderweb. We waited for him to start eating us alive.

"We're going to take you one at a time," he said. "My officer here is going to make sure you don't compare notes while you wait your turn. And your stories better hang together."

"I don't feel so good," Holly said.

"Boo-hoo," said our friendly police chief.

And that's how I spent the rest of the afternoon; telling my side of things, rewalking every single step I'd taken, explaining what I'd touched, all the little details that I hated having to remember. After that, I put special emphasis on asking why it had taken so long for the cavalry to arrive, a topic I considered extremely important.

"It's your fault your department responded so slowly," I said to Johnny Jay. "You can't discriminate against me by refusing to respect the importance of my phone calls. I had a real emergency on my hands. I pay taxes just like everybody else and I deserve better treatment. I ought to file a complaint. Besides, I told you Lori Spandle was the first one inside. Why don't you have her yet?"

"That's none of your business."

Right up until the end, he kept all us witnesses completely segregated with cops watching our every move. I didn't learn anything new about Lori Spandle. But I wanted to know how it happened that Tom's brother showed up in town and hid from sight at my ex's house. Really, I had a lot of questions.

Johnny Jay tried to get the final word in, as usual. "I don't want anybody involved in this case socializing together until we get to the bottom of this. And no talking about the case among yourselves."

"You can't order me to stay away from my sister," I said.

Johnny Jay didn't reply, he just dangled his stupid hand-cuffs as a silent warning.

He could take a flying leap as far as I was concerned. I'd found a murdered body in the house next door and that fact made me involved whether he liked it or not. What if a serial killer was murdering everybody on Willow Street? What if Patti and I were the next targets?

Okay, maybe that was a little over the top, but (thankfully) it isn't every day that a person next door is murdered. Lots of things go through a neighbor's mind. Like am I next? Self-preservation steps up to the plate intent on slamming a home run.

I made a to-do list:

- Find out why Lori Spandle hadn't behaved like a responsible citizen and get her in trouble.

- Learn more about Tom Stocke's background, including his mysterious brother.

- Avoid Johnny Jay like the plague.

- Hide from Mom, who was going to feed me to the wolves for getting involved in another awkward position that in her repetitive words "reflects poorly on the family reputation."

Holly was in deep, too, which helped my case with the family matriarch. Although my sister's role was minor compared to mine. And once I thought about it, I realized she wouldn't be involved at all if I hadn't called her and told her to come to the crime scene. Shoot. Mom would *not* be happy about that, either.

And what about how no one believed me last night when I found Ford's body the first time? Here it was, right in plain view. A few people owed me apologies for doubting my word. At least we now knew who the body in the cemetery belonged to. And that no one was buried in the Petries' backyard.

When I finally returned to The Wild Clover, the vendors were packing up. I couldn't help noticing how unhappy they looked.

Aggie Petrie summed it up for everyone. "I lost sales for the whole blasted afternoon, thanks to that corpse. And you"—this was her talking to me—"couldn't you have just left it there till after the festival? You're as dumb as dirt."

I sorta took offense at that, but after considering the source, I decided not to react to it. Some things just aren't worth fighting over. And I've been called worse things than "dumb as dirt."

Aggie wasn't through with me. "Speaking of dirt, I'd hate to be the one to mention garden dirt. You owe me. For ruining sales. For trespassing on our property."

Her son shot me a glare, but I wasn't sure if that was because he blamed me for their lack of sales or because his dad caught me in his yard under suspicious circumstances. Chalk one more up to Patti and her brilliant ideas. And as usual, I'd been stuck holding the bag. Or in this case, the shovel.

"I was trying to be helpful," I lied, sticking with the weak story Patti and I concocted. Or rather I came up with when I was forced to improvise. "Helping prepare your garden for the next round of planting."

"Horse hockey. Here's what we'll accept and there's no room for negotiating."

Jeez, this woman was impossible. Now she was making demands.

Eugene stood off to the side, acting like he wasn't part of this couple. Almost tame, as he usually was when his wife had the floor. Not at all like the Rambo he'd been when he drew on Patti and me.

Aggie had her cane and she was tapping it at her side when she said, "You'll let me leave my booth set up right like it is for a week. I'll sell to your customers and if I'm lucky I'll make up for lost revenue. Take it or leave it."

"I'll leave it." No way could I look at Aggie every morning for a whole week or deal with her rotten personality.

"Then I'm calling the police chief and pressing charges against you for trespassing, and I'll throw in destruction of property right along with it. And anything else that sounds good."

"I changed my mind," I said. "I'll take it."

Fourteen

The Wild Clover closes at five on Sundays. Due to all the excitement, my workday had barely begun before it was over. Luckily the twins, Brent and Trent, and Carrie Ann had kept the store and booth running smoothly, although business had been light once Ford's death was broadcast. Everybody congregated down the street, closer to Willow, where residents and visitors alike traded opinions, predicted outcomes, and hoped to overhear some of the juicier details.

The locals hadn't seen this much action downtown since two years ago when a group of kids smoking behind the post office had burned the old building to the ground. That particular incident still comes up on a regular basis, but it doesn't come close to comparing to this latest tragedy.

"I took care of Dinky while you were away," Carrie Ann said when I walked into the store. "In case you want to thank me."

"Thanks. Really. I totally forgot about her."

"A raise would be a good thank-you gift. I'm doing a manager's work half the time. You're always gone. I keep the place running."

Where was this coming from? I muttered something noncommittal. Carrie Ann's work performance went up and down depending on her sobriety, which could change as fast as Wisconsin weather. And it wasn't as though she didn't have reliable coworkers right there with her.

"Besides," Carrie Ann said, "Dinky peed on my foot."

"That means she likes you."

"I'm not so sure of that," Carrie Ann said, gathering up her purse and car keys. "You should train her better."

"I'm too busy chasing down dead people," I said.

Carrie Ann smiled then. "You've been in it up to your armpits, that's for sure. Hope you have a better evening. See you tomorrow."

Patti slipped in as Carrie Ann walked out.

"I did some digging for information on Tom," she said.

"Already? That was fast."

"An investigator doesn't let grass grow."

"Tell me."

"Before Tom moved to Moraine," Patti told me, "he lived in northern Illinois with his wife. Then one day she ran off with another man."

"How awful for Tom," I said, really meaning it. I knew a thing or two about infidelity, thanks to an ex-husband who thought it was a perfectly acceptable form of physical exercise.

"Worse, she ran off with Tom's brother."

"Ford? That's awful."

"Ford was a big-time loser."

"Sounds like Tom's wife was, too." I thought about what a jerk both she and Ford had been, then said, "That doesn't explain why Tom still wears his wedding ring. I would have thrown it away."

Patti shrugged. "That I don't know. She died from an

aneurysm a few years ago. In the meantime, Ford has been behind bars more than he's been out. Petty crimes for the most part, but they start adding up. The guy was poison."

"How did you find out so much personal information?" I asked.

"I called Tom's dead wife's sister. Once she got started, I thought she'd never quit."

And with those bits of juicy gossip, Patti bounced out the door.

Hunter came along as I was locking up. I'd planned on getting some paperwork done in my office, paying a few overdue bills, late not because I didn't have the money to pay, but because I really hated detail work. Hunter was the perfect excuse to procrastinate even further.

In the back room I shared what I knew about the situation at Clay's house, which was mostly my side of the story. Hunter knew very little. Johnny Jay had clamped down on information imparted to other law-enforcement agencies, and no one in the chief's department was talking to anybody outside, on pain of termination.

"I feel bad for Tom Stocke," I said, deciding to share a chair with Hunter. I moved to his lap, missing those high school years when we both were lean and could actually fit side by side together in a chair. "I can't imagine how Tom felt, finding his brother like that. He's never mentioned a thing about his family. Only it isn't so odd, once you know about his sordid past."

Hunter had a pained look on his face and it wasn't because I was too heavy. "Ah, man, Story, I really dislike gossiping, you know that."

"I know you do, but you'll want to hear this."

So I related all that Patti had shared about the triangle between Tom, his wife, and Ford.

"I knew there was something off about Ford when I met him," I said, "but I couldn't put my finger on why he gave me the creeps. If he was such bad news, the list of suspects could be long." I didn't really believe that. The name of a suspect had already hit me like a pile of bricks when I found out Ford was Tom's brother, but I hadn't wanted to believe it then and I didn't want to believe it now. I verbalized it anyway. "Tom did it, didn't he?"

"Stop, okay, please," Hunter said, not liking what he was hearing from me. He sighed. "You can't make an assumption like that. The entire town is going to think exactly the same thing you do once his history is made public."

"There's no other explanation."

"That we know of at the moment," Hunter added. "Things aren't always what they appear to be."

Yeah, right, sometimes they're even worse. Tom looked like a bad guy, with that crooked nose. And he dodged any questions about his past, which was turning out to be checkered. And his brother had looked even more like a wanted poster.

"What should I do?" I said. "He's seeing my mother."

"What you have to do is let Johnny Jay do his job," Hunter said to me. I hopped off his lap and moved to a metal chair next to my desk, too upset about my mother and the whole situation to sit still. Dinky, lying up against the closed door, looked up when I moved, then went back to licking her paws.

"I wouldn't think of interfering with the police chief's investigation," I said, really meaning it at that moment. "I just hope he moves quickly. This whole thing is chilling me to the center of my bones."

"I'll just have to warm you up," Hunter offered. "Come back over here." But before I could consider taking him up on that, his phone rang. When he hung up, our brief interlude was over. "Gotta go to work," he said. He saw the big question mark on my face. "No, the phone call doesn't have anything to do with what happened here today. It's county work."

"How long will you be gone?"

"Don't wait up," he said, smiling.

After Hunter left, I walked home with Dinky trotting along on her leash. As hard as I tried, I couldn't get Tom and Ford out of my mind. I made a quick salad with some of the vegetables from my garden and ate dinner outside. The garden needed attention and I thought I should look in on my bees, make sure my girls were happy. Getting back into my regular routine, and getting a little dirt under my fingernails, might clear my head so I could sleep tonight.

For the next several hours until the sunset, I worked hard. First, I cleaned up the honey house, my sweet little shed where I harvested and bottled honey products. I sterilized jars, getting them ready for the upcoming honey harvest, which promised to be a bumper crop.

Then I weeded the garden, hoeing between the rows of beets and Brussels sprouts and my greens. I like to grow mustard greens, arugula, and a wild assortment of leaf lettuces. And I love tomatoes. The tomato vines were heavy with fruit, still green but starting to ripen.

Working my muscles felt good after the stressful day I'd had.

But later when I tried to fall asleep, I still couldn't get Tom and Ford out of my mind.

Or should I call them Cain and Abel?

Fifteen

❦

Dinky and I arrived at Grams's house before the sun rose, but I knew she and Mom wouldn't mind. They're the early-to-bed, early-to-rise, get-the-worm type of women. Peeking in the screen door, I saw Grams already at the stove, making blueberry pancakes, my favorite breakfast food. She wore a brightly colored flowery robe and had a fresh daisy tucked into her bun.

I love anything with blueberries—pancakes, buckle, pie, crisp, you name it. My ex-husband had hated them, which should have been a big tip-off that there was something majorly wrong with him. Shaking Clay out of my mind, I made a mental note to talk to Milly about putting a blueberry recipe in the next newsletter.

"Come in, sweetie. Is everything okay?" Grams looked worried. My early appearance in her kitchen must have seemed like the dreaded late night phone call, the one that always brings bad news.

"I'm fine," I said quickly to reassure her, then took a seat at the table in front of a Ball jar filled with maple syrup. Grams put a steaming cup of coffee in front of me. "Where's Mom?" I asked.

"She's fixing herself up. She'll be out for breakfast soon. Want pancakes?"

"You bet."

Grams eyed me up, still suspicious. Well, to tell the truth, since Mom moved in with her, I didn't exactly pop in on a regular basis. Mostly just when they invited me, and even then I made more excuses than appearances. Mom and I crossed swords more often than the Vikings raided coastal towns. Why would I willingly go into that arena?

The only reason I made an exception this morning was that I wanted to save my mother from Tom Stocke. I couldn't let her continue to see him until this whole business was behind us. I might say a lot of negative things about my mother, but deep down I love her immensely and would never stand back and let someone dangerous near her.

"Hey, sweet puppy," Grams said to Dinky. "Want a treat?" And Dinky trotted right over to where she knew Grams had a stash of liver snaps.

While I was waiting for Mom and pancakes, Holly called my cell, giving me the same kind of scare I'd just given Grams. My sister isn't usually functional until closer to noon. I hustled outside for privacy and confirmed that Holly was fine except she couldn't sleep because yesterday's drama continued in her dreams. Or nightmares.

I told her why I was over at Mom's, and that led to relating the inside information I had on Tom thanks to Patti.

"Mom isn't going to be happy with you if you interfere," Holly said. "Not one bit."

"What else is new? I just want her to be careful around Tom, that's all."

"I've been analyzing Mom, and I'm pretty sure she's been depressed."

"Depressing, you mean?"

"No. Depressed. She has all the symptoms of someone suffering from depression. Ask her if she's been sleeping. Or if she's had suicidal thoughts."

"I'm not asking her that." I really wish my sister would give up with the psychoanalyzing stuff. She had me almost convinced I really was passive aggressive. I sighed into the phone before saying, "She's always been like this."

"Only since Dad died."

"She's a pessimist, that's all. She can't help it. She'll always be like this." As I said it, I couldn't help noticing I'd started to sound just like my mother. Mom didn't believe that people could change. Was I thinking the same way? Jeez.

Holly went on, "Don't you notice how nice she's been since dating Tom?"

Now that I thought about it, Mom hadn't given me any grief recently except our brief encounter over the observation beehive. Was Holly onto something?

"So you think she just needed a little romance in her life?" I said. What a simple solution to the conflict between us that would be. "If she has a love interest in her life, then she'll be sweet and loving to me?"

"That's what I think. You better leave things alone."

"Let her go out with a possible killer?"

"I would," my sister said and hung up.

Grams stuck her head out the door. "Your pancakes are ready," she said.

Behind Grams, I saw Mom come into the kitchen. She already had her makeup on. And she was wearing a brand-new shade of lipstick, cranberry colored.

"Hi, Story dear," Mom said from the doorway, causing me to trip and fall on the steps, banging my left knee. "It's those things you wear on your feet," she said. "Thongs are the worst footwear."

"We call them flip-flops now," I said, bouncing up,

going in, and sitting down at the table. "Thongs are skimpy underwear."

"What's the reason for this lovely surprise visit?" Mom had a smile on her face. Now that Holly had pointed it out, I couldn't believe the change in her.

"Is Mom sick?" I asked Grams. "Why is she in such a good mood?"

"She's been like this since the other night." Grams flipped a pancake in the air. "Since her last date with Tom Stocke, but she's keeping the juicy-fruit details to herself."

Mom actually blushed. "And the poor man just lost his estranged brother in a horrible, horrible way," she said, all sadness and concern now. "Has there been any new news? Did they catch the killer yet?"

"Nothing on the early morning news," Grams said. "I bet the killer is long gone. They don't stick around waiting to get caught, you know."

It was obvious that Mom and Grams hadn't come to the same conclusion I had. "Maybe someone local did it," I ventured, easing into the subject, hoping someone else in this kitchen would mention Tom before I had to.

Grams put a plate of blueberry pancakes on the table and sat down. "That's not possible," Grams said. "Nobody around here would do such a thing." That's my grandmother, never thinking a mean-spirited thought about anybody, even about the bottom-of-the-barrel kind of humans.

"That's right," Mom agreed. "Besides, nobody around here would have done it that way, leaving him in a fireplace like that. A local would have hauled him out to the woods and buried him under a pine tree. I mean, if one of them had a reason, which they don't, they would have handled it completely different."

"Was he shot?" Grams wanted to know.

"I don't know," I said. Then I thought about Grams's question, and what might have really caused his death. I hadn't seen any blood around his body. And Patti and I didn't find any blood the night before, nor had Ben been able to pick up the scent even with his keen sense of smell. If not shot, then what? Poisoned?

We dug into the pancakes, so talk at the table came to a halt, which suited me just fine, since I needed to regroup and decide how to present my warning to Mom without losing the sweet new mother sitting next to me.

Nothing simple and easy came to mind. Instead, I ate so many pancakes I couldn't move. That's the problem with pancakes—they're delicious, but they sink to the bottom of your stomach like chunks of concrete.

"The Wild Clover opens soon," Grams said. "Who's taking care of business?"

"The twins. I'm really going to miss them when they go back to college. Then it'll only be Carrie Ann, Holly, and me opening up. And you know how that goes."

Mom snorted, like the woman I used to know. She doesn't approve of my cousin. Carrie Ann has issues, nothing I consider really major or unfixable, but Mom thinks she's nothing but trouble and I should fire her. Mom should be snorting about Holly instead, who shows up whenever it suits her.

"Want me to make more pancakes?" Grams asked.

"I'd explode," I said.

"I almost forgot. I have something for you." Mom jumped up and left the room. I hated to imagine what it was. Mom's presents usually involved changing my life around to suit her image of what it should be. Like a new floor plan for the store, since she thought I could do a better job of organizing the shelves. Or a subscription to a dating service to remind me of her preemptive warning about Hunter. Maybe this time it would be old lady shoes because she dislikes my flip-flops. Or . . .

Mom came back with something wrapped in pink tissue paper. "A gift," she said, handing the package over.

"For me?" I acted like I was excited.

"Open it."

So I did. And held up a gorgeous tiger-print scarf with crystal beaded fringe. My mouth slammed open, almost hitting the table. "For me? Really?"

"It's handmade," Mom said. "The minute I saw it, I thought of you. The colors go with your complexion."

"It *is* beautiful." I fingered a topaz bead, then wrapped the scarf around my neck and loosely knotted the fringed edges. I was pretty sure Mom had bought it from Aggie Petrie, because it was the same style as the one I'd admired on Milly, only a different print. I quickly rationalized that I could keep it since Milly had said Aggie's daughter-in-law made them, and I didn't have a problem with Alicia like I did with her in-laws. "It's beautiful," I said.

Mom smiled again. She was breaking records today.

"Have you been sleeping okay?" I asked Mom.

"Like a rock. Why?"

"No reason." Okay, here it came, time to spit it out. "Mom, tell me about Tom. Are you two really an item?"

Mom actually giggled. "We're just friends at this point," she said. "I'm going over to his apartment in a little while to see how he's doing. He's distraught about his brother, as you can imagine."

"What do you know about Tom's history?"

"Enough to know he's a decent man, with integrity and honor."

Grams got up and brought over the coffeepot. "He wears a wedding ring," she said. "What's the story behind that?"

See, Grams can say things any old way, just blurt them out, which is my style, too. But if I did that with Mom, right away she'd bristle and get all snappy.

"He was married once," Mom said. "But his wife died from a dreadful disease. He wears his wedding ring because he's loyal to her memory, to the woman she was before she got sick."

"What a nice man," Grams said.

So he hadn't told Mom about the part where his wife ran off with his brother.

"Let me get my camera and take a picture of you looking so smart, Helen," Grams said. "It's about time you found a man to have fun with. And, Story, don't take off that beautiful scarf yet. I want a picture of you wearing it."

At that point, I gave up. What else could I do? Burst her bubble? Without the full support of my sister and grandmother to interrogate my mother and demand she stop seeing Tom, I decided to crawl back into my shell. At least for now. If Tom Stocke *had* brutally killed his brother in a fit of revenge, then maybe Ford asked for it. Or it could have been an accident. Who knows at this point.

In any case, that certainly didn't mean that Tom would harm Mom.

From now on, though, I was going to keep an eye out for trouble from him. Luckily, since Tom worked at his antique store during the day, all I had to worry about was nighttime.

"Are you two going out tonight?" I asked Mom, acting all nonchalant while I wrapped the scarf back up in the pink tissue paper.

She didn't answer, but by the Mona Lisa smile she had plastered on her face, it was a sure bet.

Sixteen

I parked my truck behind The Wild Clover and wad-
dled around to the front of the building, still stuffed from
Grams's wonderful blueberry pancakes. She had offered to
dog-sit for Dinky, so I was free from that responsibility for
the entire day.

As a small business owner, I'm here to say that sometimes I really feel the weight of the burden I carry, especially
when I'm forced to work with family members. Mom's
adjusted attitude and her scarf gift, which I actually like for
once, gave me a temporary high. But the thrill was fading.

I felt grumpy because Holly's Jag wasn't behind the
store, and she'd promised to be on time in the future. While
hiring Carrie Ann had been my idea from the very beginning and I was prepared to accept full responsibility for
any problems my cousin created for me, Holly had been
forced on me by Mom and that stupid contract I'd signed
when I borrowed money to pay off my ex-husband. So now
I had to put up and shut up and I didn't like it one bit.

I felt even grumpier when I discovered that Aggie and Eugene Petrie had already set up for business, and they'd expanded from one table to two, doubling the amount of junk from the past weekend.

"Wait just one minute," I said. "You can't do that. Twice as big was not part of the deal."

"Eugene," Aggie said, smirking at me, "would you get another table out of the van?"

"Another table! Eugene, stop right there. This wasn't the deal!" Eugene slowed and was about to do just as I said, until Aggie got through to him with a more commanding voice than mine. "Eugene, that table. Now!"

This was *not* going to endear me to the other business owners in Moraine. I'd caved to Aggie's trespassing charge threat, but I'd been so mad at the time, I didn't take into consideration how it would affect anyone else. We'd tried so hard to keep the festival revenue in the hands of our residents, and here I was, looking like I was welcoming the competition. Maybe I should just take my medicine, let nasty old Aggie Petrie press charges, and make Johnny Jay's day.

Now I knew exactly how it felt to be between a rock and a hard place. And it wasn't a pleasant experience.

Carrie Ann came out of the store to watch. "Uh-oh," she said right away. I followed her gaze and saw Tom Stocke heading our way and looking upset. I immediately felt defensive about how having Aggie here must look to him.

"Can I have a word with you, Story?" Tom said.

"This isn't my fault, Tom," I said before I could corral the Fischer blame game words. They'd just slipped out automatically. "I take that back. This is my fault, but I can explain."

Tom looked at Aggie's tables as if he were seeing them for the first time. "Oh, that," he said. "I have bigger problems today."

"I'm so, so sorry about your brother," I said next, rather

awkwardly, because I was sorry he even had Ford for a brother in the first place.

"I'm sorry, too," Carrie Ann said from the doorway.

Aggie was in the process of ignoring our existence. Out of the corner of my eye, I saw her putting sales pressure on one of my regular customers. And really hoped she didn't drive away business. I hadn't thought of that before.

"I want to talk to you about yesterday," Tom said to me. "What you saw, what you think might have happened. Since you found him and all." He had pulled me aside, out of earshot, and kept his voice low. "We need to go over the facts."

The last thing I was about to do was share any information with Tom Stocke. He was the number one suspect in my book. So I used that stupid directive ordered by Johnny Jay. "I can't talk to you. The chief would have my head on a platter. Remember what he said about staying away from each other?"

"I forgot all about that," Tom said. He didn't look so good—hair plastered in spots where he'd slept on it wrong, red and unfocused eyes—but if I'd just lost a sibling, I'd probably look even worse.

"Johnny Jay was pretty clear," I said.

"Sorry. Forget I mentioned anything."

"Who's minding your store?"

"I didn't open. I just can't. Not after what happened. Finding Ford like that, well, it brought back lots of bad memories. Horrible ones."

I couldn't imagine how awful his wife's treachery must have been for him. Infidelity is an ugly, soul-wrenching thing to have to go through. I knew exactly how he felt. My ex-husband should have had *philanderer* branded on his forehead for eternity. And imagine if my sister had run off with the sex addict? That would hurt even worse. And finding out the other man was his own brother . . . Maybe Tom could plead self-defense. Or temporary insanity. Against my will, I felt my heartstrings tugging for him. Money didn't buy happiness and Tom's millions weren't going to comfort him now.

Tom probably didn't even plan to kill his brother. Total blinding rage must have taken over.

"You should turn yourself in," I suggested. "No jury is going to convict you."

"You think I killed my brother?" Tom had a haunted look in his eyes. "I didn't even know he was in Moraine. You have to believe me."

"I'm trying, Tom, but nobody else around here knew your brother at all. None of us had a reason to want him dead."

"Somebody did. Nobody is going to believe me when I say I didn't murder my own brother. And that crazy woman, Patti Dwyre, has been stalking me. She's threatening to write up a big piece in the newspaper."

Before we got any further, I heard a siren coming our way, growing louder fast. Johnny Jay's police chief car zipped past the store and slowed. Then it turned down the street where I lived.

"Always in a great big hurry," Aggie said from her junk-laden tables. "I've seen him using his touch-button toys just going to lunch. What a waste of taxpayers' dollars. Self-important caveman. What a show-off."

Finally, a subject Aggie and I could agree on.

Tom muttered something under his breath and took off in the opposite direction as though Johnny was out to get him. So much for Tom running against Grant Spandle for town chair. What a pipe dream that had been.

Another police car roared past, making lots of noise, too. It also turned down my street.

This couldn't be good.

"Better make sure nobody blew up your house," Aggie suggested.

I studied the obnoxious blackmailer and couldn't help

thinking I'd just been threatened by her again. Unfortunately, I gave her the satisfaction of watching me run down the street, just in case my house really was involved in some way.

For some reason Noel, the tween explosive expert, popped into my head.

As it turned out, Patti had been the one who called for help and it really did have something to do with firepower. She and Johnny were standing in her backyard. They were both looking up at Patti's favorite room, the one from where she scoped out gossip and *Distorter* news with her telescope. There was a small hole in the center of the window.

"What are you doing here, Fischer?" Johnny Jay said. "Don't you have anything better to do?"

"Actually, I want Story to see this, too, Chief Jay," Patti said. "She's my closest neighbor. We have to stick together."

Tim, Johnny Jay's oldest police officer on the force, raised the window from the inside and stuck his head out.

"Telescope is smashed to smithereens," Tim said. "My guess is a high-powered rifle."

"Damn," Johnny Jay said. "Everybody ought to know they can't fire a rifle in my town."

"That's not the point," Patti said, scowling at Johnny, then to me, "the chief thinks it was a stray bullet."

Johnny Jay nodded. "But once I catch him, he's going to get nailed for firing a rifle. Nobody does this and gets away with it when I'm in charge."

Johnny should be getting all blustery about what had happened to Patti's window and telescope. Instead he was more concerned about the choice of weapon selected by the shooter. We all are aware that rifles, because of their long-range power, aren't legal in our area. Everybody knows that. But there's always somebody horsing around with a rifle when they shouldn't be. This, though, was different.

"After what happened on this block yesterday," I said to him, "with a dead man and a killer running loose, you can't assume this was accidental."

"Really! And who went and made you the new chief of police?" Johnny Jay said with enough sarcasm even Lori Spandle would have caught it going by. "But since you're here, you saved me a trip to your store to pick you up."

Oh no, not again. The man hauled me down to the police station every chance he got. I'd been waiting for the ax to fall even though I'd given him a fully detailed written and verbal statement at the scene.

"Don't you need a warrant?" I said, even though I knew what he would say.

And he did. "I can get one, if you want to go in cuffs instead."

"What about my window and telescope?" Patti demanded.

Johnny scratched his jaw like he was pondering her question. "I expect a few people in town will be relieved about the loss of your telescope, Dwyre," he said. Which was true. Me, for example. I didn't appreciate that thing one bit. "But you can file a claim with your insurance company. Report will be ready by tomorrow. You can pick it up then. Let's go, Fischer."

"I'll meet you at the station," I said. No way was I voluntarily driving anywhere with him. And I knew he couldn't force me. Legally that is, although Johnny bent the rules to suit himself.

He glanced at Patti. In the past, she'd managed to capture a few of his more aggressive actions on video. I could tell he was remembering, too, and didn't want to go through that again. "Suit yourself," he said to me. "But don't make me come looking for you."

With that, he strolled to his car and drove off.

Tim came out and left, too.

Patti and I studied the window.

"Coincidence?" she asked.

"Maybe," I said, doubting it.

"I'm not so sure. And to top it off, I could have been up in that window when the rifle was fired. My eye could have been shot out. My life is definitely in danger." Then Patti grinned, a wide, happy smile. "Somebody's out to get me. I'm a real, honest-to-goodness reporter now."

"I don't know how you can be enjoying this."

"Come on, give me five."

Patti made the universal gesture of high five, and reluctantly I slapped my palm against hers. "Glad I could be here for your shining moment," I said.

"Me, too."

"Where were you when it happened?" I asked her.

"Around."

"Really?" Call me too nosy to resist. I could tell by her dodgy eyes that she'd been up to something worth knowing about. "And I thought we were best friends."

"Okay, okay, I was looking around inside over there."

She pointed to my ex-husband's house where yellow police warning tape was plastered all over the door. "I'm pretty sure they were done there anyway," Patti said. "Somebody just forgot to remove the tape."

We looked at each other. "And?" I said. "Find anything?"

Patti dug around in her pocket vest and handed me a hickory nut. "I found this by the front door."

I do my best to follow Patti's lines of thought, and I usually do a pretty good job. But this time, she had zoomed to another planet and was speaking Martian.

Here's what I know about hickory nuts:

- They grow in Wisconsin woodlands.

- President Andrew Jackson was called "Old Hickory" because he was so tough, and hickory wood is so hard it's even used for ax handles.

- Shagbarks, named for the distinctive way they shed bark—in long, ragged strips—are the most common hickory trees and produce the best tasting nuts.

- The nuts are encased in hulls that fall apart when they're ripe enough to eat.

- And they are heart healthy, filled with nutrients like protein, potassium, and vitamins A and C.

- Pecans are close relatives, so you can use them just like you would use hickory nuts.

- Right now, in August, they are beginning to fall from the trees and will continue to drop through September.

"Then I found this one under my window." Patti handed me another one, exactly the same as the first—still in its hull, a little smaller than a golf ball, just beginning to crack open.

I like to think of myself as a naturalist, loving all living things. The proof is in my backyard. I raise honeybees for lots of reasons, but one main reason is because they are threatened, and I hope to make a difference in local crops, which are fertilized by bees raised by people like Stanley and me. My garden is a source of outright pleasure for me. To watch a seedling sprout and grow into a mature plant bearing gifts is a joy to behold.

That might be why I finally caught up with Patti's thinking. "There aren't any shagbark hickory trees on this block," I said.

"Right." Patti slammed me on the shoulder as a reward for my hard brain work.

"Maybe a squirrel dropped it there," I guessed. "They're starting to forage and bury food for winter."

Reluctantly Patti admitted that possibility. "Still, I think someone left them as warnings."

"Have you been nosing around anyplace else that you shouldn't?" I asked Patti.

"Of course, it's part of my job."

"Well, watch your back," I said, returning the nuts and leaving her standing in her backyard. Not that I was too worried. The woman has been known to carry wasp spray to fend off potential attackers. Who knew what else she had hidden in that vest she always wore?

Seventeen

When I got back to the store, I found DeeDee Becker, the kleptomaniac Honey Queen, squaring off with Holly in the entryway. They had a sizable group of spectators because The Wild Clover is a gathering place for the locals, especially when there's something as gruesome as a murder in our backyard to gossip about. When something this big happens, the community rallies around our Main Street businesses, clinking glasses at Stu's bar, whispering in the library, and speculating in line at my store. Then the rumors and innuendos really fly.

Whatever had caused this altercation between DeeDee and my sister was an added attraction for them.

Holly saw me and said, "I'm throwing her out of the store, and you're not going to believe why."

DeeDee still wore the Honey Queen crown on her head. I wanted to knock it off, but by some miracle I managed to rein myself in. I felt like snorting fire at her, burning up the stupid crown. This was the first year for an official Honey Queen. It should have been me, not DeeDee.

"I represent Moraine," DeeDee said. "Grant said I have the key to the town and can go wherever I please. That includes The Wild Clover. You can't throw me out."

"You're taking this Honey Queen thing a little too seriously," I told her. "Besides, the weekend is over and so is your reign."

"I get to do this until next year's festival when I crown my successor."

I really wanted to crown DeeDee right now but not in the way she meant. "And what purse-sized items inside my store have your attention today?" That wasn't nice of me, but the woman ran around with a suitcase for a purse and liked to load it up with freebies. And there it was right on her shoulder, probably completely empty in anticipation of a Wild Clover windfall.

"Tell Story why you're here," Holly said to DeeDee.

"I have to inspect your honey products and make sure they meet code," DeeDee said to me with a whole lot of presumptuous authority.

The gall of the woman!

"Take her away," I said to my sister.

DeeDee resisted, so Holly got her into a headlock. The crown went flying, and in the blink of an eye, my wrestler sister had DeeDee and her big tote bag on the ground.

"I'm telling Grant," I heard DeeDee shout as she got to her feet and snatched up the tiara.

Noel was watching from the sidelines. He had a fistful of honey sticks. With his free hand, he gave me a thumbs-up. I liked that kid more and more all the time.

Carrie Ann was behind the cash register, ringing up a few customers, the ones who weren't too busy watching the wrestling show to shop. Holly stepped in to help her. "I'm going to be gone again today for a little while," I said.

"What else is new?" Carrie Ann said. "You haven't been around much. Lucky for you, you have me to watch your store while you're away. I tell you, I'm management material."

Everybody wants to be the boss—Carrie Ann, Holly, Mom. As long as the going is good. But just let things get sticky and they all go running. Well, maybe not Mom, but she doesn't handle situations like a normal person, either.

"This time I don't have a choice," I said. "Johnny Jay has more questions for me. Believe me, I'd rather stay here. And I appreciate everything you do."

"We'll take care of everything," my cousin said. "Don't worry. Right, Holly?"

Carrie Ann slung a goodwill arm across my sister's shoulder. "Holly might not always be on time," she said, "but when she finally shows up, she's like having two more people on the schedule. And she keeps the riffraff out as you just saw. We'll handle things together."

Holly has a work ethic? I was amazed. My sister? Really? I would have to start paying more attention.

I stood there, in the middle of my store, my legs refusing to take even one step toward the door. Johnny Jay and his lockable interrogation room were waiting for me. I was starting to feel beat up, abused, and generally unfit to handle Johnny in my usual fashion.

All the nasty people in my life had been in my face for the last two days—Lori, DeeDee, the police chief, Aggie Petrie, Mom (before she transformed into super mother). The very last thing I wanted to do was spend another minute with any of them, especially with Johnny Jay.

So I decided not to go.

I called Hunter from my office. "The chief is bothering me," I said. "He demanded that I show up at the station."

"Want me to meet you there?"

"No. I'm not going."

Hunter sighed into the phone. "He's investigating a crime. You have to cooperate."

"Yes, but I did that already. I told him everything I knew. I cooperated perfectly fine."

"Don't you watch cop shows?"

"Sometimes."

"The police always want witnesses to go over their stories more than once. There's a reason for that."

"To try and trip them up. See, he's after me."

"To make sure they don't know something important that they might have forgotten."

"Believe me, I didn't forget a thing. Will you tell him that?"

"No. If I step in, he'll go after you harder."

"Fine," I said, knowing that was true.

Then I told Hunter about Patti's window and that the telescope had been shot out.

I didn't mention what our esteemed police chief thought, about it being some thoughtless, trigger-happy mistake. I wanted to see if Hunter came up with the same dumb rationale. And I definitely didn't mention the hickory nuts because then he would think I was . . . well . . . nuts.

After I finished, Hunter didn't say a single thing for what felt like a long time. Finally, he said, "I'll call and talk to Patti. Unofficially, of course."

And that scared me a little, because he wasn't taking the incident lightly at all. If Hunter had explained it away like Johnny had, I would have been annoyed. Now I felt scared. This felt much worse.

"That would be great," I said.

"Keep your cool with Johnny, okay, precious?"

"I love when you sweet-talk me," I said, feeling wanted and loved as I hung up.

In a perfect make-believe world I wouldn't have any problems. Or if I did, Hunter would solve them for me. Unfortunately, in the real world, a woman has to look out for herself.

So during a lull in business, I took a break from the
store, walked home, and stopped briefly to admire my beeyard, where all my honeybees were humming in a happy
way, implying no more hive robbers were around. Then I
tugged my kayak into the river. Whoever shot through Patti's window would have had to have been on the opposite
side of the river, judging by the angle.

Patti had two windows in that upper room. One looked
out directly at my bedroom window. The other window
faced the river. That's the one that was blown out.

I waded into the cool water of the Oconomowoc River,
not caring that my flip-flops got wet, which was one of the
beautiful things about my preferred footwear. Then I
scooted into the kayak, careful not to tip it.

The river was lazy today, not much more than a ripple
here and there where bugs slid along the surface. I paddled
over to the opposite side, got out carefully, pulled my kayak
up onshore, and studied the situation, angling a little so my
vision lined up straight with Patti's window.

From the bank of the river, the terrain sloped up. I
climbed it, keeping one eye on Patti's window, picking my
way through the brush and trees until her house was out of
sight. That meant the shot had probably been fired from the
area between the brush on the top of the hill and the river-
bank.

Next, I studied the ground on the way back to the river-
bank, looking for anything that might point to the culprit.

Not a thing.

Next, I looked around for shagbark hickory trees.

None along the bank of the river, but I hadn't expected
any. Most of them grew a little more inland where squirrels
buried their nutty treasures then forgot all about them. We
should be grateful for the little pests because they help
more trees grow. But I've also found my tulips growing in
the woods, thanks to squirrels digging up my bulbs and
replanting them.

Nothing here seemed out of place.

But when I crossed over to my side of the river and hauled my kayak up onshore, I found something that made my heart race faster and my blood pressure spike through the roof.

Because one solitary hickory nut was lying next to my back door.

And it had been smashed to smithereens.

Eighteen

❦

"Why me?" I asked Patti. "I shouldn't be getting hickory nuts. I can see why you might, but why me?"

We were in The Wild Clover at the end of aisle three after I'd finally tracked Patti down on her cell phone and asked her to stop by.

"We know too much," Patti said to the why-me question. "Now we have to be eliminated."

"That's a little dramatic, don't you think?"

"What if it has to do with that Ford guy?"

"You weren't even with me when I found his body. If it had to do with him, I'd be the only target, not both of us. That doesn't make any sense."

We stopped to think.

Holly came around the corner and said, "We can hear you two up at the register. Milly and Carrie Ann want to help you brainstorm. You might as well come up front."

Well, wasn't that embarrassing? You'd think by now I'd

know better than to have a private conversation out in the aisles. We shuffled up.

"Hickory nuts?" Carrie Ann said.

"For the next newsletter," I said lamely. "Milly, can you whip up something with them?"

"I know just the thing," Milly said. She had an armload of fresh flowers and was arranging them. "You've been collecting hickory nuts?"

"Not voluntarily," I said.

Then my cell phone rang. "I'm outside with Ben," Hunter said. "Come out."

"You come in," I said.

"No way. The town's biggest gossipers are in there. And why are the Petries holding a rummage sale outside your store?"

"I'll explain later. I've just been threatened."

"Fine, I'll be right in."

That's one of the things I like about Hunter. He's flexible when he has to be. In more ways than one, but we won't go there.

Trent had been stocking fresh produce. He came up front at my request and took over the register. The rest of us, including Hunter and Ben, crowded into my office. Patti and I took turns, or rather, cut each other off randomly, so the story was a bit convoluted. "Then Patti found a hickory nut outside my ex-husband's house," I just had to add toward the end, forgetting that my boyfriend didn't know that part. Hunter snorted. I hadn't planned on telling him about the hickory nuts for exactly this reason. But I was in too deep to retreat, so I ignored Hunter's amused expression. "And she found another one by her shot-out window. Then I decided to explore on the other side of the river, but I didn't find anything unusual. When I got back, someone had left a smashed hickory nut by my door."

A moment of silence ensued.

"Why hickory nuts?" Carrie Ann finally said. "That's

really stupid. I mean, if I was trying to scare somebody, I'd leave bullets or a knotted noose or a brownie with a note that said, *Eat this and die*."

Hunter looked momentarily startled, like he thought she really meant it in a literal way. Hunter wasn't too sure about my family members and what they might attempt.

"Carrie Ann's just giving examples of more effective scare tactics," Holly told him when he continued to stare at our cousin.

"Hickory nuts are all over the place right now," Milly piped up, using common sense, something a lot of people lacked. "You probably have a hickory nut–addicted squirrel on your street. You could be making a mountain out of a molehill."

"We don't have any hickory trees on our block," Patti pointed out.

"Who knows how far a squirrel travels before it buries a nut," came the reply. Milly wasn't one to give up easily.

"I wonder when the nut was left by my door," I said. "I didn't notice it before I went out in my kayak, but that doesn't mean it wasn't there."

"It wasn't," Patti said matter-of-factly.

"How would you know?" I asked.

"I just do." Patti looked away.

Then Hunter spoke up and let me down by saying, "Everybody's on edge right now and maybe slightly over-reacting. I suggest relaxing, going about your business, and"—he glanced at me—"cooperating with the police chief. Johnny Jay might not be everybody's favorite, but he's thorough and dedicated. He'll wrap up the case with the right suspect behind bars."

I looked around the room. Neither Milly nor Hunter believed that Patti and I were in any harm. Holly would support me regardless, even if I said little green men were on my roof. But that's just because she's my sister and has to. Even Ben avoided my eyes. Or so it seemed.

After everyone else cleared out, Hunter gave me a hug

and a top-of-the-head kiss and left me to reflect on the past few days. Maybe Milly was right. And Hunter probably knew best. After all, he was a cop. By the time I finished thinking things through, I had almost convinced myself that the hickory nut threat theory was pretty ridiculous.

Except if I wanted to psychologically mess with someone, I wouldn't make it obvious with bullets or brownies like Carrie Ann had suggested. I'd go the more subtle route. Leave my victim with enough doubt to make her uncomfortable and nervous. And best of all, who would believe her when she ran around telling everybody she'd been threatened with hickory nuts?

Nobody, that's who.

Holly knocked on my office door and came in before I could invite her, which defeated the whole purpose of having closed doors and the courtesy of knocking. "We're getting complaints about Aggie. She's accosting customers."

A lightbulb went on in my head. I remembered what Hunter had said when he first saw her tables outside. Something about a rummage sale. Yes, that was it. "Can they hold a rummage sale on Main Street without a permit?"

"Got me."

I called the town hall to check, and my cheesy grin gave Holly the answer without her even having to ask. "You can't turn around in this town," she said, "without paying to do it."

"I'll have Trent call the police station and report them. They'll respond if he's the one who asks them to. We can't let Aggie Petrie ruin business."

A little later I heard commotion outside. I tried not to gloat, I really did, but I wanted a ringside seat to see the coming attraction. We all headed for the sidewalk, employees and customers, all of us.

Johnny Jay and Officer Sally Maylor, who is a decent cop and loyal customer, were trying to explain the rules about having a permit to Aggie and Eugene. Their son Bob was there, too. He had a box open and was transferring more handmade scarves to a table. Aggie was swinging her show cane. "I have permission from the store owner and that's all I need."

"No," Sally said, "you still need a permit."

Eugene turned to me. "Can you write us up one?"

Johnny Jay rolled his eyes. "Fischer can't help you. You have to apply at town hall. Come on, pack up and get out of here."

"Over my dead body," Aggie said to him.

Johnny told her he could accommodate that request.

Something must've snapped in Eugene, because he jumped between his wife and the chief and shoved Johnny Jay.

Sally smacked Eugene with her nightstick. Not hard, but with enough force to get his attention.

Aggie whacked Sally in the back of the legs with her cane, causing Sally's knees to buckle. She went down, but came up swinging.

Then it got really rowdy.

I could tell Bob was torn between his loyalty to his parents and the possibility of doing jail time. Since he had a record (or that was the rumor anyway), I'm sure the last thing he wanted was cop trouble. He backed away.

By the time the dust settled, Aggie and Eugene were handcuffed and locked in the backseat of Sally's squad car.

I couldn't believe what I'd just seen. Amazing really, if you think about it. Most of us are relatively afraid of Johnny Jay, but those two Petries waded right in without even once considering the consequences. Johnny Jay was going to roast them alive over a slow fire.

Better it was somebody other than me for a change.

Bob started putting the scarves back into the box.

"I want all those tables taken down. You have ten minutes," the police chief said to Bob, who nodded and picked up speed, jamming things into boxes haphazardly.

"Where are you going, Fischer?" Johnny said to me when I turned to re-enter my store.

"Johnny Jay, last I looked this was a free country. I can go wherever I want. And I don't even have to ask your permission."

"Look what I have for you, that little present I mentioned earlier. Since you didn't bother showing up down at the station, I'm here to present it in public."

I really didn't want to turn around. I whispered to Holly, who was ahead of me, "What does he have?"

"Handcuffs," she said.

And that's how I got locked up in an interrogation room with Aggie and Eugene Petrie.

Nineteen

"A whole street full of people heard the police chief threaten my wife," Eugene said from his shackled position at one end of the table.

"I think he meant it figuratively," I said from the other.

I really hadn't believed Johnny Jay when he'd threatened me with handcuffs for not showing up at the station to answer more of his dumb questions. But here I was! And putting me in the same room with these two was just plain mean.

"We're countersuing," said Aggie, who was in the middle. "He can't just chain us up like dogs."

"You shouldn't have hit him with your cane." That was me.

"Why don't you shut up," Aggie said.

We sat in silence for a while. The only good thing about this unpleasant situation was that the Petries couldn't attack me even if they decided to get physical. I swear I saw rabidlike froth on Aggie's lips. But they weren't nearly as intimidating in handcuffs and leg irons, although in my opinion Johnny Jay went way overboard with restraints this time.

At least he'd left *my* legs free. That was a plus.

"If you get out before we do," Eugene said next, directing his gaze my way, "bail us out."

I wanted to say, "Over my dead body," but I had a pretty good idea what his response would be. Instead I said, "Bob and Alicia will get you out."

"You owe us," Eugene said.

I made a mental note: In the future, no more nasty characters in my life. I would surround myself with people who made me feel good. Only happy ones, nobody else. People like:

- Grams (always sweet and kind)

- Holly (usually a great friend)

- Carrie Ann (upbeat most of the time)

- Hunter (makes me feel good all the time)

- Stanley (to talk bees and honey)

- Patti (wait, scratch that)

- And even Mom (if she kept up the good vibrations)

Aggie grinned slyly. "I bet you wouldn't be in here in the first place," she said to me, "if you hadn't had sex with the dead guy."

"What?"

"Sure, pretend you didn't."

"Where did you hear a ridiculous thing like that?" Just imagining myself with Ford made me sick to my stomach.

"I heard your sister tell that real estate agent all about it."

Then I remembered. "Oh, that." I tried to laugh it off, but the sound coming out of my mouth was more like a weak whimper. Aggie had overheard Holly messing with Lori's head. My sister's trick to get Lori chasing after Ford had worked in a sort of twisted, bizarre way we couldn't have anticipated. "She was only kidding."

"Uh-huh."

"Really."

"The police chief should hear about your sleazy little tryst, if he hasn't already. Maybe Eugene and I can make a trade, negotiate with him—information on you and the dead guy for our freedom and all charges dismissed."

"Don't forget I caught you digging in our garden," Eugene pointed out.

"I wasn't digging in your garden."

Just then, I heard keys jingling in the lock and Johnny Jay walked in. "Fischer," he said. "You're up first."

"I should go before her," Aggie said. "When you hear what I have to say, you'll lock her up for good."

Johnny Jay ignored her. Thank God for small miracles, as Mom would say.

A few minutes later, he and I were in a different room, smaller and much quieter without big-mouth Aggie making all that threatening noise.

"I don't know what I can tell you that I haven't already told you," I said. "It's all in the written report and we've been over this before."

"New facts came to light and I'd like to shine a bigger beam on them. And on you." He chuckled like he'd made a funny joke. Now, he kicked back and swung his feet up on the table, which I thought was rude. The bottoms of his shoes were facing me. He had a wad of something disgusting squashed on the right one. After staring at me for a few minutes, he said, "What was your relationship to the deceased?"

"Ford? Nothing at all," I said. "We didn't have any kind of relationship. I only met the guy once for a few minutes. I went over to the house thinking Clay was back in town and he answered the door." Since Johnny Jay would try extra hard to trip me up, I thought I better revise my statement. "I take that back, I saw him twice after that. Both of those times he was dead."

"You didn't happen to see him go from alive to dead, did you?"

"Very funny."

"I have a witness who says you had sexual relations with him."

"You were listening in when horrible Aggie came up with that outrageous lie?" I couldn't believe we were wired for sound in the interrogation room, but it stood to reason, knowing Johnny.

The chief shot me a look. "I'll follow up with her when I'm through with you. But I have another reliable witness who made that exact same claim."

I knew exactly who that was.

"Lori Spandle isn't a reliable witness," I said. "She's been out to get me since high school." I could have mentioned that Johnny Jay has been out to get me since then, too, but I didn't want it to sound like sour grapes. "Where is Lori anyway? I really need to talk to her."

"I never mentioned my witness's name, so back off. I should get your sister in here. She's the one who spilled the beans about you and the victim," he said.

"Yes, bring her in right now so we can clear this up."

"She'd stick up for you, wouldn't she? She'd lie right to my face." He sneered. "Here's one possibility: You and the deceased start getting all hot and heavy and he does something you don't like, maybe something especially kinky and he won't stop, so you end up killing him. Or maybe you like what he's doing, but get carried away, if you follow my drift. Pretty soon, you realize he's dead. The whole thing could have been an accident. Either way, he's not around anymore and you don't know what to do with the body. So you stuff it into the fireplace."

I had to interrupt at this point because the whole thing was so unbelievable. "That is the stupidest . . ."

"Pipe down. Killers do strange things in a panic. Anyway, once he's dead, you calm down and come up with a better plan. Send Lori Spandle over there, let her discover him. You know her pretty well, know how she reacts to a crisis; not too good with them, is she? She does exactly what you think she'll do. She runs away. But what you didn't plan on was that she decided to keep her mouth shut. Partly to save the last few hours of her husband's festival. Partly because she feels responsible because she rented to the deceased, and she doesn't know how to handle it."

Talk about a twisted story. Lori Spandle hasn't taken responsibility for a single thing her entire life. What a crock.

"I need my cell phone back," I said. "I get to make a phone call." If the chief *and* the town chairman, *and* his loosey-goosey wife were all working together to put me behind bars, I was in really big trouble.

"What do you think of my theory?"

"I'm not saying one more word to you, Johnny Jay." Then I thought of something. "Actually, I do have one question: Exactly how did Ford Stocke die?"

"You don't get to ask questions." He swung his feet down to the floor and stood up. "Now, I'm going to let you loose for now, but don't leave town. I'll be watching you."

And with that, he let me go. Officer Sally Maylor drove me back to The Wild Clover. After a few minutes of silence in the squad car I asked, "How did Ford Stocke die?"

Sally pantomimed turning an imaginary key on the side of her lips and tossing it away.

I sighed. Johnny had an iron grip on his officers.

When I reentered The Wild Clover, the store was full of customers. They collectively turned to me with questioning expressions on their faces.

"Everything's cool," I said to them. "Aggie and Eugene

are still in jail. But me? No big deal. A misunderstanding between the chief and me. But what else is new on that front, right?"

Holly came forward and gave me a big sisterly hug.

Since I had an attentive audience, and the rumor about me and Ford was bound to get out, if it wasn't already, I decided to head it off by announcing it right up front. Total transparency was my new motto, one I'd been thinking about since accusations started flying at the police station.

"There's a nasty rumor going around—" I began, only to have my cousin cut me off.

"We haven't heard any new rumors yet," Carrie Ann said. "And I'd know because I've been checking customers out, *managing* things." I didn't miss my cousin's extra emphasis on managing. I ignored her, however, and continued "—that claims I was romantically involved . . . er . . . um . . . more like sexually involved with the dead man," I said. "Please, please don't believe a word of it, because none of it is true."

Holly glanced up sharply and asked me, "Who started *that* vicious rumor?"

I narrowed my eyes and did a short stare-down into my sister's eyes, sending a message as privately as possible. "Oh," she said, catching on that it had all started with her. "Uh . . . oh no."

And just when I thought my whole life sucked, that it was heading for the storm sewer to mix with who knows what kind of disgusting sludge and waste, my friends and loyal customers came to my rescue.

"What a lie!" Carrie Ann shouted with passion.

"Whoever is spreading that one around is going to regret it," someone else said. "Just let them open their mouth to me just one time! I'll set them straight."

Heads nodded in unison.

"We're behind you, Story," Milly said. "All the way. Aren't we, gang?"

Murmurs of agreement swept through the store, from front to back and even sideways in one giant wave.

To my battered and abused ears and downtrodden soul, their voices were like one big, beautiful, mountainous roar of confidence.

It was all I could do not to break down and start sobbing with joy.

But a few renegade tears slid down my cheek and I lost my voice for a little while.

Twenty

✷

Soon after, my cell phone rang and Grams's sweet voice said, "I love this little dog."

"She's looking for a home. You know Norm isn't coming back."

"I would take her in a heartbeat," my sweet grandmother said, "but . . ."

There was always a but when it came to Dinky.

". . . she isn't very well trained. She peed on my brand-new slippers."

"That means she likes you."

"I'm sure it does," Grams said, always looking for the best in everything. "But I can't have that going on. Your mother almost had a conniption fit when it happened."

I thought about what Carrie Ann had said earlier about Dinky needing training. But what if she wasn't trainable?

"If I can break her of that bad habit, will you adopt her?" I was excited at a prospective new home for my foster canine. I sensed a sale. Not that I would actually try to sell

Dinky. She was definitely a giveaway. But it would be great to have her close by, to be able to visit. She had plenty of flaws, but she had grown on me.

"You don't know anything about training dogs," Grams pointed out.

"No, but Hunter does and he'll help me."

"Tell you what, you fix Dinky's peeing problem and you've got yourself a deal. But don't mention it to your mother. I want to surprise her."

Oh, that would really make her do cartwheels. Mom wasn't exactly an animal-friendly person.

"Where is she, anyway?" I asked.

"At Stu's Bar and Grill with that nice man Tom."

"Oh Jeez." I'd forgotten all about keeping tabs on those two.

"What's wrong, sweetie?"

"Nothing. Gotta go. Can you keep Dinky until tomorrow?"

"Sure thing," Grams said, agreeing like I knew she would.

Trent had worked a split shift today, so he was back at the store and agreed to lock up later. And better yet for me, business was slow enough that he felt he could handle it alone until closing.

"Call me if you need me," I offered. "I can be back here in five minutes."

I quickly headed home, changed my clothes, and wrapped my new tiger-print scarf around my neck, which I knew would please my mother.

The full moon was already visible in the sky as I hurried toward Stu's. We still had an hour or more of daylight and the moon was already out, waiting to prey on those of us with weak wills and unruly minds. And what if I qualified? Was that what had happened to end Ford's life? Had Patti been right about the forces of the full moon driving someone over the edge?

Spooky!

As I reached the corner of Main Street, I caught sight of Lori's car coming toward me from the north side of town. Her car slid into a parking space in front of the bar. I picked up speed when I saw her crawl out and stand up.

Lori saw me and tried to jump back in her car, but I pulled her out by the back of her too-tight sweater.

"We have a little unfinished business," I said to her. "We need to talk."

"I don't have anything to say to you." Lori twisted around to check her sweater. Then she turned to face me. "And look what you did to my sweater. You stretched it out of shape."

"That's nothing compared to what you did! For starters, you didn't do a background check on Ford. You rented out the house right next to mine to a chronic jailbird. I'll see your license to sell real estate revoked for negligence."

I didn't have a clue what it would take to get her license lifted, but I vowed to find out. Lori didn't look too worried, though, which wasn't a good sign.

"I'm warning you, Fischer," she said. "Back off."

I decided to finish plotting the destruction of her career later. Right now I had a bigger bone to pick with her for telling Johnny Jay I'd been sleazing with Ford Stocke. I stepped closer.

Lori was all red, like she gets when she's mad. "Back off right now," she warned me again.

"Not until you reassure me that you're going to reverse the damage you did to my reputation."

Lori smirked. "What reputation?"

I wanted to kill her so bad it took all my willpower not to reach out and choke her. I didn't need a full moon to have an overwhelming desire to finish her off once and for all. Normally, I'm not a physically violent person. I'm really not. But I'd had a really bad day and a chunk of it was thanks to Lori. Later I would blame the overhead Transylvanian lunar moon for my next move.

I grabbed a bunch of her precious sweater, right between her big boobs, and yanked her closer, if that was even possible. "You want stretches," I yelled. "You'll get stretches."

We were nose to nose, breath to breath, eyeball to eyeball.

Lori grabbed my brand-new scarf with both hands, getting a good grip on each side and jerking it tight around my throat. She tripped and we both went down. By now I was pretty sure we were in the middle of the street, but I was seeing red, partly because of lack of oxygen to my brain, partly because I was flaming mad.

I had her. She had me. First she was on top, then I was.

"Let go," I managed to croak. We both still had firm grips; me on her sweater, her on my scarf and I wasn't breathing so well.

"You first," she said back.

We both gripped harder. I tried to get a leg over her torso, which I hoped would give me an advantage. She got an elbow free and tried to swing it into my nose. I blocked it. To anyone observing, we must have looked like a giant lunatic pretzel.

Pretty soon, firm hands grabbed both of us and pulled us apart. I had a chunk of Lori's hair in my fist. Her sweater was stretched so far her bra was popping out. Some of the beads from my scarf bounced away, which really ticked me off.

Then I noticed a bunch of Stu's customers out on the curb, watching the whole thing. My eyes landed on two people front and center: Mom and Tom. Mom had a hand clapped across her mouth like she was mortified. Tom pulled her close to him in a show of manly support and protection.

"Well, Lori deserved it," I called out to Mom right before she turned and hurried away. "She ruined my new scarf."

Twenty-one

Tuesday morning at The Wild Clover, I wasn't imagining all the snickering going on behind my back. It was definitely real. In the light of day, my actions last night seemed juvenile at best. I regretted what had happened in the middle of Main Street. Boy did I ever. It's just that something came over me and I totally lost all self-control.

The worst part was that nobody who came into the store talked about it out in the open. Which made me squirm even more.

Bits and pieces of other information slowly began to surface, sharing the limelight with my public meltdown. Tom Stocke's entire life story for one, thanks to blabby Patti. Nothing I hadn't already heard, though—his wife running off with Ford, Ford's ongoing problems with the law, and Tom's quiet move to Moraine to bury the past. Until the past followed him here and got itself buried instead.

A catfight in the street should have been overshadowed by that juicy news, but by the sly and amused looks I was getting from my customers, I knew I was competing with Tom for top news story.

His friendly association with my mother came up, mostly behind my back, too, but my staff clued me in. My perfect mother, who'd spent her life worrying about what the neighbors would say, and blaming me for what they *did* say, was now fodder for gossip herself. At least when she eventually reverted back to her old snarky ways, I would have some ammunition of my own next time she fired a round. After last night, I suspected that round had to be right around the corner.

The senior citizens arrived to play sheepshead, Wisconsin's official state card game, in the choir loft, a friendly, cozy nook I'd converted into a gathering place. This was their regular card day, but they usually played in the afternoon.

Grams, an avid card player, said it best as she came in carrying Dinky. "We want to be part of the conversation and there's sure a lot going around." She handed the dog over to me, saying, "And here's your adorable Dinky back. Let me know when she's trained, sweetie." Grams winked to let me know the deal was still on.

The seniors were mixed on whodunnit. Everybody hoped the killer was an out-of-towner who was gone for good. Of course, Tom's name came up as the one and only other possibility, but many of the crusty old-timers thought his brother had gotten his just deserts, whether Tom did the deed or not. A small-bit criminal who stole his brother's wife didn't garner the same compassion as your average murdered citizen.

Stu walked in the door for his daily newspaper and had a silly smile on his face when he spotted me. He didn't mention the fight, though. And he had news we hadn't heard yet. "Aggie and Eugene Petrie are out of jail on bail."

"Their sidewalk rummage sale days are over, though," I said. "I hope they learned their lesson."

What goes around, comes around. Words my sister and I had heard plenty while growing up. Sometimes it's true. Actions, words, whatever—they all have a way of boomeranging back at you when you least expect it.

Aggie is a perfect example. She shouldn't have threatened me the way she did. If she hadn't blackmailed me into letting her set up her junk tables outside my store, she wouldn't be in trouble now.

After rearranging a fresh batch of red and yellow heirloom tomatoes, I came around a corner and caught Holly, Carrie Ann, and Patti whispering together. When they saw me coming, they pulled apart with guilt written all over their faces. Patti quickly hid something behind her back.

"What?" I asked. "What's going on? I know you're talking about me."

They looked at each other then burst out laughing. All of them were laughing so hard they couldn't talk, tears running down their faces.

"What!"

Still unable to speak, Patti handed over two pictures that had obviously been printed out from a computer.

"Where did these come from?" I demanded, staring in disbelief. Somebody had captured Lori and me in full motion. On the ground, trying to rip each other's clothes apart. It wasn't a pretty sight.

"It's all over the Internet," Patti said.

By the time my three "friends" got themselves under control, another wave of customers came through and we had to split up to take care of business. But before that, I ripped up the damaging photos and threw the small pieces into the garbage can. It didn't feel really great being on the outside looking in. Now I knew how P.P. Patti felt her whole life. I always thought she deserved her outcast status. Today, I deserved mine.

When I had a chance, I said to Holly, "You three have your fun. Me? I'm taking an early lunch. If anyone wants me, I'll be at the library." I paused, then added, "On second thought, everybody just leave me alone."

I grabbed a plastic bag with my scarf inside it and stomped down the street.

Where I promptly ran into DeeDee, sporting an enormous red, white, and blue tote bag slung over her shoulder. "You stay away from my sister," she warned me with a snarl. "Or you'll have me to deal with."

"Yeah, right," I muttered and kept going.

Moraine's library is tiny, but well stocked. I hoped to find a how-to book there that would help me figure out how to replace the missing beads. The library is run by Emily Nolan and her daughter, Karin. While the Harmony Festival was a town-hall-run event, all the other community attractions are planned and executed by small committees. The library sponsors most of them, many taking place on the lawn in back of the library when weather permits.

Besides children's events like story times, we have several book clubs and special visitor talks. Events bring the town together in shared camaraderie and focused missions. At an invasive species discussion in the spring, we were all motivated to attack and kill garlic mustard and buckthorn. We even ran a contest to see who could destroy the most. And not too long ago we had a fabulous chocolate tasting. Then there was music—jazz, folk, country, whatever.

But I wasn't at the library to talk about any of those things.

As I came up to the front desk, I saw Emily and Karin working hard to control their mouths, their lips curling up on the corners. But being the serious librarians they are, both of them stayed in control, unlike the treacherous trio back at the store. Did every single person in town know about Lori and me?

What a dumb question.

I pretended that nothing was wrong, though, and explained about the beads missing from my scarf.

"Let me see it," Karin said, taking the scarf and laying it out flat on a counter.

"Great scarf," Emily said.

"Mom bought it for me."

"It's beautiful," Karin said. "Just a few missing beads. It's really not that noticeable."

"It is to me," I said.

Karin studied it a little more. "You don't need a book to fix this. I'm pretty handy with this sort of thing. I can do it. Where are the beads?"

"I looked for them this morning," I said, which was true. I'd returned to the street and hunted for them. "Now what?"

"Do you know who made it?"

I nodded. "Alicia Petrie."

"See if you can get more beads from her. Leave it here. I'll match up the bead thread in the meantime."

"I really appreciate your help," I said. "A nice gift from Mom is something to cherish."

After that, I sat down at a picnic table behind the library. Holly popped around the corner.

"Go away," I said, wrapping my arms across my chest in classic ticked-off mode.

"Listen, we need to talk."

"Make it short, as in text-speak," I said. Then realized how insensitive that was. "Sorry. I didn't mean that."

"You're going to get even crabbier with me when you hear what I have to say, but hear me out. And don't interrupt till I'm done, okay? You've been acting weird ever since you found out Mom was dating."

I opened my mouth to set her straight. The problem wasn't that Mom was dating. It was *who* she was dating. Wasn't it?

Holly held up a warning finger. "Let me finish. Dad's been gone five years, but to me it's like he died five minutes ago. Sometimes, I even forget he's not here and when I remember, it hurts like heck all over again. I bet Mom feels the same way. And I bet you do, too.

"So seeing Mom with another man is difficult. Believe me, I have all kinds of emotions bouncing around inside of me. I don't like it. Part of me thinks it's the right thing for her to do. Another part of me feels like she's cheating on Dad. But look at Mom. How happy she is. Tom is making her feel good about herself again. She's positively glowing. And she deserves to feel that way. Story, it's been five years! We have to let her start living again."

Tears welled in my eyes and I didn't fight them.

"I miss him so much," I said, wiping at tears.

"Me, too."

"You're getting really good at that therapy stuff."

Holly patted my hand in appreciation then said, "You had a fight with Lori because you were angry about Mom and Tom."

"I don't think that's true."

"Did you know Mom was inside the bar?"

I nodded.

"And when was the last time you and Lori got physical?"

"Last year. When she tried to spray poison on my bees."

"Then you were defending your hive, protecting them because they couldn't help themselves. Why did you fight this time?"

I thought about the reason. Lori had made a stinky comment about my reputation. But I'd put up with much more than that from her without snapping. "She said I was sleeping with Ford."

"Are you mad at me, too? Mad enough to fight with me? Because you know I'm the one who started it."

"I'm not exactly happy with you."

"I'm really sorry. I had no idea how that one comment would take on a life of its own and bite you in the butt."

And in that second, all the meanness and bitterness and

anger washed right out of me. A simple apology from Holly had done the trick. I thought over some of my own actions recently and decided to make some amends, too.

"I'm going to apologize to a few people myself," I said, giving my sister a big hug.

Twenty-two

Tom Stocke's antique shop was located between Moraine's new post office and a seasonal corn stand, where Country Delight Farm operated a successful business on weekends selling fresh corn on the cob dripping with pure Wisconsin butter.

The sidewalk outside Tom's store was jam-packed with various items he hauled out every morning to entice potential customers. Every night he hauled them back inside.

I'm not much of an antique collector, but I had to pause to admire a Schwinn bicycle in perfect condition. Then I realized I was stalling and went inside where I saw mahogany and wicker, spinning wheels and toys, glassware and crocks, a Popeye tray next to two cartoon character metal lunch pails. Almost too much to take in all at once.

I found Tom at the back of the store, sitting in a wooden rocker. And he was cleaning a firearm. Like the one that shot out Patti's window and telescope. That's the first thing that popped into my head even though I couldn't tell one type of gun from another. But didn't Tom complain to me recently about Patti's snooping? In the past, I had intentionally overlooked the fact that Tom had a wanted poster face, mainly because of his mellow personality. If I've learned nothing else in life, I *have* learned not to judge a book by its cover. Although, on second thought, haven't I picked up lots of books because they had cool covers? Only to find sometimes that the insides didn't measure up?

Anyway, right now, I saw Tom in a whole new criminal-element light. It's amazing how a weapon in somebody's hand can change your perspective on their capabilities.

"Hi, Story," he said, looking up and seeing me before I could hightail it out of his store.

"Is that a rifle?" came out of my mouth, because suddenly I forgot why I'd come here in the first place.

"Pretty, isn't she?"

I couldn't peel my eyes away. "Is it an antique?" It looked old even to my inexperienced eyes. Not exactly like something you'd see in a war movie, not the kind that had to be loaded with gunpowder. But cowboy flicks had firearms that looked a lot like the one in Tom's lap. Where was Hunter with his weaponry knowledge when I needed him?

"She's not exactly an antique," Tom said, moving it to his knee so the barrel pointed at the ceiling. My eyes swept the immediate vicinity in case he had bullets close by. I didn't see any. "She's vintage."

"Oh, right," I agreed, like I had a clue what the difference was between antique and vintage.

He gave the weapon a final swipe with a rag and propped it against the wall. "What brings you here?" he asked.

For a panicked second or two, I still couldn't remember. Then it came to me.

"I came to apologize for my bad behavior last night. You must think I fist fight on a regular basis, but I don't. Really I don't. And I'm sorry I upset you and Mom."

Tom stood up. I realized how tall he was, as though I

was seeing him for the very first time. He literally towered over me. I started backing up, not willing to turn away. My imagination took off with visions of him grabbing that rifle and using it on me.

"I appreciate that," he said. "We've been retail neighbors for five years. I know you aren't normally a rabble-rouser."

I recognized *rabble-rouser* as one of Mom's more descriptive words. She must have called me that last night after witnessing her oldest (and dumbest) daughter behaving like a maniac. "Well, thanks for accepting my apology," I said.

"You're welcome."

Then I noticed something else. He was wearing the same blue button-down shirt he'd had on the night I first saw him and Mom at Stu's. "I see that bloodstain almost came completely out."

Tom looked down at his shirt, to the faint outline where he'd supposedly "cut" himself the same day I'd lost a body that turned out to belong to his brother.

With that I blew out of the antique store, went around to the back of the corn stand, and called Hunter. The first thing he said was, "I heard about last night. If you wanted to get physical with someone, you could have called me."

Great. Even Hunter had found out!

"Where are you?" I asked. "I need you down at Tom's antique store right away."

Of course he asked why. I told him about the rifle, about it maybe being the same kind that had shot at Patti's house and about the washed out bloodstain. Then, tipping my head and looking up over the corn stand and antique shop, I spotted another piece of condemning evidence.

"*And* he has a hickory nut tree in his backyard," I finished. "Right behind his apartment."

"Well that tree thing cements it." Did I hear amusement in his tone?

"You have to handle this."

"Call your police chief, Story. I'm working."

"He's not taking my calls."

"Just don't call 9-1-1. Call the nonemergency number."

"Pleeeeeze?"

Hunter sighed into the phone. "Exactly what do you want me to do?"

"Just check out the rifle. Figure out how to match its bullets to the one over at Patti's." Hunter wasn't always this dense.

"Story, you've been watching too much *CSI*. Can't you stay out of it?"

"Pleeeeeze?"

"All right. I'll go over and talk to Tom. But I'm not accusing him of anything. If I sense something wrong, I'll contact Johnny."

"Can you come over right now?"

"Why not? I don't have anything better to do."

"I heard the sarcasm."

"You owe me."

I grinned in spite of the grimness of the situation. My debts to Hunter were mounting. We'd have to come up with some kind of payment plan, and I had just the thing. But it would have to wait.

Speaking of waiting—he sure took his time. It felt like forever before he pulled up in his SUV. He saw me hiding out behind the corn stand, gave me a wink, and strolled into Tom's store. I got into his SUV and shared the passenger seat with Ben. "Hey, big guy," I said to my canine friend. "What's new?"

He gave the end of my nose a big slurpy tongue kiss. I stroked his ears and neck.

"I sure hope Hunter agrees with me that Tom has some explaining to do." I continued to talk things over with Ben, explaining why I'd gone to Tom's store in the first place and what I stumbled over while inside. I'm positive Ben understood all of it.

A little later, Hunter came out and got in the driver's seat. He stared straight ahead. His face was twitching.

"Well?" I wanted to know, tugging on his sleeve. "Say something. Anything."

Hunter turned to face me, and like the rest of the people in my life today, started laughing. And he wouldn't stop.

"Ben," I said. "Tell Hunter I don't appreciate being laughed at."

Ben gazed at me, then at Hunter.

Hunter wiped his eyes with the palms of his hands.

"Did you see the rifle?" I asked. "Did you?"

Hunter nodded, and I could tell he was choking back another laugh-out-loud response.

"And?"

"It's a Daisy air rifle."

And he cracked up again.

Twenty-three

This much I knew for sure—my knowledge of guns was extremely limited, so when Hunter finally got himself under control, he had to explain what a Daisy air rifle was. Although the *air* part had already clued me in that it couldn't have shot out Patti's window from across the river.

"It's a kid's BB gun," he said. "They still make one called the Red Ryder, but most of them are collectibles now." Hunter burst out laughing again.

I got out, slammed the door, and walked back to my store.

I wanted to tell my mother to stop seeing Tom immediately, but I still couldn't believe the transformation in the woman I'd been at odds with for so long. All it took was a little romance to soften her crusty, hard edges. But why couldn't she have picked a different man?

I called her, but instead of making demands that she ditch Tom, I said, "We're a little shorthanded at the store. Can you help?"

Now, those who know me might find that request a little bizarre on my part, since I've been spending years trying to keep my mother out of my store. And for good cause. But how else was I going to keep tabs on her? She agreed to come over, and arrived soon after.

"You asked Mom to come in and work?" Holly said, stomping into the back room. "What are you, nuts?"

"It's very temporary," I said.

"Do you know what she's doing right this minute?"

I suspected that I really, really didn't want to know. "Dusting?" I guessed. "Reorganizing the toilet paper display out by the door?" She'd done that before.

"No. She's taken over the cash register and she's giving away honey sticks with every purchase."

"That isn't like Mom," I said.

"This is the new Mom, remember? What will she give away next?"

Was Mom about ready to give away the store? "Trust me," I told my sister. "It's a temporary situation."

"Where are you going?" Holly noticed when I shut down my computer, something I had to do these days to keep Carrie Ann from playing social media games all day.

I picked up Dinky, grateful for summer and the twins. Running the store *and* the beeyard was tough when they weren't there to pitch in. "Since we have extra staff, I'm going home to work in the beeyard," I said. "Want to come?" Like Holly would ever say yes.

Holly turned and walked away. "No thanks," she said over her shoulder. "I'll help Mom hand out free honey sticks."

Outside, I spotted Johnny Jay poking around in the cemetery. So! He'd finally figured out that Ford hadn't been killed in the fireplace, that Tom's brother had died someplace else. Gee, too bad he had such a late start when he could have been right on top of the case if only he'd listened to me. Leaving Dinky leashed to a hook on the side of the store, one I'd specifically designed for dog owners, I slithered along the building to get a good look without him seeing me.

A few kids ran past, right in front of him. One of them jumped over a headstone.

"Hey," Johnny Jay yelled at them, but they kept going. "What's the use," I heard him mutter to himself. What's the use is right. If he'd believed me in the first place about the body in the cemetery, he could have handled it properly. But now so many people had been in and out of there, he'd never find clues even if they reached out and tapped him on the shoulder.

He was standing at the center of the actual crime scene. I was convinced of it. Ford Stocke had been murdered right there next to the crabapple tree. Then he was hauled away almost right in front of my eyes. If the killer got away with this murder, it was all on Johnny Jay's thick-skulled head.

I saw Stanley Peck drive up, so I went back to the front of the store, and invited my beekeeping friend to join me in the apiary. Stanley's never in a big hurry, especially now that he's a widower and retired. He fell into step with Dinky and me.

"How much longer will Noel be in town?" I asked Stanley.

"He'll be around till next week. He's working on something top secret. I'm afraid to ask what."

"At least he isn't into drugs."

"Drugs might be more wholesome," Stanley said. "I worry about him. He's had one or two accidental explosions."

"Put him in riot gear," I suggested.

The honey house in my backyard is one of my favorite places on earth. It's where I've spent long hours immersed in the sweet aromatic smell of honey, creating different forms of this liquid gold to offer to my customers. I was proud of my product. Honey isn't wasted nutrients like sugar. It has many great B vitamins as well as calcium, iron, potassium, and more.

And honey has honest-to-goodness healing properties *and* naturally retains moisture. So lately, I've been experimenting with it in special beauty treatments, like skin lotion and cleansing scrubs. I haven't perfected those enough to sell them yet, but I'm working on it.

Before Stanley and I entered the honey house, I released Dinky from her leash. We watched her sniff around.

Then Stanley pulled something out of his pocket and handed it to me, saying, "I found a bead. Holly said it might be from a scarf you own."

Sure enough, the bead Stanley held out looked very similar. "Close, but not quite. This one is silver," I said. "Mine are topaz. Where did you find it?"

Stanley looked sheepish. "I cut through the cemetery earlier," he said. "I used to walk all the way around out of respect. But since everybody else does it . . ." He let the sentence die out.

The location surprised me. "I wonder how it got there." Stanley shrugged.

Then we heard a strange sound coming from the other side of the cedar hedge, the one that separated my house from Patti's. Stanley and I looked at each other, both of us listening hard to a growly, moany sound. Then a weakly voiced, "*Mmmhhhmm*."

Dinky heard it, too, and barked.

"What *is* that?" I said to Stanley, figuring it out as soon as I said it and doing a Patti-style leap through the shrubs.

My neighbor was on the ground facedown, wearing plaid pajamas. And she'd been tied up tight. And gagged with duct tape. And her eyes were wild. She squealed when I pulled off the tape—a little too roughly, but I was worried.

Stanley whipped out a pocketknife and cut away at the rope, being careful not to cut Patti.

"Oh no! I can't move," Patti said when she was released

from the bindings. "I've been like this for hours and hours and my muscles are paralyzed."

"Just relax," Stanley said. "We'll work 'em slow." Then to me, "You better call the cops."

"Do I have to?" I said. "Can't you handle this?"

"Make the call," Stanley said.

"No, don't!" Patti yelled. "We don't need cops."

"Make the call," Stanley said again, overruling her.

So while he coaxed Patti into a sitting position, I used my cell phone to call the nonemergency police number, since my word was as good as toilet paper in emergency dispatch.

"They're sending somebody over," I said when I hung up, relieved that they had taken me seriously this time. At least I hoped they had. I was even more relieved when Officer Sally Maylor showed up instead of the chief. By then we had Patti propped up on her back steps with a glass of water in her hand. Sally wanted her to fill out a report.

"I can barely move my hand to drink this water," Patti said. "How can I hold a pen and write? I'm still getting over the shock of thinking I was paralyzed."

"I'd think you'd be more shocked at being tied up so long," I said, taking the glass from her. "What happened?"

Sally butted in, "Let me ask the questions, Story. Okay?" But nobody needed to ask anything from that point forward, because we couldn't have stopped Patti if we tried.

"This morning the delivery truck brought the new telescope I ordered," she began. "Which I was expecting, and paid a whole lot extra to have shipped extra fast. I was in these jammies, so I called out the front door and told the driver to leave it by the back door.

"The box was big and I was trying to get it through my door when I was attacked from behind. Someone grabbed me and before I knew it, I was all tied up on the ground. That was around nine o'clock."

She really *had* been tied up for hours.

"Did you get a look at your attacker?" Sally said.

But Patti wasn't focusing on Sally. She jumped up at that point, forgetting about her paralysis. "It's gone! My new telescope is gone and I didn't even get it out of the box. What kind of crazy lunatic is running around this town? You'd think a place like Moraine would be safe, but no!"

"So," I said, cutting her off before she got too far off topic. "Did you see who jumped you?"

Patti shook her head. "I might have passed out."

"Since when do you pass out?" I asked her. To my knowledge the only fainter in our bunch was my sister Holly.

"I could have been drugged," she suggested.

"Let's take you into the hospital and have you drug tested," Sally said.

"No, thanks, I take that back. What if I was choked until I passed out?"

Sally studied Patti's neck. "No marks."

"Well, whoever it was sure knew how to use rope," Patti said, obviously embarrassed that someone had trussed her up and she hadn't been able to do a single thing to stop it.

"You didn't see anything?" Stanley said. "Not one detail that might help Sally?"

"Not a one."

"Aren't you supposed to be observant?" I said. "Since you're a reporter and all?"

Patti shrugged that off, but she had a theory about the type of individual who would attack an innocent woman like herself.

"I'm sick and tired of all those do-gooders who still think they are entitled to private lives. This is the age of transparency and they need to get with the program. Nobody has the right to stop me from gathering personal information!"

Sally and I exchanged looks of disbelief, then Sally

stood back with her arms crossed and said, "Patti, you and that damn telescope have obviously made a few enemies and one of them really doesn't want you to set up another observation tower. We'll check around, but our chances of catching the guy are slim."

"I wonder if my homeowner's policy will pay for another telescope," Patti pondered.

"My point is," Sally said, "maybe you should give the telescope obsession a rest."

"And give in to aggression? No way! Next time, I'll be ready."

"Next time," I said. "You might be dead."

Twenty-four

It wasn't until later in the day, after I'd spent some much-needed time catching up in the honey house, that I remembered the conversation with Stanley and how he had found a bead in the cemetery. I'd shoved it in my pocket when we heard Patti moaning from her side of the cedars.

I fished it out and held it up. What did Stanley have, X-ray eyes? Because it wasn't that big. Although it was crystal, so maybe the sun caught it just right and Stanley spotted the reflection.

And it wasn't until even later, after I'd closed up the store and walked home under a rising full moon with Holly and Dinky, that I remembered something else: Dinky had gobbled up something that night in the cemetery. I'd tried to stop her, but I'd been too late. And she'd upchucked it after we got home. At the time, I hadn't thought anything of it, since she tended to eat just about anything and everything.

But what if it was an important clue? I didn't have any

solid facts to support that assumption. The idea presented itself out of nowhere, just rose up and struck me in the head like a sudden bolt of lightning.

Before I got a chance to follow up on that thought, P.P. Patti arrived at my house wearing her pajamas and carrying a pillow and a duffel bag.

"After what happened to me," she said, "I can't stay home alone."

What could I say? Nothing, that's what. I had a houseguest whether I wanted one or not.

I'd already taken the trash outside, so I hustled out there with Holly and Patti trailing behind. I pulled out the top garbage bag, got down on my knees, opened it up, and rummaged around. It really smelled ripe.

"What are you doing?" Holly asked, holding her nose.

"I have to check something out." There it was. I came up with the wadded paper towel I'd used to clean up Dinky's gooey mess.

"I'm going to be sick," Holly said when I pried it open and she got her eyes on semidigested stomach stuff.

"If you had a dog," I said, "you wouldn't be such a sissy. Besides, I have natural ruggedness that I must have inherited from Mom."

Wow. That came out of nowhere. My ruggedness statement was a huge improvement in my attitude toward my mother. Before today, I would have shuddered to think I shared any qualities, good or bad, with her. This was a giant step in the right direction. And unlike Holly, I didn't need a shrink to tell me I was on the right path.

Studying the paper towel, I spotted something solid in the drying out blob, something round. I palmed it and swiped at it to clean it off.

"A silver bead," I said with a little frog in my voice. "Exactly like the one from my scarf, only a different color."

Holly and Patti wanted to know what was so important that I'd pick through dog barf, so I told them how Stanley had found a silver bead in the cemetery and here was another one from the same place.

"The bead Stanley gave me could have been dropped anytime," I said. "But this one"—I held Dinky's gobbled treasure up between my fingers—"was in the cemetery when Ford Stocke was killed. We have an important time-line."

"So what?" Patti said. "Unless Ford Stocke choked to death on a bunch of beads."

"We still don't know cause of death," I realized, closing up the garbage bag and returning it to the trash can.

"Maybe," Holly said, as we went back inside, "Alicia used those same beads in other scarves. Or maybe one of the Petries walked through there with a stack of scarves and beads dropped to the ground. I agree with Patti. No big deal."

I made a phone call to Mom just to confirm that I wasn't barking up the wrong tree. "The scarf you gave me," I said. "Came from Aggie Petrie's sale booth, right?"

"Yes. Why?"

"Um . . . eh . . . I love it so much I'd like to get another one. For a friend."

"Oh, isn't that sweet." I almost thought I was talking to my grandmother. I was tempted to say, "Put Mom on the phone."

After I hung up, I said to Holly and Patti, "Have either of you heard anything about a murder weapon? Or how Ford was killed?"

They both shook their heads.

I made another phone call. This time to the medical examiner, Jackson Davis.

Jackson and I were friendly enough that I had him on speed dial. We'd bonded one night at Stu's bar during an Irish wake, and since then he shares tidbits with me. Jackson's job is to fit together all the missing pieces. It's a big jigsaw puzzle to him. He might have an easy time stamping "dead as a doornail" on Ford's forehead, but next he'll have to figure out exactly what had happened to make him that way. Not only would he figure out what caused Ford's death, but hopefully Jackson would have some insight into even more details that might catch his killer.

I'm slightly embarrassed to admit to myself that I'm not above having a morbid fascination when it comes to tragedies and major dramas. We humans are wired that way, even though most of us won't admit it out loud. But I'm not the only one in this town who is fixated on crime shows on television or who slows down to gawk when I come across a car accident.

Holly made sandwiches for us while I talked about this and that with Jackson. Finally I got around to the reason for my call. "Did you finish the autopsy on Ford Stocke?"

Jackson chuckled. "Are you pumping me for information again?"

"You know me. Snoopy Story. But I have a personal interest in this case. My mom's dating Ford's brother."

"As a matter of fact, I *did* complete the autopsy. I just finished giving a verbal report to the police chief and the next-of-kin."

"Tom Stocke?"

"Right. He's the closest relative."

"Can you tell me if Ford was killed inside the house where his body was found?"

"That I can't do, because it's an ongoing investigation."

"Can you tell me what caused his death?"

"That's not a secret."

Oh good. I had been ready to go into my promise-not-to-tell speech, which usually only worked when Jackson was tipping a glass or two at Stu's. And even then it wasn't easy getting him to talk. So the "not a secret" part was a relief. "How did he die?" I asked, hearing the eagerness in my voice. Darn.

"In layman terms or . . ."

"Layman," I interrupted.

"Strangled," Jackson said. "Strangled until dead."

I felt my stomach pitch. "With what?"

"Can't reveal that, either. The chief wants to withhold certain details."

After I hung up I didn't feel like eating the sandwich Holly put down in front of me.

"What's wrong?" she asked.

"You're not going to believe this," I said.

"Try me."

"He was strangled."

"With a scarf?" Holly practically shouted.

"Jackson wouldn't say."

"Bring it on," Patti yelled, excited over the latest bit of news.

With that war cry, Patti made herself at home. Holly stayed overnight, too, since her husband Max was out of town as usual. The three of us sat up late, talking through possibilities and various scenarios while sipping wine.

I drank more than usual.

And ended up dreaming about beads, barf, and bullets.

Twenty-five

The next morning I had a monster headache. Patti and Holly were sharing a bed in the spare room and didn't wake up when I peeked in. Dinky's head poked out of the covers between them, but she nestled back down. The hairless dog loved the warmth of a nice thick blanket more than anything else.

After having a light breakfast of coffee and toast with honey butter, I went right to The Wild Clover where I found Carrie Ann in the back room playing games online.

"I thought I shut down that computer," I accused. "And I have a secret password. How did you get online?"

Carrie Ann's eyes were definitely darting. "Uh—uh, you forgot to shut it down?"

She had the password! How had she found it out? Before I could continue my interrogation of the computer hacker, a siren wailed close by. So of course we had to go investigate that instead.

By the time Carrie Ann and I burst through the front

door, Johnny Jay's chief car and two other squad cars were parked just down the block, in front of Tom Stocke's antique store. And when they got out of their vehicles and approached the building, they did it cautiously and furtively like they didn't want the occupant to know of their approach. Which was ridiculous considering all the noise they'd made coming into town.

The antique store wasn't even open yet, so they slunk around the back side of the building where we couldn't see them anymore. But we didn't have to. They were obviously heading for Tom's attached apartment and, based on their serious body language, weren't paying a friendly social call.

If that wasn't enough bad news, I saw Grams's Caddy come down the street, do a U-turn in slow motion, and pull up next to Johnny's car. I heard the crunch of metal connecting with metal. When Grams pulled forward, the car's side mirror came loose, dangling from a few wires.

Mom got out of the passenger seat with a covered dish in her hand. "For cripes' sake," she said, shades of the old Mom popping to the surface. "Next time, I'm driving. You better get out of here before the chief spots you."

Grams, taking Mom's advice, peeled rubber, something I didn't know she could do. The only bad part was that she took off while Mom's passenger door was still open and it banged against one of the squad cars before slamming shut.

"Unbelievable," my cousin said as we watched Grams disappear. Then Carrie Ann said, "I'll cover at the store." And she took off.

I was already moving in my mother's direction.

Mom was staring at the three cop cars as though she was trying to absorb the implication. By then, I was at her side. "Where are you going?" I asked her.

"I'm taking breakfast to Tom." Her head continued to swivel. "What's going on here?"

"I don't know. The cops arrived a few minutes ago and headed around back toward Tom's apartment."

"This can't be good."

"No, it can't," I said. "Why don't you come to the store until we find out what's happening?"

"Why would I do that," Mom said, "when I can just go to Tom's and find out firsthand?"

She had a good point.

Mom started marching. I followed.

Officer Sally Maylor was guarding the door to Tom's apartment. She wasn't a large woman but I always thought of her as a tough, strong woman if she ever had to be. I imagined she had all kinds of weapons at her disposal— mace, a nightstick, a stun gun, a firearm, and lots of legal authority to apply them as necessary. But Sally had always treated me well and I didn't want that to change.

Mom wasn't about to let Sally stop her, though. "I'm going in," she said, trying to hand her dish to Sally. "Here, hold this."

"Sorry, Helen. I have my orders. Nobody gets inside."

"We'll see about that," Mom said, pulling out her own authoritative tone. She edged closer. Sally looked ready to act.

"Helen, I have two choices," Sally said. "I can let you in, in which case I'll lose my job. Or I can keep you out and stay employed. Guess which one I'm going to pick?"

"Tom's okay, though?" Mom asked, sounding worried now instead of bossy. "He isn't hurt, right?"

"Tom's health is fine," Sally said. I'd already figured that out since no ambulances or fire engines were outside the store.

I grabbed Mom's arm. "Come on. We'll wait out front. Let's not get Sally in trouble."

Mom didn't look like she was going to back down, but after a moment of hesitation she did.

While we waited, I took a few minutes to survey the damage to the chief's vehicle. From the front end, I said, "We have to cover for Grams, or Johnny Jay is going to make sure her driver's license is taken away from her."

"That might not be such a bad thing," Mom said. "She's going to kill somebody at this rate."

"Not at her regular speed of five miles an hour she won't. Just don't tell her to floor it next time she does something like swipe Johnny Jay's car."

The side mirror would have to be replaced. Lucky for Grams, there was no telltale sign of paint from her car. Not a trace on the other squad car, either, which only had a little bitty scrape. And if anyone on the street or inside one of the businesses had witnessed the incident, they wouldn't tell on her. Johnny Jay wasn't their favorite guy. Grams was everybody's darling. So my grandmother was home scot-free.

I took the opportunity to apologize to Mom for my behavior outside of Stu's when I'd gone to the mat with Lori Spandle. She set her breakfast dish on the hood of Johnny's car and hugged me. Two apologies down, two to go. Because as much as I dreaded the idea, the new kinder me realized that I had to make things right with the Petries, too. Lori Spandle and Johnny Jay were my lifelong enemies and for right now, they could just stay that way. But I didn't have any real quarrel with Aggie and Eugene, although Aggie did her best to pick fights. In the customer service business, I've learned to grovel when necessary.

I tried to prepare Mom for the inevitable. "I'm pretty sure Tom is going to jail."

"I don't think so."

"Three police cars? It doesn't look good."

But she refused to listen. "I just hope they finish before Tom's breakfast gets cold."

Carrie Ann arrived on the scene again, saying the twins had punched in. She patted Mom on the shoulder and gave me a worried glance.

Finally, they brought Tom out and as I'd suspected, he was handcuffed.

What followed was classic television-style romance between Mom and Tom.

"I brought you breakfast," Mom called out, holding up the dish and making her voice peppy even though her face was white. Then to Johnny she said, "Let the man at least have his breakfast first."

"Save it for me, Helen," Tom said, giving her a big grin, sort of forced considering the circumstances. "I'll eat it as soon as I get back. Everything you make is so delicious."

"Shut up and get in the car," Johnny Jay said to Tom.

"Hurry back soon," my delusional mom said. "I'll be waiting."

"Miss you already," Tom said as he got in the backseat of the squad car. Johnny Jay slammed the door and went around to get into the driver's seat.

"What the hell happened to the side of my car?" he yelled, proceeding to take the Lord's name in vain in a few combinations I'd never heard before.

Nobody said anything.

"Well, if this doesn't beat all," he said. "Somebody had the nerve to swipe my car in broad daylight while I was right around the back of the building." He uttered a few more angry swear words.

After examining his vehicles from all angles and putting pressure on the bystanders, which didn't get him any further, Johnny Jay glared at me, then at Mom, then at the dish in Mom's hand.

"How did you get here, Helen?" he asked her, knowing as well as the rest of us that Grams drives her around most of the time.

"She came with me," I piped up and lied, committed to my grandmother and her continued freedom to travel as she pleases.

Johnny Jay cursed some more but eventually got into his

car and slammed the door, causing the mirror to fall all the way off. As they drove away, Tom turned around in the backseat and locked eyes with Mom until the chief's car disappeared from sight.

My heart ached for Mom after seeing how devoted she'd been to Tom. They really had something going, something powerful. Not once did my mother question his innocence. What would happen to her newfound faith in mankind if Tom turned out to be guilty?

After that I really, really, really didn't want Tom Stocke to turn out to be a murderer.

Twenty-six

My mom had never dated anybody other than my dad. He was number one in her book from high school until his death. And even beyond.

Then Tom came along.

If Tom killed his brother, that would be a bitter pill for her to swallow. Not to mention she might revert to her old bitter-pill personality, and that would be a setback for the entire family.

Tom Stocke had a lot going against him.

For one, he was a big man, large enough to pick up Ford and carry him a good distance if he had to. So if Tom had watched me stumble across his brother in the cemetery before he managed to accomplish whatever he was trying to do, he could easily have made off with the body as soon as I went inside the store.

Then there was the blood on his shirt. If it turned out to be Ford's, Tom was toast.

And if they found the murder weapon inside his apartment or store, Tom was burnt toast.

After careful thought, I decided Tom didn't stand a chance.

"I might as well come to the store and help out," Mom said. "Until Tom gets back."

I didn't like that one bit. Not only because Mom might reorganize all the shelves or give away the store, but because customers would be gossiping up a storm, making all kinds of crazy accusations about the Stocke brothers. That was the last thing Mom needed, and I told her as much.

"This will all be cleared up very soon," she said. "In the meantime, I'll set any misguided customers straight with their facts."

The only positive thing about her working was that I'd get some other errands and projects done. I tried calling Alicia Petrie from a listing in the phone directory. When an answering machine picked up, I left a request for her to call me back.

Planning to get a little paperwork out of the way, I sat down at my desk with the door closed. But before I tackled the stack in front of me, I remembered something about my conversation with Tom's brother.

When I'd asked Ford how long he planned to rent Clay's house, he'd said, "Just for the weekend. By then we'll be done."

We'll!

One sleeping bag. One camping chair, one everything. So what had he meant?

Who was the other person, or persons? And where were they?

I hadn't caught that at the time, mainly because I was so freaked-out that Lori Spandle might actually have let Ford sign a long-term lease. The only part I'd really absorbed was "for the weekend," which was a major relief.

I went up front and questioned Mom. "You've heard the gossip about Tom, right?"

Mom nodded. "It's all over town."

"And the part about Ford running off with his wife? Is that true?"

Mom nodded again.

"Do you know if Tom and Ford were in contact before this happened?" I asked. "I mean, did Ford know that Tom lived in Moraine?"

"Apparently, because he showed up. But it was a surprise to Tom. They hadn't spoken in years."

"Did Tom have any idea what Ford wanted?"

Mom shook her head. "Tom's such a good man he didn't want to think bad thoughts, but I'm pretty sure his brother was after his money."

I'd forgotten about Tom's lottery score! He'd lived so simply. He must have banked the entire wad. And the money would have grown since then.

"If Ford was after Tom's money," I said, "how would he get his hands on it? After what he did with his wife, Tom wouldn't willingly share his wealth with the jerk."

Mom looked both ways to make sure nobody was close enough to overhear us. "The only way?" she whispered. "He'd have to inherit it."

"But that would mean . . ."

Mom nodded. "Tom would have to be dead."

"He was going to kill Tom?" I stared at Mom.

"Maybe," she said, leaving me standing there with my mouth open.

I shut it and scuttled back to my hole in the wall.

Self-defense might actually work as a real defense! I could imagine the whole thing.

Ford tried to kill Tom. Tom defended himself. Too bad he panicked. He should have turned himself in right away instead of disposing of Ford's body in a fireplace. Now look at the mess he was in. And it was way too late to convince Johnny Jay that it had been an accident. Tom was looking at manslaughter, if he was lucky.

If Ford was going to kill Tom, then the *we* meant he had a partner.

The only thing that might help my mom's new boyfriend was to expose that partner. Once he surfaced (or she), that person would have to tell the cops the truth—that Ford's intention had been to eliminate his brother and make off with his money. Then Tom could plead self-defense for sure.

I called Patti's cell phone. She didn't answer. Instead she walked in without even knocking. Patti wore her pocket vest crammed full of various tools associated with her new trade. Her homemade press pass dangled from her neck, and she wore a pair of black shades.

I wondered if last night's wine had affected her as much as it had me.

"Where's my sister?" I asked her.

"Sick," Patti said.

"The rest of us had to get up and go."

Patti shrugged and plopped down in the chair next to my desk.

I told her what I knew about Tom's arrest and why I thought Ford had a partner floating around somewhere.

Patti hung on every word, then said, "I have my own problems, too, you know."

"Like what? I thought you'd wanted to work with me to solve this. Look what it could do for your career."

"First I have to track down my attacker. Until then, I feel like a prisoner. I'm used to total freedom of movement and now? I'm a shell of the woman I used to be."

"You'll be safe as long as you don't order another telescope." I couldn't believe what came out of my mouth next. "Besides, you can stay with me as long as you want."

Before I could stuff those words back in and gulp them down, Patti perked up and said, "Okay. It's a deal. I'll help you and you help me."

"Any more hickory nuts?" I asked.

"None so far. But I have a lead on the murder weapon."

"You do? Who told you?" With Patti, asking for credentials was important.

"I can't divulge my source. That would be unethical. All I know at this point is that brown fibers were found on Ford's neck."

"Like threads from a scarf?"

"Maybe."

Patti could be making up stuff for all I knew. "So how are we going to find Ford's partner in crime?" I said.

"That's a tough one," she said. "How are we going to track the kook who tied me up and left me for dead?"

"You weren't even close to dead."

"I might have been if you hadn't come along to rescue me." Patti finally took off the dark sunglasses. Her eyes were bloodshot. "Do you think it was an outside job or an inside job?" she asked.

"Which one are we talking about? Ford Stocke?"

"No. My attacker."

"Inside," I said, convinced that Patti's assailant had been someone she'd ticked off. And that meant a local resident. "Someone is watching you, making sure you don't get another telescope."

Patti nodded. "That sounds reasonable. But I can't figure out why. It's not like I can see the whole town from that window. My view is seriously restricted." She sounded disappointed with her limited ability to snoop.

"No more telescopes," I repeated in case she wasn't listening. It seemed like a no-brainer to me.

"What about Ford's partner?" she asked. "Inside job or outside job?"

"Since no one else was staying at the house with Ford, I'm going to guess inside. Whoever it was didn't need a place to stay, so the partner lives in the area. I'm not sure how to start looking, though."

"I'm going to find out the name of the person who delivered my telescope," Patti said. "Maybe they saw something."

Right then, Alicia returned my call, I explained about my scarf, and we arranged to have me swing by.

"I'm going over to Alicia Petrie's. You check out the delivery company."

And with that, I hung up and set out to investigate.

Twenty-seven

Alicia Petrie lived right next door to her in-laws, Aggie and Eugene, so I planned on killing two birds with one stone. First, I'd talk beads with crafty Alicia, then I'd go over and make things right with crabby old Aggie.

I drove my truck slowly up Rustic Road, taking time to watch the ducks and Canadian geese floating in the marshy areas along the road, smelling freshly mowed grass through the open window. The aroma of cow pies drifted into the truck, reminding me of the country, but in a good way. Pig farms are something else entirely. They stink to high heaven. But cows make me think of lazy days, lying faceup in the grass, creating images out of the clouds overhead.

The outskirts of Colgate came into view over a hill. I turned off the main road toward Lake Five and parked between the two houses owned by the Petrie family.

Alicia opened the door when I rang the bell and said, "If you want permission to dig in the garden, you'll have to talk to my father." Then she laughed so I'd know she was joking.

I put on a happy face.

"Come in," she said, opening the door wide. "Do you want coffee?"

"Sure."

Alicia, unlike her mother-in-law, was all kindness and consideration. How she could stand living next door to Aggie and dealing with her every day was beyond me.

With a cup of coffee in my hand, I learned more than I needed to know about scarves. Sewing is not my forte. Or knitting, or crocheting, or anything else where I have to have handy hands. In fact, I failed a beginners sewing class Holly talked me into taking with her. She still brings it up occasionally.

But I pretended interest because it was obviously a passion for Alicia.

When she wound down, I said, "All I need is a handful of topaz beads to fix it. By the way, I absolutely love that scarf."

Alicia picked up a large sewing kit and rummaged through until she found the beads she needed, then she handed them to me. "Take extra, just in case," she said. "And thanks, I'm glad you like it. I almost always use crystal beads, and I weave them in carefully so if they get snagged, the whole works doesn't unravel. I'm surprised you lost so many at once."

"Me, too, but it was my own fault, not yours," I said, moving along quickly, thinking what a living witch Lori was. "What other colors do you use? Silver?"

"Sure, I use silver. And rose and blue opal, a lot of different colors. I can customize to your taste."

"Any silver beaded fringed scarves for sale at the festival?"

Alicia sipped her coffee. "Probably. I sent Bob over with several boxes of scarves. Why?"

"No reason." Then I tried to think of a way to ask if he'd walked through the cemetery with silver beads and what he was doing there, but nothing I came up with sounded right.

We exchanged some more small talk, then I thanked her for the coffee and her time and walked over to Aggie's front door.

While I waited for Aggie to answer her door, I couldn't help noticing lots of hickory nut trees in their yard. Shagbark trees, dropping hulled nuts all over the ground.

I knocked again.

Aggie answered the door. When she saw me, she scowled. I looked down at the small, snarky woman. She grabbed her cane, which had been leaning against the wall right by the door.

"What do you want?" she said.

"To apologize."

"For what?" Her nasty eyes stared into mine.

"For what happened to you, you know, getting arrested and all."

"Why apologize? Unless you were the cause of it. Were you?"

The last thing I was going to admit to was calling the cops to squeal on Aggie for not having a rummage sale permit. I'd only wanted her gone from in front of my store so she couldn't damage my business. And if things had gone as planned, if she hadn't started swinging that cane like a club, that would have been all that happened.

"Well?" she said waiting for my answer. "Don't tell me you're the one behind all our legal problems?"

"Of course not," I said, deciding quickly that I'd played only a minor role.

Her eyes narrowed into small slits.

"Listen," I said. "We got off to a bad start."

I could have mentioned that it was all her fault for making nasty comments, and then threatening me. Instead I said, "I hope we can be friendly in the future."

"Are you going to testify at our trial? Tell the judge

about witnessing police brutality and how I didn't do a thing to deserve what I got?"

"You hit a police officer with your cane!"

"Forget being friends then," Aggie said.

"*Friendly.* I said I hoped to be friendly. Not friends. There's a big difference between the two."

"And there's a difference between a toad and a frog, but they both eat bugs and poop out what's left."

I wasn't sure how toads and frogs and their bowel habits fit in, but with Aggie I couldn't be sure of anything.

"Make an effort, Aggie," I said. "I'm reaching out here."

"You can reach out with a shovel in your hand," Aggie said. "There's a pile of bark chips in the backyard. You can spread those around my bushes. Then I'll forgive you."

"You're a tough nut, Aggie," I said, watching her face for possible clues to the hickory nut stalker. No such luck.

The chip pile in the backyard was the biggest I'd ever seen in my life. There must have been twenty yards of mulch. Next to it was a large wheelbarrow. Aggie still clutched the cane even though her step was brisk and steady. While I surveyed the enormous pile, she disappeared into the toolshed. Pretty soon she popped back out. "Where did that shovel go?" she muttered. "Did you take it when you trespassed in our yard?"

"No, I left it stuck in the ground." I pointed to an empty spot in the garden. "Right there."

"Well, it's gone now."

I almost opened my big mouth and suggested we should check with Alicia, maybe she or Bob had borrowed it. But that would be like digging my own grave. If we found the shovel, I'd have to use it. Good thing that idea didn't cross Aggie's mind.

"You'll have to go get a shovel and come back," she said.

Yeah, right, like that was going to happen. "I'll see you later then," I said, meaning in some other lifetime. Aggie Petrie was impossible.

As I pulled out onto the main road, relieved to have escaped Aggie's clutches, a delivery truck came over the hill with its directional signal flashing. When it turned in front of my truck onto the lake road leading to the Petries,' I glanced at the side—Speedy Delivery. My eyes swept past the driver. Then I jerked my head back in astonishment.

Because Bob Petrie was driving the truck.

Twenty-eight

I called Patti's cell phone on the way back to my store. Unlike on my leisurely drive over, gawking at waterfowl and inhaling the scent of mowed grass were the furthest things from my mind. I had bigger fish to catch and one of them had just swum past me, heading for the lake.

Part of me was looking out for myself, I'll admit. Because once we nailed Patti's attacker, she would go home. If Bob had made the delivery, he might have seen something of significance. Or he even could have been the one who tied up Patti.

"What was the name of the delivery service that dropped off your new telescope?" I asked her when she answered her cell phone.

"Speedy Delivery," Patti said. My heart soared. Finally, a lead! Bob Petrie, here we come. Then she let me down hard. "They do almost all the deliveries in our area."

Subconsciously (and consciously) I guess I knew that.

"I found the driver," she said. "He didn't see anything

out of the ordinary. Nothing suspicious before, during, or after the delivery. No one at all around my house or even walking on the street. No cars. Nothing."

I decided that was one of the most observant delivery guys I'd ever heard of. He was missing his calling. He should have been a detective. "How did he remember so much?"

"Simple. I know how to get information out of people. Interrogation is part of my job."

"Did you recognize him?" Patti had been in Moraine long enough to remember faces, if not everybody's full name.

"What does that have to do with anything?"

"Just curious."

"I didn't actually meet him in person," she said. "We talked on the phone. Why?"

"What was his name?"

Silence on the other end while Patti thought. "I guess I didn't get it. I called the delivery office. Some woman said she'd check the records and someone would get back to me. He's the one who called. What's going on?"

"Meet me at the store."

Mom and Carrie Ann were meeting, greeting, and checking out customers. And even though Mom hadn't been up to her usually shenanigans when it came to disrespecting the way I ran the store, she'd managed to insert herself in a new way.

My staff all had on adorable pink bib aprons with "The Wild Clover" stenciled across the front.

Mom was busy at the moment, so I went to the back of the store. The twins were stocking shelves and arranging produce bins. They, too, had on pink aprons, though both of them looked extremely uncomfortable.

"We tried to tell your mom that guys don't wear pink," Brent said.

Trent nodded in agreement. "But she said a real man can pull off pink."

"She's right," I said. Hunter had a pink shirt and looked hot in it. I told them that and I could tell they felt slightly better, since they had a lot of respect for Hunter. "And you two," I continued, "are going to break female hearts wearing these."

Next I looked for my sister. Holly was nowhere in sight, which annoyed me. Don't we all wish we could stay in bed when the mood suits us?

I went back up front. "Mom, the aprons? You did that?"

Mom beamed. "It's a surprise I've been working on since the beginning of the year. I made them myself. Look," she pointed out details on the one she wore. "Clover pink to match The Wild Clover, a pen pocket, adjustable neck, and easy-to-reach patch pockets."

I'm proud to say I've rounded an important corner in my quest to live peacefully with my mother. Before, I would have been blowing steam just because she hadn't asked my input. Today, I thought they were really cool. Pink aprons that reminded me of clover were perfect.

"They're sweet," I said out loud, giving her a big hug.

"Wouldn't it be cute to add a few purple clovers to each one?" she said. Everybody agreed. Well, except the twins.

I put on the apron Mom handed me and thought about how I'd struggled to come up with the perfect name for my store. Deciding to call it The Wild Clover had been a good idea, since my honeybees and I love the stuff. Not only does clover grow wild in our yards, it's an important Wisconsin pasture crop and it blooms all summer, not just for a few weeks.

The blossoms are edible and taste sweet. Just ask any cow or foraging bee. And they are high in protein, which we all need to operate at our very best. Dried seedpods and flower heads can be ground into flour, although I'd have to be desperate to bother with that. Or it can be steeped for tea, which is more my style.

Next Mom said, "Where's Holly?"

Finally, Mom was about to realize just how unreliable her youngest daughter could be. I loved Holly to pieces, but family members working together was a big mistake waiting to happen. Plus, Mom thought Holly could do no wrong. Ha! My sister was about to have her flaws exposed right out there in front of everybody just like the rest of us.

"She's sick, Mrs. Fischer," Patti said, coming in and ruining the moment by covering for my sister. "We had a girls' overnight at Story's house and she doesn't feel good this morning."

Mom looked concerned. "I better go check on her."

"She's fine," I said.

"You should be more compassionate," Mom said to me. "Your poor sister is *ill*."

My head throbbed from alcoholic excess, too. Why should I care about Holly? Did she care about me right this minute? No, she didn't. Plus, she got to stay in bed.

Mom took off her apron, folded it neatly, and headed out to mother Holly.

"We have a situation," I said to Patti as I closed the door to the back room.

"We sure do. I'm clean out of leads to my attacker."

"Wait till you hear this." I went over my visit with Alicia, sort of skimming the surface. Investigation work, I was discovering, was a good part cerebral, like a giant mental puzzle. If only my head didn't hurt so much.

I finished with, "Then as I was pulling out, Bob Petrie drove past in a Speedy Delivery truck."

"So?" Obviously Patti had lost a few brain cells last night, too.

"So, he very well could be the driver who delivered the telescope."

"It doesn't matter if it was him. Or the police chief. Or

whoever. Because the driver didn't see anything suspicious."

"Maybe," I said, putting my own recent suspicion into words, "just maybe, the driver of the truck was the one who attacked you?"

Patti and I stared at each other, now firing on the same cylinder.

"He'd know what he was delivering," Patti said. "It said right on the box."

I nodded.

"Bob Petrie? But he doesn't even live in Moraine. I thought we decided my attacker had to be someone who didn't like me for professional reasons."

"Have you ever given Bob any reason to dislike you?"

"He doesn't even know me."

"Huh."

I'd been worrying over the events of the past few days. About how everything was rotating in a big loop around the dead-end street I lived on. Patti and I were the only ones on our block. Aurora and her garden center were across the street, but her house and outbuildings were set back. So really it was just me and Patti.

"The Petries have been like toilet paper stuck to my flip-flop," I said. "As hard as I try, I can't get rid of them." I thought a minute. "You better call the delivery service office again and get the name of the driver. With my luck it really was Petrie."

While Patti was on the phone, I called Holly's phone to tell her to suck it up and get into work. She didn't answer.

Patti hung up and said, "You were right on the money. It was Bob Petrie."

I thought about Aggie's hotheaded son and all the rumors about his previous run-ins with the law.

"Now what?" I asked.

"Now I go after him."

"You did say you're a good interrogator."

Patti grinned. "Bring it on!" Then the grin faded. "You're coming, too, right? That's what friends do, right?"

I sighed. "Right," I said.

Twenty-nine

The next several hours were busy, so Patti went off on her own with a promise to return soon.

Stanley Peck came into the store looking for his grandson. "Anybody seen Noel around?" he asked.

Carrie Ann answered. "Did you check the ammunition dump?"

"We have an ammunition dump?" Stanley said, gaping at her. "And I didn't know about it?"

"Gee, Stanley," Carrie Ann said, laughing. "You're getting gullible in your old age."

"Well," I said, "if the county had a live ammo and explosives storage facility, Noel would be volunteering there."

"Which reminds me," Carrie Ann said. "I haven't heard any explosions lately."

Stanley pulled a shopping basket from a stack and said, "That kid's been working nonstop, barely takes his head out of that notebook of his. But he wasn't around when I got up this morning and he hasn't come back since."

"He must be testing his experiment," I said. "I'm sure he's fine. None of us have seen flames shooting in the air or heard exceptionally loud noises."

"Noel needs a friend," Stanley said. "Somebody to spend time with instead of always being alone. It isn't natural."

"He seems perfectly normal to me," I said, not believing my own words but wanting to make Stanley feel better. Besides, what's normal anyway?

With my reassurance, Stanley headed down an aisle toward the beer cooler.

Sometimes I enjoy guessing what my customers will put in their shopping baskets and carts. Aurora, who specializes in otherworldly things, comes in to buy soy in all its forms, along with tofu, milk, beans, flour, nuts, and tart juices like cranberry without any added sweeteners. She's easy to guess.

Patti purchases quick energy boosters in case she doesn't have time for meals while she's stalking potential story leads. That means energy bars and certain specialty drinks containing enough caffeine and sugar to fuel a rocket ship.

Speaking of turbo power, if Noel did come in, he'd buy drain cleaner and ammonia, no food at all except maybe a fistful of my root beer honey sticks.

Right now a tourist passing through Moraine was at the checkout. I bagged for Carrie Ann—breath fresheners, a diuretic, and celery. This one had an eating disorder for sure. Which gave me an idea. So I asked my cousin, "Was anyone in right before or during the festival buying bleach, latex gloves, and black trash bags?"

"How would I remember a thing like that?"

"Just curious. If you remember anything significant, let me know."

I searched for the twins and asked them the same thing, but if anyone really had purchased crime-scene cleanup supplies, none of the staff remembered.

Mom came back from nursing Holly and she was toting a yellow cloth bag. I recognized it as mine, one I used instead of paper or plastic to save the environment.

"How's Holly?" I asked.

"I gave her painkillers. She's going to stay in bed a little longer."

"What's in the bag?"

Mom said, "All those hickory nuts piled up by your door. I put them in this bag so I can get them over to Milly for her recipe."

I opened my mouth. Nothing came out. Mom opened the bag so I could see how many she'd gathered. Lots. More than a squirrel could pile up in a week, maybe in a month.

"Did you see anybody over at the house?" I managed to croak.

Mom looked at me weird. "Just Holly," she said.

"Other than her."

"No. Are you okay?"

I nodded.

And if I thought things couldn't get worse than a pile of suspicious nuts, Lori Spandle strutted in to prove me wrong. Once, in the past, Lori had entered the store wearing a bee veil when she was recruiting residents to rise up against my beehives. She hadn't won that round. Today, she had the nerve to come in wearing a hockey helmet with a face cage.

We exchanged pleasantries.

"I have to wear this just in case you lose your temper again," she said. "You're a menace to society."

"Nobody's forcing you to come into my store."

"I need to know what you're up to next, check out what's going through your twisted little mind. This is the only way."

"And you think that helmet is going to protect your pea brain?"

"Watch it, Fischer." Lori flounced past me to the fruit aisle. I followed.

"A quick question," I said. "When you rented Clay's house to Ford, did he mention anyone else would be with him?"

She squeezed a lemon, then another. "No."

"Does my ex know how badly you messed up?" I said. I really had wanted to call Clay and tattle on Lori's incredible lack of good judgment, but I couldn't stand the thought of speaking to him. Besides, he'd probably defend her.

"Don't you have anything better to do than pry into my affairs?" she made the mistake of saying, since affairs were her specialty.

I didn't have to respond. My smirk said it all. I turned on my heel and walked off, thinking she looked utterly ridiculous in that helmet.

Patti returned with a full report on Bob Petrie. She filled me in while I walked Dinky around the perimeter of the cemetery. "I CCAP'd him," she said, pronouncing it c-cap. CCAP stands for Consolidated Court Automation Programs and is a website where Wisconsin governmental agencies upload information about cases in circuit courts. And they update it hourly to keep it as current as possible. So if a person has been in legal trouble, anybody can find out about it, unless it involves sealed records like underage individuals or adoptions, that sort of thing. Any other records are wide open.

"He isn't a habitual traffic offender," Patti said. "Speedy Delivery probably checked with the motor vehicle department and cleared him for hire without investigating any further. But he's been in trouble for petty theft, disorderly, and vandalism."

"What a nice guy," I observed. "Perfect profile for what we're looking for."

"And he's getting off work just about now."

"Let's go wait for him at his house."

On the way over, I told her about the hickory nuts my mother found at my doorstep. "Are you as confused by those nuts as I am?" I asked her.

"A threat of some sort. And I still can't believe I let that guy get away with my telescope."

"Your hands were tied," I said, meaning it literally as well as figuratively. "It wasn't like you had a choice. Any more info on the murder weapon?"

"Just brown fibers so far."

We came over the hill into Colgate and parked close to the road leading to the lake. And waited.

"What should we do when he shows up?" Patti asked. "Run him into the ditch?"

I hadn't thought that far. "We better stop him before he gets home," I said. "Otherwise we'll have to deal with all the Petries and we won't accomplish a thing other than get run off their property. Or get put to work spreading bark mulch."

"Spreading what?"

"Never mind. Do you know what Bob drives when he isn't working?" I asked a bit late in the game.

"No."

"That's problematic."

"I'll walk out in the road and flag down every car," Patti said, twisting around and peering into the back of my truck. "I could use one of those construction flags. Do you have one?"

"No. And if he's the guy who tied you up, what makes you think he won't recognize you and run right over you?"

"Good point."

"You're the experienced investigator," I said, using finger quotes around the *experienced* part.

"I'm thinking. Shhhh." Pretty soon she said, "If we had an ax we could chop down a tree, fell it right across the road. That would bring him to a stop fast. Then I could blast him with one of my sprays."

I glanced over at her vest, the one with all the little pockets. And wondered about the contents.

My phone rang. It was Hunter.

"What's new?" he asked.

"Not much. Just sitting around talking to Patti Dwyre."

"That ought to be interesting."

"It always is."

Then I remembered about Grams and her conditional offer to adopt Dinky. "I need help training a dog," I said.

After a slight hesitation, he said, "Not Dinky. Please don't tell me you want to train Dinky."

"She needs work."

Hunter laughed. "She had to be the runt of the litter. Only a runt could be that stubborn."

"I have to do it. It's doable, right?"

"We might have to spend long, intense hours together."

"Let's get started soon," I suggested, then hung up. The sooner the better.

Patti said, "For a minute I thought you were going to tell him about Petrie and ask him, in a simper voice, to take over for you."

"What do you think I am? A helpless female?"

Just then, a white van came over the hill, one just like the van at the Petrie booth during the festival.

Sure enough, Bob Petrie was behind the wheel.

But we reacted too late to stop him from turning down his road.

Thirty

"We're implementing Plan B," I said, starting my truck.

"Which is?"

But I was already in motion, tearing after Bob. Tires squealed. We peeled.

We caught up with him before he got out of the van. Patti jumped out. "Bob Petrie," she said, flashing her press pass. "We have a few questions to ask you. Please come with us."

Bob looked startled. So did I. My hasty plan hadn't included putting him in the truck with us.

But the whole situation could have all worked out for the best, because he refused.

Except Patti kneed him between his legs.

"@%#&," I said, the four-letter word slipping out. Then I got out of the truck and ran around to the other side where Bob was down on the ground between my truck and his car, sucking frantically for air.

"Help me load him," Patti said.

"No way. We can't kidnap him."

"He's the guy! The one who attacked me!" Patti was grunting from the effort as she tried to get him up off the ground and into the truck.

"Are you sure?"

"Never been surer. Now help me!"

Bob continued to roll around, absorbed in his own problems.

"I have a better idea," I said. "Put him in his own vehicle, and you can drive it. We can't leave it here for his family to see."

"Okay."

Between the two of us, we managed to get the job done, stuffing fetal-prone Bob into the passenger seat. I didn't even want to think of the consequences of our actions. There wasn't time. Any minute Aggie or some other family member was going to hear us or see us if we didn't move out fast. Plus, very soon Bob was going to get his cojones under control and he was going to brain Patti.

Besides, there was a method to my madness. This time, if we were caught (and that was pretty much a given, considering the way we were carrying on), Patti could be the one to face the music in Johnny Jay's locked interrogation room.

A few minutes later we tore out onto Colgate's main thoroughfare, me in the lead driving my truck and Patti following in Bob's van.

Grams's property wasn't too far. I headed there. In the rearview mirror I saw Bob's head swing up. Then some kind of commotion between them before Bob's head disappeared from view. I wasn't even going to ask what she'd done to him.

We turned into the field Grams rented out to a local farmer. He'd planted corn this year, rotating annually between corn and alfalfa. The corn was a whole lot taller than knee-high, almost ready to pick, which meant we were concealed from view. I kept to the far edge of the field, bouncing along, scraping against the closest row of stalks until I was sure we were out of sight.

Patti pulled up, got out, ran around, opened the passenger door, and did something to her prisoner, then slid into the seat next to me.

My head swiveled toward the van. "You can't leave him alone in there," I said. "Won't he drive away?"

"He's handcuffed. Besides, he has a temporary vision problem."

I couldn't believe what Patti was capable of. I needed to remain in her good graces for eternity, so she didn't practice her methods on me. Or else I needed to run away from her as fast as I could. Whatever my future choice would be, I was stuck with what I had at the moment. "How do you know for certain that Bob was the one who attacked you?"

"I smelled him," Patti said. "Then it all came rushing back."

I thought about that. She'd groin-punched Bob, kidnapped him, and handcuffed him all because of his smell. This was *not* a good thing.

Patti must have sensed my doubt because she said, "Haven't you ever noticed a person's smell? Until they weren't there anymore, you didn't think that person had a particular scent of their own. But then you put your head down on a pillow they'd used. Or you picked up a piece of clothing they'd worn that hadn't gone through the wash yet. And suddenly you breathe in something familiar. You smell *them*."

Patti's little speech had a touch of poignancy to it. Don't tell me P.P. Patti actually had a soft, tender side?

Not that you'd know it by her recent actions.

And more amazingly, I understood exactly what she meant. That exact thing had happened when my grandfather died. He had his own little den where he smoked his pipe. After he died, I'd go in there just to smell him. Grams would, too. That room was where we felt closest to him.

"Okay," I said. "What's Bob's scent? What tipped you off?"

"Sort of a cross between peppermint or menthol . . ."

"Like the stuff you rub on your skin to make a sore muscle feel better?"

"That's it! And garlic. And stale cigarette. He smelled exactly like those things the other day and he still smells like them. I'm going to make him spill his guts."

I trotted over to his van right behind Patti, who had her own special scent—she reeked of determination. What if she got even more extreme?

Bob didn't look so good. He'd just endured one of every man's worst nightmares. Patti must have sprayed him with something toxic, too, because his eyes were all red and he couldn't stop blinking. And his hands really were hand-cuffed.

"Help!" he croaked when he saw me. "Is she going to kill me? I didn't do anything. Please believe me."

Patti leaned in close to him. "You tell us the truth," she said. "And we'll let you go."

Bob looked frantic. I backed away and considered taking off, leaving Patti behind. She'd done it to me in the past, so I figured I was justified if I did. I made up my mind. Any more torture and I was outta there.

"Now," Patti said to her captive, "do you recognize me?"

Bob nodded.

"From where?"

"I delivered a package to your house."

"And then you grabbed me from behind and tied me up and duct-taped my mouth."

"I didn't do that part," Bob said.

I edged closer.

"Who did?" Patti wanted to know.

"I don't know. Somebody called the main office where I work, just like you did. Looking for me." Bob's face twitched. I assumed it was some kind of aftereffect. "I was finishing up for the day, clearing my paperwork when the call came in."

"And?"

"And they said there was some cash in it for me if I let them know if you had any deliveries come through. Your house is in my delivery area, so I said, sure, cash was always appreciated."

"How much?"

"A hundred."

"Did you collect?"

"Not yet."

I couldn't resist joining in. This was so cool. Patti really was making him talk. "All you have to do," I said to him, "is give us your contact information. The number you called."

"It wasn't a phone number," Bob said, his eyes never leaving his tormentor, Patti. "E-mail."

"What's the address?" Patti said, getting out her flip notebook and pencil.

Bob rubbed his eyes with his free hand. "Are you going to let me go if I tell you?"

If it was me, I'd also be asking him about Ford and feeling around for clues that he might be Ford's partner. I looked forward to my turn to interrogate him.

"We'll let you go," I said, "after a few more questions."

"But," Patti said, adding a caveat, "tell anybody about this and I'll start screaming rape. You hear me?"

"I hear you loud and clear," Bob said.

"I should have been given a chance to question him, too," I said as we drove back to the store.

"What questions didn't he answer?" Patti asked.

"You don't even remember, do you? All you could focus on was you and your own problems."

"A violent stalker isn't a major neighborhood problem?

Next time it might be you on the ground all tied up and dying a slow death."

"I wanted to find out if he knew Ford. Remember that? Murder trumps stalking in most people's priorities."

"You could have asked."

"Yeah, sure," I snorted out in a whine.

Because right after Patti removed the handcuffs, Bob got out of the van, and she kneed him again. No discussion with me in advance, no sign whatsoever. Just blam.

"I had to incapacitate him," she said. "So we could make a clean getaway."

"He's never going to answer questions from us ever again. Not after what we did to him. And I bet he's going to press charges."

"That guy is such a wimp," Patti said, "considering he's supposed to be a criminal. He's a pathetic example of his profession. Did you see how he opened up? I really rattled his cage. He's not going to press charges against us unless he wants a rape charge to add to his rap sheet."

I was still bitter about the outcome. "If you'd given me equal time, I would have answers, too."

"We know he's involved in stealing my telescope," Patti said.

"He tried to blame most of it on somebody else. He could be lying."

"He wasn't."

"He sure started talking fast. Shouldn't he have resisted for a while?"

Patti grinned, and it wasn't pretty. "You don't need to know everything," she said. "It's better that way."

Okay, then.

Back in my office, away from the queen of torture, I keyed in the e-mail address that Bob had given us and sent a blank e-mail to see what would happen.

It bounced right back with a message informing me that the e-mail account didn't exist.

Figures. Did that mean it had never existed? Or that it wasn't available any longer?

Had Bob lied?

Or was Patti's opponent really good at covering his tracks.

Either way we were back to square one.

Thirty-one

According to the local news reports, we were in for a few days of bad weather, even a possible tornado, which always brings customers stampeding in for staples. The most popular household items at times like these are milk, eggs, bread, and beer. But the number one choice for the more intelligent among us is toilet paper. There aren't many substitutes for that particular item. Mom, in the spirit of things, had stacked the toilet paper up front so no one would forget to buy it.

I could almost sense and smell the storm approaching from the northwest. Still, when I heard the first burst of thunder, I thought Stanley's grandson was up to his chemical tricks. Until I went outside and saw the sky. Ugly clouds were forming on the horizon. For those lucky enough to live in twister-proof territory, a tornado is an enormous, destructive funnel cloud whirling from the ground right up to the clouds. Wisconsin is on the outer fringe of Tornado Alley, but we get more than our fair share of that kind of weather.

There's a big difference between a tornado watch and a tornado warning. A watch suggests conditions are ripe for a twister to form. A warning means one has been spotted and you better run for cover. Hide in a basement or in an interior room. If you don't have shelter, dive into a ditch and start praying. Because one of those funnels can pick up a house and move the whole thing just like in *The Wizard of Oz*.

In the past, we couldn't believe anything our weather forecasters told us. If they said one thing, we could count on the exact opposite. But lately, they were getting better at predicting what was coming, even approximately when it would hit.

Another thing I've noticed about approaching storms—whether snow, hail, rain, or thunderstorms—is the upswing in camaraderie among Moraine's residents. Having to batten down the hatches lends a certain excitement to the air. There is no subject better than impending bad weather to spark conversations in the checkout line and aisles to bring us closer together as a community.

I'd been watching the sky from the entrance when suddenly, the town's siren went off announcing a high alert.

"Into the basement," I ordered my customers and staff.

Carrie Ann burst out of the back room and scampered for the stairs.

Stanley Peck ran in as customers continued to file down into what used to be the church's gathering place. "Noel's missing," he said, sounding on the verge of panic. "I have to find him."

"Get downstairs, Stanley," I said, noticing how dark the sky had become in the open door behind him. Black and scary. "Hurry. I'm sure he's hiding out somewhere. There's no time." Stanley hesitated, so I punted, invoking Holly's name even though she wasn't in the building. "My sister and I will use whatever wrestling techniques required to get you down there. Don't put us in that position."

Reluctantly, Stanley stomped down with the rest of the customers to wait out the storm.

Next, I called down to Mom. "What about Grams?"

"I warned her. She's in her cellar," came the reply.

Holly burst into The Wild Clover with Dinky in her arms.

"Take this animal," she said, pushing Dinky at me. "I can't stand her another second."

Dinky hated storms more than anything in the world. She could hear thunder before any of us humans. She was so tuned-in, she could be a celebrity weather dog. As soon as she started shaking, that was our cue to pay attention.

Holly and I went down the basement steps.

I did a mental count of family and friends. Everyone was clustered around my craft table, the one I used for teaching classes related to honeybees and their by-products. Patti wasn't with us, but she was resourceful and had lived in Moraine long enough to know the signs of a serious storm. Stanley sat at the far end of the table, looking worried.

Dinky clawed her way under my arm. I wrapped her in a fleece I'd left on the back of a chair and that seemed to calm her.

I wandered over to Stanley and said, "Any kid as smart as Noel, who can create chemical reactions like he can, will know how to survive a tornado. In fact, he'll probably harness its energy."

Stanley gave me a weak but appreciative smile. "If anybody could, it would be him."

"He's taken shelter. I'm sure of it."

"But where has he been all day?"

"We'll find him as soon as the storm lets up."

By now, we could hear full gale forces outside. A clap of thunder and the lights flickered and went out. I heard the backup generators kick on.

Hunter called my cell. "Where are you?"

"In the basement of the store. The power went out, but we're safe. Where are you?"

"Safe, too. Don't worry about me. I'll call you when it's okay to come out."

"Is Ben with you?" My favorite K-9 better not be at Hunter's house in his outdoor kennel.

"He's here. I'll get back to you."

The sounds from above us were deafening. Dinky burrowed deeper into the jacket. I wished I had a great big cuddle blanket to hide under. I could see the outlines of the others in the basement, but just barely.

Mom said, "I told Tom I'd stop by his house and pick up a few things for him. A change of clothes, something to read . . ." Her voice broke.

"When we get out of here," I said, "we'll go over together."

"I'd hoped Tom would be back tonight."

"At least he has the money to make bail."

"Bail!" Mom said. "This isn't going to go that far. You make it sound like he's going to actually be charged with a crime."

"Of course he won't," Holly said, meeting my eyes over the top of our mother's head.

Thirty minutes later, Hunter called to say the coast was clear, that the storm hadn't produced any funnels after all. Stanley tore off in search of Noel. Other than a few toppled Adirondack chairs in front of the store, The Wild Clover hadn't suffered at all. All good news so far.

The electricity hadn't come back on, so I called to report it, thankful for the generators that would make sure the coolers stayed cold. There wasn't anything else to do at this point but close up and check periodically to see if the power was back on.

"Stanley Peck can't find his grandson," I called Hunter back and said. "We're going to look for him. I hope he's okay."

"Who's 'we'?"

"Me and Holly and Mom."

"You're with your mother?" Did I hear incredulity in his voice? And why did my protective reflexes kick in?

"She's a changed person," I said, a bit defensively. "Nothing like the old Mom. You should re-meet her."

"I have to see this. How about now? Ben and I will help search, if that's okay."

"Great. Meet us at Tom Stocke's apartment."

"Why there? What's going—"

I interrupted. "I'll explain later," I said.

Thirty-two

By the time we left the store, dusk had settled over Moraine. Dark clouds were swirling above and the air smelled thick and musky. Without a full moon to guide the way and with all the lights out on Main Street, we wouldn't have been able to see a thing if I hadn't brought two flashlights from the store to shine the way. We stepped carefully around tree branches that the wind had blown to the sidewalk.

Holly, Mom, and I walked around to the back of Tom Stocke's antique store. Mom let us inside his apartment with a key she plucked out of a flowerpot. I wondered how long she'd known where to find the key, and if her relationship with Tom was moving a bit fast for my comfort level. Then I shook it off. My comfort level shouldn't matter.

Tom looked like he was living a simple life for a man who'd won the lottery. Just the basics, no frills. He'd even incorporated antiques from his store into his small living quarters. I noticed a few white sales stickers dangling from furniture.

"I'll put a bag together for him," Mom said, flashlighting her way into his bedroom. "You girls wait right there in the kitchen."

"She seems to know where everything is," I said to Holly, a bit accusingly.

Holly sat down at Tom's table. A tin antique-looking box filled with fresh-cut daisies was in the center. It had Mom written all over it. In fact, were the flowers from Grams's garden?

"I think I'll look around a little," I said.

"Mom said to wait."

"I can't sit still."

With the light from the flashlight to guide me, it took only a few minutes to cover his kitchen and living area. Saying the place was small was a huge understatement.

"Where does this door go?" I said coming back into the kitchen and muttering to myself as I opened it.

The basement.

I flicked my light on the steps ahead of me and tiptoed down so Mom wouldn't hear. The stair's wooden floorboards didn't cooperate. They creaked under me. I heard a *psssttt* sound coming from my sister, her response to me for not listening to our mother. I chose to ignore it.

How could I resist an opportunity like this? When else would I have a legit reason to be inside a murder suspect's digs? If I was going to help Tom with his self-defense plea, I needed all the information I could get.

"What are you doing?" my sister hissed after following me down. "You left me all alone in the dark."

"Shush!" I whispered back.

I swung the flashlight beam up and down and across, my eyes sweeping over the unfinished basement; concrete floor, cement-block walls, everything neatly stored on shelves, labeled boxes, a workstation, nails and screws in mason jars, a washer and dryer, all the standard stuff homeowners keep in their basements.

Walking toward the opposite wall, I spotted another entrance to the basement from the outside. The slanted outer door, steep crumbling steps, and wooden shelves and cupboards along the wall told me that area had been used as a root cellar. Fruits and vegetables had been stored there at one time.

Based on Grams's cellar design, which was much like this one, I knew the outer door could be padlocked from the outside and probably was.

To my right, a door led to a utility room and I assumed that was where the furnace and water heater were. The door was closed and padlocked.

Mom's voice came from the top of the stairs, sounding thunderous. "Are you two girls down there?"

Holly and I stared at each other. The basement stair squeaked and before we could answer, Mom joined us. "What are you doing down here?" she demanded as soon as she reached the bottom step.

"Snooping," Holly said, which I couldn't believe she'd just admitted. What was my sister thinking?

"We were not," I lied. Mom frowned, so I did a quick reversal. "Okay, maybe a little."

Holly, who could read Mom better than I could and knew what to say at times like these, said, "We're curious about Tom. After all, he seems to be very important to you."

"And we want to get to know him better," I said, scoring my point, too.

"Isn't that sweet of you," Mom said, her tone softening, again sounding just like Grams, only a little more delusional.

Right then, we heard Hunter's voice above us. "Story, where are you?"

"Down in the basement," I called, seeing a flashlight beam appear at the top of the stairs.

Hunter came down. "Do you have permission to be here?" the cop in him couldn't help asking.

Mom told him why we were inside, finishing with a slam dunk. "I even cleared it with the police chief." She beamed. "And how are you, Hunter?"

Mom has never, ever approved of Hunter Wallace. Not when we were hot and heavy in high school. Not even after Hunter stopped drinking and became a good cop. Not even now, when she knew we were seeing each other again. She always had a cold, disapproving way of looking at him that perfectly matched her icy tone of voice.

Except now.

"How's your family?" she asked. "I hope everyone is well."

Hunter didn't miss a beat, although he had to be as stunned as I was. "Everybody's doing great. Thanks for asking."

"Our family likes to get together on Sundays at my mother's house," she went on. "You know where that is. Would you like to join us for dinner sometime?"

Hunter's eyes met mine. He grinned. Probably because my mouth was hanging wide open in utter astonishment. I didn't have much of a poker face, which is why I stay out of the store's sheepshead card games. But really. My mother had just invited my boyfriend to dinner. I had to be dreaming. Any minute I'd wake up.

"Sure," Hunter answered her, still smooth. "Thanks for the offer."

I found my voice. "Holly and I thought we'd look around," I said to him, partly for Mom's benefit. "We wanted to make sure everything was locked up tight. The last thing Tom needs while he's away is a break-in, somebody stealing his antiques." I tested the root cellar door. It was locked.

"He'll be back tomorrow," Mom said with total confidence. "Nothing to worry about."

In case Hunter was about to burst her imaginary bubble with the plain truth, I jumped in with a fast subject change. "What's behind this locked door, Mom?"

"A furnace," she said vaguely.

"Why does it need a padlock?"

"Tom's safe is also inside. He told me all about it. He said he cemented it to the concrete floor inside the utility room and locked it up tight."

"That's a lot of effort on Tom's part," Holly said, taking the words right out of my mouth. "What's in the safe? Gold bullion?"

"That's Tom's business," Mom said. "Not ours."

I stared at the locked door. Who goes to those lengths unless they are guarding something valuable? Like gold. Or the *Mona Lisa*. Or a queen's jewels. Or stacks of cold cash.

"Mom," I ventured. "Tom must have a banker, somebody who looks after his money. Where does he bank?"

Hunter glanced sharply at me, following my thought pattern.

Mom started bristling at the banker question. "What's with you? For cripes' sake, he isn't after my money, if that's what you think. Not that I have much to go after, but Tom doesn't need financial help. He still has all of his lottery money stashed away. His antique business is healthy, and he has no debt. There, are you happy?"

"We're just looking out for you," Holly said.

"I don't need any looking out for. I'm perfectly fine." Mom glanced down at the bag dangling from her hand. "I have to get these things to Tom."

With that, we climbed the steps, relocked the outer door, and put the key back in the pot.

Out on Main Street, Hunter and I watched Mom and Holly walk down the street toward the store, the night darkness swallowing them up.

"I see what you mean about your mother," Hunter said in awe. "Talk about a complete personality change."

"Isn't it incredible?" I agreed. "Holly says it's because of Mom's feelings for Tom Stocke, that all she needed was some romance in her life."

I really wished she'd found true love with somebody

other than a murder suspect, though. For example, Stanley Peck would be a perfect choice. He's an available widower and doesn't have a murdered brother. And he isn't in jail. But I could wish on every star in the sky, if they were visible, and it wouldn't change a thing.

Then Hunter said, "Story, you aren't going to stick your nose even further into the Ford Stocke murder, are you?"

I gave him an eye-roll, hoping he could see it in the dark. "Of course not. I'm just helping my mother with a few things." I didn't mention that those "things" involved hoping to prove Tom had acted in self-defense. Instead, I brought up Bob Petrie. Not that I could tell Hunter the whole story. Dating a cop has its own set of problems. Hanging around Patti has even more. I couldn't tell Hunter that Patti kicked Bob in the crotch, kidnapped him, threatened him, then kicked him again. I had to keep quiet because, like it or not, I had become her accomplice. I sort of circumvented that part.

"Bob Petrie was driving the truck that delivered Patti's telescope," I said. "He's been acting suspicious. He might have been involved in the attack on Patti."

"Patti's a piece of work. Stay away from her."

"But it happened on my block. Bob's been in trouble in the past and some of the things he told us made me very suspicious. Check Bob out for me?" I asked. Patti had worked the CCAP site, but Hunter had better resources. "Run a background check."

Hunter shook his head. "I'm not touching this one."

"Johnny Jay isn't bothering to investigate at all. Unless Patti's attacker trots into the station and admits it, we aren't ever going to be safe again on Willow Street."

Now Hunter rolled his eyeballs. I caught it clear as day, even though it was pitch-dark. "Fine. I'll see what comes up on him," he agreed. Then he did some kind of strangled thing with his throat, then said, "You know I never tell you what to do, right?"

"That's what I love best about you."

"We respect each other just as we are, right?"

Now, we were beside Hunter's SUV with Ben eyeing us from inside. "Right," I agreed, sensing a *but* coming.

"But . . ." he said, "this time, just once, I'd like to . . ."

I silenced him the only way I knew—moving in close so our bodies touched, lifting my face to his, my eyes sending a promise he couldn't mistake. When our lips came together, I felt an electric connection, one I experienced every time we kissed.

As Grams would say, you catch more flies with honey than with vinegar.

Men are so easy.

"Come on," I said. "Let's go over to Stanley's and see if he found Noel."

When we got inside the SUV, Ben licked my face in warm welcome. I put my arms around the big guy and hugged him tight. We took off through the night with only our headlights to guide us. The town seemed a scarier place without streetlights.

Apparently only our local area had lost electricity, because as we approached Stanley Peck's place we saw lights in the houses we passed. I wanted more than anything to find Noel sitting at the kitchen table, writing in his notebook.

Johnny Jay's police car was in Stanley's driveway. I remained hopeful. "Maybe he found Noel and brought him home," I said, jumping out.

My promising good mood was short-lived. Because, inside the house, Stanley was filing a missing person's report.

"He hasn't been gone that long, Stanley." Johnny Jay wore the same old attitude he'd had last time we met up. "If it wasn't for the storm and all, I'd tell you to wait a little longer."

"You sure do like to wait, don't you?" Stanley said with a matching attitude, risking ticking off Johnny Jay, but I had to silently applaud his boldness. Anyone who carries a concealed weapon and doesn't like the chief is a friend of mine for life. "But this is a kid we're talking about here. I don't know why I'm even bothering to report it. You're useless."

"A little respect for the law, Stanley," Johnny warned.

"Respect goes both ways."

Johnny noticed us at the door. "Fischer. Wallace. We're busy here. Take a hike."

"No. Don't. Come in," Stanley said, visibly relieved to have friendly support. "Noel's still missing. I looked everywhere."

"We're here to help search," I said. Hunter opened the screen door, which creaked loudly, and we went in.

"You can't predict what a kid that age will do," Johnny said to Stanley. "He's probably mad at you over something and making you pay for it. Did you have a fight?"

"No." Stanley shook his head adamantly. "We never have a harsh word between us. Ever."

Johnny Jay threw his personal opinion into an already emotional situation. "That kid causes all kinds of trouble in town. Blowing stuff into the air, running wild, now this. You should keep him in line better."

Stanley gave him a disgusted look and said, "Noel's a good kid."

Hunter joined in. He stayed respectful even though Johnny Jay didn't know the meaning of the word. "Maybe we can all work together," he said to Johnny. "Stanley, let's go over some of the places you searched already so we don't cover the same ground. Story and I will help you. And chief, you might have a few ideas where to look, too."

"I'm through here. I'll let you know if anything turns up," Johnny said and abruptly walked out.

"He's a real team player," Stanley said with a thick coating of sarcasm.

Then he filled us in on the places he'd looked, which

turned out to be pretty much everywhere I would have thought to check.

"Does he have any friends close by?" Hunter asked. "Someone he might be visiting?"

"He keeps to himself," Stanley answered. "Don't get me wrong, he isn't lonely, just preoccupied with his experiments." Stanley couldn't have been sadder. He hung his head. "I can't call his parents and tell them I lost their boy. We have to find him."

"You don't have a single lead that might help us?" I asked.

"Let's take a look at his room," Hunter suggested. "Maybe something will jump out at us."

Noel had been staying in one of Stanley's spare rooms and his junk was scattered everyplace. It had a distinctively unpleasant odor to it—dirty-sock smell combined with lingering chemical fumes. My eyes watered as I took in the sights: beakers, funnels, kerosene, the place looked like a chemistry lab after a class of a dozen students finished with it.

"What about his notebook?" I asked, since I'd never seen Noel without it.

"Gone, too," Stanley said. "But that doesn't surprise me one bit. I'd be even more worried if he'd left it behind."

Hunter swung his head across the room, checking it out as only a cop can. He opened a few drawers, stuck his head in the closet, lifted a pile of dirty clothes with the toe of his Harley boot. "You said some of his things are missing."

"His backpack for one thing."

I remembered the day before the festival, when Noel saved me from a round of words with Mom. He'd had a backpack with him.

"Can you tell if he packed any clothes?" Hunter asked. In the mess, I didn't see how Stanley could.

Sure enough, he shook his head. "Noel forgets to change his clothes unless I remind him. I'm most worried because he takes that backpack when he's done tinkering with his equations and ready to put the experiment to the test. What if he blew himself up?"

Just as we were discussing trying to track Noel with the help of Ben, Patti called my cell phone to whine about staying at my house all by herself. I brought her up to speed regarding Noël and told her to go to bed.

Stanley pulled out one of Noel's dirty T-shirts to give Ben a sniffing start. Right then, I heard the screen door creak open.

And there stood Noel, as good as new.

"Where have you been?" Stanley wanted to know. From the expressions flicking across his face, I could tell he was vacillating between mad and glad.

"I lost track of time," Noel said. "Then the storm hit. I got down in a ditch when the siren went off."

My eyes took in the twelve-year-old kid.

The storm had only recently passed.

But Noel was perfectly dry.

Thirty-three

At the crack of dawn, I went outside with Dinky to visit my honeybees, who were still bedded down waiting for the sun to shine. I inspected several frames, pleased to see an abundance of honey in the comb cells. And no signs of any more hive robbers.

I'd already done some early harvesting in July. Based on what I was seeing for the late harvest coming up soon, this year I'd have a bumper crop. Right there in the beeyard I ate my breakfast: I dipped my fingers into one of the frames that had an overabundance of honey, then picked a small ripe Roma tomato, nibbled on that, and topped it off with raspberries from one of my berry bushes.

Life was sweet.

I heard my back door open and my roommate Patti joined me, already fully dressed for the day.

My taste buds lingered over the heady combination of honey, tomato juice, and mashed raspberries while I considered Patti. She was turning out to be a serious problem

in my life. I'd taken the blame for more than a few of her
screwups, including jail visits and interrogations by Johnny
Jay. She used unethical techniques bordering on torture
and abuse. In her book, the means justified the end. She
gets results any way she can. The woman had lost her
moral compass. But friends should talk things out, right?
Besides, the maniac lived next door, so I didn't dare totally
alienate her. Imagine what she could do to me?

"We need to clear the air, Patti," I said, plopping down
at my patio table. With a wary expression, she sat down
across from me.

"What happened yesterday has me very upset," I began.
"I don't know how things got so out of hand."

"I agree," Patti said.

I stared. "You do?"

"Absolutely. It won't happen again."

"Really?" This was easier than I ever dreamed.

"Really. Next time we'll get every single bit of information out of the big wimp. You can even go first if you want."

Okay, then, this wasn't going well after all.

"I can't be your partner anymore," I told her. "You're
methods are too cruel."

"Cruel?"

"Maybe that's the wrong word."

No, it wasn't , but . . .

"I see where you're coming from." Patti leaned forward.
"You're a sensitive woman who can't handle the icky stuff.
From now on I'll take care of the unpleasant part of our
partnership, and you can be the brains behind the operation. How's that?"

I liked that brains part but said, "I want out."

"Out of what?"

"Out of . . . um . . . never mind." I'd have to figure out
how to extricate myself without a fuss. "That's fine for now."

At least next time she resorted to dubious methods, I
wouldn't have to witness any of it.

"What's on the agenda for today?" she asked.

"Work at the store. Keep my ears and eyes open."

Patti stood up and said, "I'm off."

"Where to?" I asked.

"You don't want to know."

After Patti left to spread her reign of terror, I fed Dinky, showered, dressed, and walked down the street with Dinky sniffing everything along the way. I paused in front of the store and took a moment to enjoy the beginning of a new day. Then I heard a horn toot and saw Grams pull up in her Cadillac Fleetwood. Since The Wild Clover wasn't open yet, there weren't any cars obstructing my grandmother's path. This time, though, she misjudged the curb by a good four feet, stopping way short.

Mom got out, assessed my grandmother's parking job, and said, "You can't park there. You're in the middle of the street."

I didn't hear what Grams said, but apparently she got her way, because Mom slammed the door shut and headed for the store. She dug through her purse. "I couldn't sleep so I thought I'd open up."

I watched her pull out a key chain with a wad of keys, search through the mess, select one, and insert it into the keyhole. Until now, I didn't know she even had a key.

I decided not to comment on that, though, and instead followed her in.

"Does Tom belong to a political party?" I asked while we turned on lights.

Mom gasped in shock.

In Moraine, as in any small town, talking politics is the kiss of death, a big social no-no. Sex and religion are absolutely acceptable topics of conversation (if we really want to stir the pot). But differing political views have ruined friendships and family relationships.

Owning a business where people gather and share, I've learned a few things about personality types, political parties, and how sometimes I can peg a person's affiliation just by what they do for a living, or how they live their lives.

We have a diverse and active mix of residents and some of them tend to get overly rabid regarding their stances. Moraine has its share of fanatics on both sides of the fence. And even though we don't talk about it, we have a pretty good idea who sits on what side.

Still, nobody comes right out and asks like I just did.

"Well?" I said, waiting for Mom's answer.

"You certainly are showing a lot of interest in Tom," she said. "After what I've had to put up with from you, I now understand why you resent my interference in your own life so much. I'll never stick my nose in your business again. And you'd better do likewise."

Did my mother just tell me to mind my own business?

"I'm trying to help him, Mom."

"That's exactly how you get yourself in so much trouble—interfering in other people's business."

"Please, Mom, just answer the question. It's important."

"No!" And with that, she stomped away.

Grams popped into the store.

"Hi, cutie," she said, giving me a hug. "Your mother couldn't sleep, so she came in early. Hard work is what she needs to get her mind off her troubles."

"I thought Mom was in denial," I said.

"She's hopeful."

"Does Tom have anybody we should notify?"

"Your mother said he doesn't. Ford was it. Isn't that sad?"

Before I could get distracted, I put the political question to her, too.

"Libertarian," she said without even hesitating.

Bingo, I thought.

Libertarians are seriously into individual rights. They distrust the government more than any other party and are fiercely independent to the point of resisting any interference from government whatsoever.

Stanley Peck is a libertarian. Because of our friendship, he's told me about all the weapons he buried in the ground in case the government tries to take them away. Bearing arms is big with the libertarians. "Nobody's getting my guns," he says often. "I'll shoot the SOB first."

I'd seen Tom with a rifle, even though it was only an air rifle. And I'd bet he had a few antique guns in his store. For all I knew, he might have some buried in his backyard, just like Stanley.

So based on the Libertarian point of view, I imagined Tom's home would be his castle. And he might distrust banks.

I had to snort at that. Who really *did* trust banks?

Without any evidence that Tom kept his money in a bank, I had to think it was in that safe in the basement.

All of it.

And that's what Ford was after. Ford was his brother. He'd know Tom's quirks. Once he found out about the lottery win, he'd be after it.

I couldn't help feeling pleased with myself. "I have an errand to run," I said to Grams. "Want to keep Mom company in the store until I get back?"

"Do you have any of those tasty anise squares left?"

I laughed. "You know I do."

"Then I'm in." And Grams took off in the direction of the candy bins.

In Grams's youth, Moraine had had a candy store on the corner of Willow and Main, and it had carried all the penny candy Grams and her friends could eat. So when she found out about the store I wanted to open, she demanded I have a candy corner, which she insisted I fill with all kinds of special items like:

• taffy—black jack, Turkish, saltwater, and Laffy Taffy

• hard candy—anise squares, mint twists, and root beer barrels

- bubble gum—Bazooka, Cry Baby, Gold Mine, and Big League Chew

- chewy candy—banana splits, Bit-O-Honey, candy corn, orange slices, and caramel cubes

- suckers—Dum Dums, Blow Pops, Slo Pokes, and Charms pops

- and all the fun miscellaneous—candy lipstick, wax bottles, and satellite wafers

I made an instant decision, right there on the spot. Dinky and I walked down the street, looked both ways, and crept along the side of Tom's antique store.

The key was exactly where Mom had left it in the pot. It turned easily in the lock. I picked up Dinky and slid inside.

Tom's apartment had a feeling of permanent emptiness to it, an eerie silence that put my nerves on edge. The entryway and kitchen faced the east, so dawn's first light sent ribbons of sunshine streaming through the window. The refrigerator kicked in, its motor startling me and making my heart skip a beat. From my arms, Dinky licked my chin as though she sensed my trepidation. I put her down and wrapped the leash around a chair leg. She'd have to wait for me there.

Last time I'd wandered through Tom's apartment without a goal. This time, I was looking for two things: evidence of a bank account with a recent balance, and a key to the locked utility room, so I could search it.

I don't know much about murder, but I've watched some television. There really aren't many reasons to kill somebody. Leaving out organized crime hits and crazy serial killers, I can think of three big reasons to commit murder:

- Revenge. In Tom's case, he could have killed his brother in retaliation for stealing his wife.

- Greed. That was totally out. Tom had plenty of money.

- Self-protection. Tom could have killed his brother because his life was in danger. Or his assets were.

So applying the same set of motives to Ford, what were his possible reasons for coming to Moraine:

- Revenge. Nope. He was the one who messed up Tom's life, not the other way around.

- Self-protection. But then he would go into hiding, not show up where he wasn't wanted.

- Greed. Ka-ching.

In my opinion, Ford was definitely here to steal from his brother. Or blackmail him for cash. Or murder him for his inheritance. Whatever. It had to do with Tom's big lottery win.

Some days I'm really dense and can't see the forest through the trees. But today I paused to consider the possibility that Ford's mysterious partner could have played a much more major role in all of this than I'd originally thought.

Whatever the case, I was about to toss Tom's apartment.

His place was small. I could do this fast. Nobody would know what I was up to. Patti didn't have me on her radar. Nobody did.

The kitchen gave up nothing worthwhile. It had typical bachelor equipment and gadgets—toaster, coffeemaker, microwave, electric can opener, toaster oven—all lined up in a row on the counter. Not much in the drawers or cabinets, either.

Bathroom and living room. Nada out of the ordinary, only the basics.

Next, the bedroom. And since he was dating my mother, it better be as dull as the rest of his apartment. It was, thank God.

He didn't have a desk or a pile of bills lying around. A two-drawer file cabinet in the closet contained tax returns from prior years and other important papers. But not a single bank statement, extra checks, or any keys.

In the basement, I gazed at his tool work area in dismay. Canning jars filled with nails and bolts and whatnots, tools hanging from Peg-Boards, a workbench with drawers crammed full of antique restoration materials.

It would take me a lifetime to go through all of it looking for something as tiny as a key.

Dinky started whining from the kitchen, letting me know she'd had enough alone time.

I'd failed to accomplish one of my goals. I hadn't been able to search the locked room.

But I'd accomplished the other.

I was pretty sure Tom Stocke didn't have a bank account.

Thirty-four

❦

Back at the store, Mom was holding down the fort. Grams and her car were gone. Several customers were shopping inside. I shooed Carrie Ann away from the back room computer where she was "updating inventory like a manager-in-training would if she was about to be promoted."

I went up front and worked with Mom and Carrie Ann while ideas churned inside my head. What if Tom caught Ford inside his house? They struggled. Things got deadly. Tom strangled his brother. Suddenly Ford was dead, and Tom was frantic. In a panic, he grabbed a garbage bag and dragged Ford's body through backyards and alleys, staying in the shadows. As he passed through the cemetery, he saw me coming with Dinky, ran and hid, then came back and finished what he started by returning Ford to the house he was staying at.

And stuffed him in the fireplace, thinking he'd burn him later.

If I was a jury, that last part especially would make me want to throw a few more logs on that fire and roast Tom.

I hoped there was a better explanation for why Ford was in the fireplace.

Just then, Lori Spandle came into the store still wearing that stupid hockey helmet. I had just deposited Dinky in the back for a little nap. Which was a good thing, since dogs weren't allowed in the store and Lori would try to cause trouble for me if she knew.

"What were you doing inside Tom Stocke's house?" she demanded.

"I wasn't," I lied. Lori was almost as bad as Patti at snooping where she didn't belong.

Of course, my mother overheard us. "What do you mean you weren't in his house?" she said to me, then to Lori, "She helped me gather up some of Tom's things, not that it's really any of your business."

Lori's helmeted head swung toward Mom. "You weren't with her this morning," she said.

"Story?" Mom said, raising an eyebrow.

"I forgot my cell phone over there," I stammered, digging it out of my pocket and flashing it.

"A whole bunch of us are taking bets outside," Lori said.

"Bets?"

"Over what stupid kind of lie you'll try to feed us to explain this one."

My heart leaped into my throat. What would I say to them? How could I explain?

Mom glared at Lori, giving her the same evil eye she usually reserved for me. "You have some nerve," she said. "Causing trouble at our store!"

Our store! I didn't miss the implication, but I had other issues to deal with at the moment.

I hustled over to the front door and popped my head out. Absolutely nobody was outside. I gritted my teeth, clenching them hard so I wouldn't explode and say something I'd regret later. I really wanted to rip that helmet off Lori's head and thunk her with it. Or jab a honey stick through the face cage and poke her in the eye.

I caught the smirk she gave me as she turned toward the aisles. I considered banning her from my store right along with her sister.

Lori was turning out to be the bane of my existence. Even over Johnny Jay. She sure knew how to push my buttons, even worse than the police chief. Maybe Hunter would help me figure out how to shut Lori up for good, get her permanently out of my face.

While I walked to the library with replacement beads, I thought about whether Patti was right about me being overly dependent on Hunter.

Holly has a few irrational fears, but when she's faced with other kinds of conflict, my sister tackles the problem head-on. She might be scared silly of bees, but that woman can take down an opponent in such a way and so fast that she'd make Hulk Hogan proud. Give her a fight and she's all over it.

And Patti. What a tough woman. She whines incessantly, that's true, but give her a mission and she's every bit as aggressive as V.I. Warshawski, only without the skintight outfit and high heels.

Then there's Carrie Ann. She's had her internal demons, but she fought them and won. And she isn't afraid of conflict, either. She'll wade in and defend herself or anybody she cares about.

All three of my friends are survivors who tackle life head-on.

What about me? Was my relationship with Hunter making me too soft? Was I leaning on him too much, letting him fight my battles for me? Oh my gawd! I was!

How many times have I called him for help? I tried to count and gave up.

I entered the library and greeted my favorite librarian.

"Hi, Story," Emily said. "Any word on Noel?"

"He's back. The kid got preoccupied with some project and lost track of time."

Emily beamed. "That's wonderful news! And what's the word on Tom Stocke?"

"Emily, you probably know more than I do. You get as much inside information here at the library as I do at The Wild Clover."

"Only sometimes. And it's been quiet this morning. I hadn't heard the good news about Noel yet and nothing new on Tom, either. I haven't even seen the police chief cruising past. It's like the calm before the storm."

"I hope not." My eyes swept through the library. "Where's Karin? I have beads for the scarf repair."

"She stayed home today with a summer cold. The worst kind, those summer colds. They last forever." Emily took the beads from me. "The scarf's still here. I'll put these beads with it and take the works over to her later today."

"There's no rush. Wait until she feels better."

Emily had reading glasses around her neck, hanging from a gold chain. She slipped the glasses on and checked a shelf below the counter. "Now I remember," she said. "I left it on my desk."

While Emily hustled away, I looked for a book, something in the self-help department.

As soon as Emily returned, I said, "Can you recommend a book to help with aggression?"

"Somebody at the store acting out?" She shook her head. "Bullies are a big topic these days."

"No, I meant for me." I felt like I was admitting a deep, dark secret. "I need to toughen up. Get more aggressive."

Emily laughed lightly. "You mean you want to become more assertive?"

"Right."

What had started as a little chuckle on her part turned

into an all-out laugh. Weren't librarians trained to maintain a certain dignified and compassionate composure, not laugh right in somebody's face?

"What?" I said, feeling offended.

"Story, you have enough spunk for a roomful of people."

"I do?"

"If you had any more, this town wouldn't be big enough for you."

I decided to take that as a compliment and gave Emily an ear-to-ear grin.

But then she said, "I don't know where your scarf went. I'm almost positive I put it on my desk. But now it's not there."

Thirty-five

I stopped in front of Tom's antique store on the way back to The Wild Clover, and stared at the closed sign. If Tom went to prison for murder, what would happen to his business? I pictured a sale sign in the window and Lori working it for all it was worth to get a big commission. What if Aggie Petrie bought it? I shuddered at the thought of that woman as a business associate.

And what about Mom? Would she revert to the sharp-tongued, judgmental, pessimistic woman from my past? Right now, like Grams had said, Mom was hopeful, still convinced that Tom would go free, that justice would pre-vail. She'd have a reality check soon. Then what?

I turned my eyes to the street just in time to see a Speedy Delivery truck approaching. When I spotted Bob Petrie behind the wheel, I stepped off the curb to flag him down.

He ignored me, pretending like I didn't exist. I stepped out further into the street.

I never would have tried a stunt like that if I didn't have

witnesses on the sidewalk. After our last encounter, Bob would have run me down for sure if he thought he could get away with it.

The truck screeched to a halt.

Walking quickly around to the driver's side, I heard the door locks slam into place. The window came down a fraction of an inch. "Stay away from me," Bob said.

"We need to talk."

"Where's crazy Dwyre?" Bob's head swung around looking for Patti.

"She's not here. I only want to apologize for any pain we caused you."

Bob was wary, but at least he wasn't speeding off. "That woman is nuts. But you didn't do anything wrong."

I really wanted to ask him if he knew Ford Stocke, and if he was Ford's partner in whatever scheme Tom's brother had been here to carry out. I just couldn't think of the right way to present the questions.

Bob had a cigarette tucked behind his visor. He reached up to get it and I almost let out a squeal when I noticed the tattoo on his upper arm.

"I have stuff to deliver," Bob said. "You're wasting my time."

"No, wait!" I said, trying to regain my composure. But Bob left me standing in his exhaust fumes.

Wondering why he had a tattoo of a hickory nut on his arm.

Before I had time to work on implications, Sally Maylor's squad car pulled up, and Tom Stocke got out of the passenger seat.

I turned when I heard my mother's voice calling his name from the direction of my store.

She trotted down the sidewalk, a big happy face, her arms extended, just like something out of a movie. They met and embraced.

"What's going on?" I asked Sally, who got out and stood next to me, taking in the scene.

"Bailed out," she said.

"Who posted his bail?"

"He did."

That surprised me, since I'd decided this morning that all his cash was in a locked safe in his basement. How did he do that?

"Cash?" I asked.

Sally gave me a hard look. "Guess again," she said.

"Check?"

"We don't take them."

"Credit card?"

"You didn't hear it from me."

So that explained it. He didn't need to get to his box yet. My hunch still might be right.

Mom and Tom finally broke their clench. Mom gave me a tiny hand wave from her cuddle position inside Tom's arm. They walked right past us and disappeared behind the antique store heading for the back apartment.

"Judge decided he wasn't a flight risk," Sally said. "Johnny Jay is hopping mad."

"I can imagine."

"The chief has a strong case."

"He must have a murder weapon then?" I'd watched enough crime dramas. I knew the drill.

"You'll have to ask him about that."

I shrugged off the dodge. "What about my mom? Is she safe around Tom?"

"She didn't look like she was in any danger to me."

Sally got back in her car and drove off. I headed for Tom's apartment.

The first thing I asked Tom was, "Do they have a murder weapon?"

Tom was sitting at his kitchen table. Mom was holding

his hand across the table. I'd never actually seen shell-shocked before, but that's how I'd describe Tom at the moment. "The police chief," he said, "thinks I strangled Ford with some kind of cloth material. They found brown fibers."

So Patti's information had been correct.

Tom went on. "Nothing in my store or apartment was a match, and the chief is getting desperate."

"He's not finding a murder weapon," my mom said, "because you didn't do it."

"We know that, Helen," Tom said patiently. "But he's determined."

"You don't have to worry anymore," Mom said, oblivious to the extent of Tom's problems. "We'll see this through."

I sat down, even though neither of them had invited me. "Did your brother ever mention Bob Petrie?" I asked him.

"Story," Mom said with some scold in her voice, "the man has been through enough. Let him rest."

Tom said to Mom, "It's okay, Helen." Then to me, "Not that I know of. Why?"

"Just fishing," I said. "But you must have some idea why Ford was holed up in the house next to mine."

Tom stared at the table, then said, "I hate to think he was up to no good. Maybe he was here to make amends."

"Oh, please," Mom said. "He was going to try to steal your money, and you know it."

"But how?" I asked her. "Not by killing Tom. That would tie up his inheritance in probate for a long time, maybe for years. Not to mention that Ford would be the primary suspect."

"I do have a whole lot of cash in a safe," Tom said, confirming my suspicion. "I think he was planning to rob me."

"We just need to prove it," Mom said, like it was an easy task.

Thirty-six

Carrie Ann was working alone. Holly had been a no-show, but my cousin was doing fine.

I, on the other hand, was far from fine.

More like seriously confused. Not to mention freaked-out at a sudden revelation I experienced on the way back to the store. If it even could be called a revelation.

It had to do with my scarf.

And brown fibers from a murder weapon used to kill a man.

My new scarf, which happened to be one with *brown* fibers, was missing from the library. While I really didn't think it was the murder weapon (or at least I tried not to think that), a scarf like mine would work to strangle a person. Lori had almost strangled me with it the other night, after all.

Had Johnny Jay taken my scarf from the library? Was he comparing it to the medical examiner's brown fibers? No, he would have told Emily if he was taking it, and she'd have told me. But what if he gave her a gag order?

And what was with Bob Petrie's hickory nut tattoo? Bob had to be the one leaving the nuts as threats, but why?

Not only did I have to extricate myself from Patti's madness, I needed to put distance between this murder case and me. Which would have been easier if my mother wasn't dating the main suspect.

I should be tending my bees, minding my store, spending time with Hunter, while the future unfolded in whatever form it chose.

Like Scarlett O'Hara, I wanted to think about these problems tomorrow. Or the next day. Or the next. Why had I gotten involved?

I decided to call Hunter and make plans with him for tonight. Hang out with him and Ben and Dinky, give the stubborn princess a few lessons in obedience, make a few well-deserved love moves on my man.

Hunter didn't answer his phone when I tried calling him. I didn't leave a message but figured once he saw that I had tried to reach him, he'd return my call. He was probably in a K-9 training session.

In the meantime, I took Dinky outside to do her business, a useless gesture since she'd already peed on the floor. After that, Carrie and I worked side by side, chatting up customers, something I really liked. I hadn't seen Patti since early this morning, making me wonder what she was up to. I'd put in several calls to her cell without a response. I kept my eyes peeled for Johnny Jay just in case he was after me for having brown fibers.

Later in the morning, Eugene Petrie came into the store, which more than surprised me. Had he ever been in The Wild Clover? I didn't think so. Without Naggie Aggie, the guy was halfway decent. He said hello, even took time for some small talk. It was all I could do not to start grilling him about his son Bob's strange fascination with hickory nuts.

But I kept quiet.

Eugene went off down an aisle.

Carrie Ann was handling business just fine, so when Hunter called a few minutes later, I went into my office for privacy. We made plans to meet at Stu's Bar and Grill later.

"I did a little research for you," he said.

"Huh?"

"On Bob Petrie."

I'd forgotten all about my request. "Tell me."

"I'm not sure how relevant this is, but Bob Petrie was in the Waukesha jail a few months ago."

"From what I hear, he comes and goes there. What was he in for?"

"Not showing up for a court appearance."

I was a little disappointed. I wanted something more obvious, like assault or battery, or anything to suggest he had a violent nature.

"What was he going to court for?" I wanted to know. "Assaulting somebody?"

"A traffic violation."

"That's it?" Pretty insignificant. Although as a full-time employed driver, his driving record would be important to his job. Not to me, though.

"There's more," Hunter said. "Ford Stocke was in the Waukesha jail, too. Those two spent time together in the same cell."

"I knew it!" I almost shouted, then remembered Eugene Petrie might still be inside the store. "Bob probably was Ford's partner."

"Story, what's going on?"

I hadn't been sharing much information with Hunter and I probably should have been. But when? If he wasn't working, I was. And he wouldn't come to the store just to chitchat, so . . . it wasn't exactly like I'd kept anything from him.

"I'll tell you everything tonight," I promised.

"Give me a quick rundown. You can fill in the holes later."

"It's complicated. It would be better if I could explain the whole thing all at once," I told him.

"Fine, save it then. We'll talk tonight."

Soon after I hung up, Holly arrived decked out in a new outfit, new shoes, new highlights—the works. I checked the time. "Only a few hours late today," I said, dripping with sarcasm. "Shopping? Getting your hair done?"

"Max's coming home tonight. I have to look good for him."

My spoiled, rich sister didn't have a clue what real work and commitment entailed. And my mother? Where was she? Oh yes, she was out smooching with her jailbird boyfriend.

A word of caution: Never, ever go into business with family members. Not that I did that on purpose. Somehow they all gravitated here after the store was a success, apparently a common occurrence in small businesses.

I sat in my office, intent on removing myself from all nuts—hickory, mental cases, and murder suspects, but I started feeling like an alcoholic who needed a drink, like a user who needed a fix. Sweat formed on my forehead. I got the shakes. I couldn't stop thinking about the murder investigation and how I could make a difference. I was sure of it. I had information that the authorities could use. If only Johnny Jay wasn't the authority in this case.

When Carrie Ann was drinking heavily, she told me how it was, that every morning she had good intentions. This was the day she'd stop. And she meant it. Every morning. Then by early afternoon, her resolve began slipping. By three o'clock the urge was strong. Just one drink, no more. By four she couldn't wait any longer. By five, she was on her third.

That was me at the moment. Back and forth with urges. The sane part of me wanted to share every last bit of information with Hunter and Johnny Jay and let one of them figure out the rest. Not that the chief would listen to me, but that shouldn't be my problem.

By five o'clock, when the twins arrived and took over, the urge to interfere was getting even stronger. I tried calling Patti again. No answer still.

I arranged a powwow at Stu's Bar and Grill with my sister, mom, grandmother, and cousin. And since I was joining Hunter there a little later, I made the meeting for an hour earlier than our rendezvous, because my cop boyfriend wasn't invited to this particular get-together.

I walked over with Holly and Dinky. As usual, Stu looked the other way when I snuck Dinky into a corner table. Mom came in a few minutes later, followed by Grams and Carrie Ann.

"I haven't had a drop to drink," Carrie Ann said, immediately going on the defensive when she saw the family assembled, assuming this was one of our interventions. Like we'd actually have one at a bar. "I'll swear on a stack of Bibles." She raised her right hand and put the other one over her heart.

"Sit down," I said. "This isn't about you."

"Thank God." She slid in.

The bar was hopping, thanks to the happy-hour crowd. Grams took a picture of Stu behind the bar before joining us.

"That Stu is one sweet man," Grams said to me. "You're attached at the hip to Hunter Wallace, another fine catch, but Stu needs a woman to spend time with. If things don't work out with Hunter, you have a backup."

"Stu has a girlfriend," I pointed out.

"Yes, but that relationship isn't going anywhere. How about you, Carrie Ann? Why aren't you after that cute man?"

I jumped in before Grams got too focused on matchmaking. Besides, I had a feeling Carrie Ann was quietly reconciling with her ex-husband, Gunnar; but even if she wasn't, would dating the owner of a bar be such a good idea for a recovering alcoholic? I thought not. Knowing this group, it would be hard to bring them back to the matter at hand once they started pairing off residents.

Stu took orders—nonalcoholic drinks for all of us out of respect for my cousin and lots of heart-clogging appetizers. Before leaving to place the order, Stu gave me a wink that made me realize he'd heard our conversation about him.

"I need help," I said to the group.

"You're pregnant," Holly said.

"No!"

"That's certainly a relief," Mom said.

"I'd go to Johnny Jay with my problem," I added, "but he hates my guts."

That comment got a flurry of active consideration. Stu delivered our drinks and said, "Johnny Jay is hot after you." Then he walked away.

"That's right," Grams agreed. "The chief is in love with you."

I snorted iced tea all over the table and grabbed a napkin to mop it up. "It's true," she insisted. "He's behaving like a little boy, being mean to get your attention."

"Whatever," I said, refusing to even consider such a ridiculous idea. "I can't go to him. So I'm telling you instead and we can all figure out what to do." That *we* part felt good. I didn't have to handle this all alone. I planned to drag them in, too.

Stu delivered our food and while we dug in, I brought them up to date on the things I knew but they didn't, starting with Ford and how I realized he had a partner of some sort.

"He made a slip when I asked him how long he'd been staying," I told them. "He said 'we.'"

That brought a few blank stares.

I plowed ahead. "Like he had someone working with him. You know, a coconspirator."

Mom said, "That's hardly evidence, Story."

I nodded and moved on to bigger and better stuff. Like

Patti's attacker, which everybody knew about, including
the hickory nuts, but it was worth repeating before I hit
them with another big tidbit. "Bob Petrie has a hickory nut
tattooed on his arm. I bet he's the one who attacked Patti.
And he was in jail with Ford! That must've been where
they plotted to rob Tom together."

Everybody stared at me.

"We have to band together to help Tom," I rushed on.
"And to help Mom."

"But how?" my sister asked.

"If we prove what I just told you, we might be able to
change public opinion's perception of Tom, maybe prove
he was only protecting himself from two known crimi-
nals."

Mom shook her head. "Tom didn't do anything wrong."

Grams agreed, but that wasn't a big surprise. She always
thought the best of everybody.

Carrie Ann joined in, siding with Mom, too.

Holly looked over at me and didn't commit to one opinion or the other.

Lately, my thoughts had been churning in the same
direction as theirs, in spite of all the evidence against Tom.
The idea that he might really be innocent zapped me like
little pricks of electric connections in my head.

But my mind argued back, bringing up a very good
point. I didn't realize I'd said it out loud.

"What do you mean, 'but he had blood on his shirt'?"
Carrie Ann said, so I had to explain what I was talking
about, how Tom showed up at Stu's with a bloody shirt.

"Oh, that," Mom said casually, exposing her index finger, which obviously had been cut and was in the process
of healing. "Tom and I had a cocktail before heading over
to Stu's that night. I sliced myself in Tom's kitchen while I
was cutting a lime. He bandaged it for me and got some of
my blood on his shirt. We didn't notice until you pointed
it out."

I looked around the table, at each one of Tom Stocke's cheerleaders. It wouldn't hurt to approach this problem from a different angle by starting with the assumption that Tom was totally innocent; not just that he'd killed his brother in self-defense, but that maybe he hadn't killed Ford at all. Hard to imagine, because lately there was just too much stacked against him.

Once I opened up my mind to the possibility, though, and painted the big picture, I had a brainstorm. I was pretty sure I knew why Patti's telescope (or telescopes in this case) had been targeted for destruction.

Thirty-seven

I muttered something vague about continuing our discussion later and hustled down Main Street. I remembered my Dinky obligation, so I used my cell phone to call back to Stu's and ask Grams to take care of Dinky, who I'd left there in my moment of brilliant enlightenment.

I tried Patti again without a response, which had me worried. P.P. Patti was usually hanging around, waiting for the right moment to swoop in and land, like a buzzard circling roadkill. No way would she disappear for this long on purpose.

At her back door, I banged hard and loud. Nothing. Then I angrily kicked a pile of hickory nuts, scattering them across the yard before turning to face my ex-husband's empty house. I had a creepy feeling that Patti's snooping had led to more trouble for her. And that Clay's house had something to do with it.

The house was locked up tight, and I didn't have a key. Theoretically, Lori and my ex should be the only ones with access. Except dumb Lori had rented out the house to a criminal element. That meant Ford had had a key, and who knew who else, like his partner, could've made copies to come and go any old time.

According to Hunter, anybody can get into a locked house without a key if they want to bad enough, and I planned on doing just that. Some people are natural experts at picking locks, using common items like bobby pins or credit cards. Based on my past efforts, which included attempts with paper clips and safety pins, I wasn't one of them. The only way in for me was through a window.

I went around the outside of the house, testing windows, and ended up smacking one of the ones in back with a hammer from my toolbox. I hadn't expected a little tap with a hammer to sound quite that loud. I held my breath like that would make a difference in whether or not I'd been caught. No one came running, which was good news. The bad news was that unfortunately, the glass in the window had cracked but not shattered. The only way in was to hit it a few more times.

I went home and returned with a towel, draped it over the end of the hammer, and banged away. Eventually the glass dropped in cascades around me. With the towel around my hand to protect myself, I pulled out large shards still embedded around the edges, then hefted myself up, and swung a leg over.

Judging by the amount of noise I had just made, I safely assumed that no bad guys were waiting inside or they would have shown themselves by now. So I swung my other leg over.

Breaking and entering was becoming my standard mode of operation. I wished I could blame Patti for that, but she wasn't around to take the rap. She'd said she was up to something and didn't want to tell me what. At the time, I felt relief; now I really wish she'd clued me in to her plan. I was worried about her.

Nothing had changed inside my ex-husband's unoccupied house in the days since I'd discovered Ford's body there. His camping gear was still scattered in the kitchen and bedroom. Johnny Jay had had the truck removed from the driveway during the initial investigation, but had left the interior of the house as he'd found it.

There's something about basements that as a general rule, men love and women dislike intensely. A certain fascination that they have, which we just don't get. Men tend to go rushing down the steps as soon as they get an opportunity. Women would really prefer not to. Also, basements in Wisconsin are damp. Mold grows quickly and spreads its tentacles over everything if you aren't careful. Then there are bugs—spiders, millipedes, stink bugs, beetles, and all kinds of other tiny terrors.

I'm a big fan of some insects, considering the number of honeybees in my backyard, but some species give me the willies.

So I considered skipping the basement.

Any sane woman would.

But if Patti were along, she'd lead the charge down stairs, though I do question her mental stability. That's why I had to go down. Because she wasn't here to make the first move, because I could hear the scorn in her voice if I told her I didn't want to. She'd taunt me about calling Hunter and having him take care of it for me, about depending on some guy again.

Patti's imaginary badgering produced enough resolve for me to tackle the basement. I didn't chicken out even when I flipped the light switch at the top of the stairs and nothing happened. Not a single lightbulb went on down there.

It wasn't exactly pitch-dark. The basement had old-fashioned ground-level windows set inside window wells, not the best source of light, but better than nothing. So I could see in a sort of late-dusk outline sort of way. I used my cell phone for a little added light, didn't stop to consider why the electricity was off in case that gave me enough of an excuse to abort my mission, and went down.

At the bottom of the stairs, I tripped over something soft and barely stayed in control, physically and emotionally. I smothered a bloodcurdling, hair-raising scream of terror, teetered in the balance, found my footing, and noted that the thing on the floor was only a crumpled blanket, not a body.

I picked it up, wondering what the heck a blanket was doing on the basement floor. It concerned me. At this point I wanted to let my instinct for flight take over, so I could run away, and come back with my family for support. My other choice involved seeing it through like a grown woman.

Before I could hightail it up the steps and out the door, I saw motion in a corner. I took a step forward. "Who's there?" I said, forcing myself forward, refusing to listen to the more cautious part of my cerebrum.

I was greeted by thrashing and snarling. A wild animal of some sort? Maybe a gigantic raccoon? Now I wasn't so sure the thing was human. In fact, I was sure it wasn't.

So I tossed the blanket over the top of the animal and kicked with my flip-flopped foot, connecting with something through the blanket. An almost-bare foot just doesn't have much power, though, and the thing didn't stop struggling. Part of its lower extremities popped through the bottom of the blanket. Only it didn't have paws or claws like I'd expected.

It had a foot and a shoe. And I recognized that shoe.

Ripping the blanket away, I came face-to-face with the rabid, foam-dripping creature.

It was P.P. Patti Dwyre.

She was tied up with tape across her mouth exactly like last time. Only this time, her eyes were taped, too. While I experienced a sense of déjà vu, I slowly removed the tape, careful not to rip out her eyelashes.

"Are you okay?" I said, fumbling with the ropes, realizing how useless my efforts were without better lighting or a knife to cut the bindings. Shining the little bit of light from my cell phone into her face wasn't helpful. She blinked rapidly and squeezed her eyes closed.

"Now I know how a blind mole feels," she said, her voice cracking. "Get me out of here."

"What are you doing down here in the first place?"

"Oh, I don't know," Patti said. "Just relaxing after a long day."

She hadn't lost her spunk or her sarcastic tongue, that was for sure.

"The knots are too tight. I'll have to go for help."

"No! Don't leave me here alone."

"I'll call for help." Remembering the phone in my hand, I hit speed dial. A phone inside one of Patti's pockets rang. At this point, I had to admit, I was pretty frazzled.

"You're calling my phone," she wailed.

"I'm shook up. Stop yelling." I tried again. For a damsel in distress, Patti sure was bossy.

"And don't call that cop boyfriend of yours," she said. "Not until you hear what happened."

I disconnected before it rang on Hunter's end. "This is ridiculous. You shouldn't be dictating terms. Do you want help or not?"

"My arms and legs are numb. I can't feel them."

"You'll get feeling back as soon as we get the ropes off, once you start moving them. Just like last time. I'm going to go upstairs and get a knife from the kitchen."

"This is an empty house. There isn't any kitchen equipment unless you dig through some of that camping stuff."

I worked the ropes again, feeling for a loose end. "I should call 9-1-1."

"No! We don't need local cops butting in."

I gaped at her. "You're roped up like a cow in a rodeo, blindfolded, and gagged. I can't even image what would have come next if I hadn't found you. Why don't you want me to get help? Who did this?"

"Just get me untied and I'll tell you the whole thing."

I gave up on freeing Patti. "Either I call for help right this minute, or you'll have to stay alone while I run home and get a knife."

"Go, but hurry."

And with that, I pounded up the basement steps.

Thirty-eight

❀

Once Patti was free and we were away from Clay's house, she seemed to take her imprisonment in stride, which was a really scary indicator of her ranking on the crazy meter. Either the woman was full-blown certifiable or her need for finding news was off the charts. Or a little of both.

It made me wonder even more about her background since she clearly had a high degree of tolerance for the most unpleasant situations. After being stuck in a basement all day, bound, gagged, and blindfolded, without food, water, or bathroom facilities, she sure had bounced back quickly.

"I suspected something was going on over there," she said from a seat at my kitchen table, a hot cup of herbal tea in front of her. "I mean, why else go after my telescope unless something was going down within its range?"

"That's exactly what I came up with," I said, although she'd certainly beat me to that realization.

"So this morning I went on another search mission.

When I went into the basement, somebody must have hit me with something because when I woke up I had a huge headache and I was all tied up and duct-taped. I never even got a look, but I heard voices. More than one person, I'm sure of it."

"Male or female voices?"

"Hard to tell. They were whispering."

"You were tied up exactly the same way as last time," I said, getting an ice pack out of the freezer and handing it to her. She applied it to the back of her head. "So it must've been the same person both times. You must have some idea who's after you."

Patti shook her head.

This was unbelievable. Patti had been physically attacked twice by a nasty and violent person, both times in broad daylight, and she still couldn't come close to identifying him? Patti wasn't a lightweight and the person who man-handled her had to be even tougher.

And stronger. Like Bob Petrie. Maybe the hickory nuts were his calling card, like what the villains in comic books always left at the scene of a crime. I told her about my exchange with Bob and how he had a hickory nut tattoo. And what Hunter had found out about our two jailbirds knowing each other.

"I knew I should have kicked him harder," Patti said, showing me a rope burn on her wrist. "Look at that. I better get compensation from *The Reporter* for my injuries."

"You should see a doctor and you should report it to the police, Patti."

"I can't. It's for the greater good. Without me the whole situation might implode."

I stared at her. "That's why we aren't telling the cops? Because you think you're some kind of superwoman, and you're out to save the world?"

"No, that's not all of it," Superwoman said. "I like to fol-low through with my commitments. Unlike *some* people."

Apparently she was referring to me. "Especially when they're in your own best interest," I said, somewhat defensively. "I brought my family up to speed on recent developments. They're going to help us." Yeah, right. Just as soon as they find time away from returning husbands, new boyfriends, and online apps.

Then I went on to tell her my theory about Tom Stocke's safe and about how Bob and Ford's plan had been blown. "I'd really like to clear Tom's name."

"He's still in the hot seat," Patti said, "and he's going to fry if we don't figure something out."

"Let's take another look at Clay's basement," I said.

So we snuck back over to Clay's house, watching the street, listening for sound. Patti headed into the basement, this time with a flashlight. I waited above.

Patti came into view at the bottom. "I think I know what hit me."

When I saw what she was carrying up the steps I almost keeled over.

"Oh my gosh," I said. "That's the same shovel you took out of the Petries' shed, the one you were going to dig with before Eugene caught us." I was so excited my next words ran over each other. "Shovel . . . Petrie . . . Aggie made me . . . bark chips . . . shovel missing." But Patti caught the gist of it.

"How can you tell it's the same one?" she wanted to know. "A shovel's a shovel."

"See the handle? It's all chewed," I said, remembering digging out a big splinter.

"Wait till I get my hands on the creep." Then Patti frowned. "But why would Bob bring a shovel over here?"

"Got me," I said, but one explanation came to mind.

Patti came to it at the same time. "That poor excuse for a human was going to dig a hole and bury me!"

"Relax," I said, not one bit relaxed. "We don't know that for sure."

I had felt a whole lot more comfortable back when I

thought Tom had killed his brother in self-defense. Back then, I didn't feel one bit threatened. But now, we were dealing with a guy with a criminal record who might have killed a man and had probably planned to kill Patti, too.

I changed into dark clothes to match Patti's standard garb, then she and I headed out. "First, let's check Bob's house for evidence," I said. "I have pepper spray in the glove compartment in case we're caught." Patti dug in the glove compartment and came out with a pocket-sized canister.

"I have a few weapons myself." Patti patted her vest. "Here's the plan. You go in first . . ."

"Why me? You should go first."

"No way. If Bob answers the door, he better not see me after our last tango. All you have to do is knock on the door. Besides, his wife already knows you, right? And you visited with her recently. She won't think it's so unusual. Just go in, make some excuse to keep her occupied, and I'll sneak in the back and look around."

I was really glad I had the easy job.

"Make sure you give me at least ten minutes inside," Patti said.

We parked out of sight and walked the rest of the way, passing Aggie and Eugene's house, which was dark. No lights. Night had arrived fast while I hadn't been paying attention. I wanted Alicia and Bob's house to be dark, too, but I already knew better.

Several lights were on inside.

I knocked on the door. Nobody answered it.

I rang the bell. Nothing.

"Try the door," Patti hissed from the shadows. "Is it locked?"

I tried the door. "Yes," I said.

"Let's go around back."

Up until now I'd have said that locks aren't really that necessary in a small town like ours. Generally, we don't have any reason to use them. But after all my breaking and entering this week, I was reconsidering the wisdom of keeping certain elements out of my house. Of which I was turning out to be one. An element.

It made me stop and think about my character. Was my moral compass going south with P.P. Patti's?

The back door was also locked. But we weren't about to let that slow us down. First we looked in every single window. Nobody was inside.

Then I said, "I'm a semiprofessional window smasher. I'll get us in."

"That won't be necessary." Patti produced several different lock-picking devices and went to work. About five seconds later, the door swung open.

"You're really good," I said.

"Practice makes perfect," she replied.

Just then my phone rang, causing Patti to glare at me. So I'd forgotten to silence my phone. So shoot me.

Carrie Ann was on the other end with an important new development. "A swat team is headed into Clay's house," she said. "I was going back to the store to play . . . eh . . . I mean finish up some computer work when I saw Hunter Wallace whiz by. I thought he was going to your house so I did a quick peek. All of a sudden, here they all came, acting like something was going down over there."

I considered the implications. Besides Hunter's job with the county and K-9 training, he works with the Critical Incident Team, a group of law-enforcement officials that respond to potentially high-risk situations. If C.I.T. was involved, it was dangerous.

"Jeez," I said, pondering possibilities. A gunman? A hostage situation? Both? Had Patti and I just gotten away by the skin of our teeth? Had Bob Petrie shown up to finish off Patti and bury her? Was he inside right now, trapped, and desperate enough to come out shooting?

I kept my cousin on the line while I related the latest to my partner. We were still standing outside.

"Hunter asked about you," Carrie Ann added. "Whether you were at home or not. He seemed worried," she said. "I told him you weren't there."

"Tell her to keep us posted," Patti said.

"Okay, thanks," I said to Carrie Ann. "If you find out any more, call me."

I hung up. And wondered why Hunter hadn't given me a heads-up. Although he was a professional when it came to his job. If there was a gag order, he'd uphold it.

"C.I.T. is onto Bob," I said to Patti. "We can turn this over to them."

"Let's take a quick look in his house anyway. We're already ahead of the cops."

So we went in, keeping the lights from our flashlights low to the ground. The only room lit up was the kitchen and a hallway. Patti headed for the basement.

When this was all over, I never wanted to see another basement.

"Well, looky, looky," Patti said from a corner.

Where we found her telescope.

Still in the box.

Thirty-nine

After that little discovery, Patti and I regrouped. "Something doesn't feel right," I said from the driver's seat of my parked truck. "Bob's been attacking you over telescopes. But why? If the plan to rob Tom is as dead as Ford Stocke, why bother?"

"I'm a loose cannon," Patti said, pulling the words right out of my head. "He can't anticipate my next move. I'm onto him and he's scared."

"But the cops already checked out Clay's house, right after Ford's murder. Suppose . . ." I paused, thinking a minute. "Suppose the plan isn't dead after all. And Bob's been using that house for a base of operation."

"Maybe. It's possible." Then Patti's eyes went wide. "Bob could have killed Ford so he didn't have to share the dough."

"Exactly. Only . . . if he needed the help, why not kill him afterward, not before?"

"Unless he didn't need Ford's help after all?"

"Not that many of us have expertise in safecracking," I reasoned, gulping back an obvious, glaringly scary possibility. "Oh God, I think I know who Bob's new partner is."

"Who?" Patti demanded.

"Noel Peck," I said. "Stanley's grandson. He's going to blow up the safe."

After that we had a major disagreement over what we should do next.

"It's going down tonight," Patti insisted. "That's why Bob isn't home. He's going to blow it right now. And he isn't going to want any surviving witnesses. That dumb kid! How did he get involved?"

"We have to find Hunter. This is too big for us. We turn over what we have and step clear. In fact, I bet Hunter already found out about Bob's plan. Or about Noel. That must be why C.I.T. is at Clay's house."

Patti had a crazy eye gleam, which should have tipped me off. "We'll compromise," she said. "Let's drive over to Tom's. We'll call Hunter on the way. I still need my story. I deserve this story."

Which was true. She'd been physically assaulted twice, tied up, and left all day in a damp basement without any creature comforts. If anyone deserved something out of this, it was her.

I started the truck. Patti yelled, "Hold on," and jumped out. She paused by the front tire and bent down, fiddling with something.

"What the . . ." I started to say, but she dove in, and yelled, "Hit it!" When I glanced over, she had a satisfied grin on her face.

"What?" I said, multitasking as I drove—clicking on the seat belt, staying on the road, and digging for my cell phone all at the same time. "You know something I don't? Dang. Where did I put my phone?"

"You crushed it under the tire when we took off," she said with a smirk. "It's in teensy tiny pieces."

"You stole my phone?" I shouted. "And put it under the tire? Are you insane?" I felt most of the blood in my body rush to my head, like a geyser about to erupt. I was under a lot of pressure. Mostly caused by the nutcase next to me.

I counted to ten.

One: Patti couldn't help herself.

Two: Not that that let her off the hook.

Three: Still, it was my fault for letting the piece of work in my truck in the first place.

Four: How many times did I have to suffer for her actions before I learned my lesson?

Five: My mother was right.

Six: I really did have to learn everything the hard way.

Seven: If anybody was hurt because of Patti's little stunt, I was going to commit a murder.

Eight: And I wasn't going to hide the deed.

Nine: Because I'd be acquitted once a jury heard the whole story.

Ten: Apparently, counting to ten wasn't helping.

"Calm down," Patti said. "You look like you're going to stroke out."

I snorted flames. "Where's your phone?" I asked through gritted teeth.

"I didn't bring it."

"You always bring your phone."

"Not this time."

I wanted to pull over and strip-search her. "Do you realize that you're totally to blame if anybody is hurt tonight?"

"You can't blame me for Bob's actions."

"No, but I can blame you for *your* actions." I shook my head in disgust. "Intentionally destroying my cell phone. What were you thinking? Was it just so I couldn't call Hunter?"

"I was thinking that you and I are going to bust a bomber."

My fingers were white on the steering wheel. I stepped on the gas.

Patti went on spewing illogical logic. "By the time you would have explained the problem to your boyfriend and convinced him to show up at Tom's house, it would have been too late. He'd want to call in backup and—"

"He's got backup with him," I fairly shouted. "He's right down the street from Tom's apartment with a team of experts!"

Why was I bothering to attempt reason with a strait-jacket candidate? Maybe it was the blow to her head with the shovel. It must have scrambled her brains. There was no other explanation.

Okay, get a grip. Deep breaths. Eyes on the road. Slow down a little. You don't want a cop car chasing you for speeding. Or wait, yes, you do.

My foot twitched and I accelerated.

"We'll be there in a few minutes," I said, seeing the out-skirts of Moraine come into view. "We need to figure out what to do about all this."

"Head over to Tom Stocke's apartment, for starters."

"You're delusional. If you're right about Bob trying to blow up the safe, I'm not going inside a building that might explode. Besides, we don't know a thing about explosives or how to defuse a bomb."

"I'm armed, don't worry."

"Oh, that makes me feel a whole lot better."

We came into town. I had my own agenda. Instead of going straight down Main Street to the antique store, I would turn onto my block and get the C.I.T. team. The two of us weren't on the same page any longer. Patti wouldn't like that one bit. She'd fuss and fume, but so what?

Hunter and his team would still be in the vicinity. If he wasn't at Clay's house, I'd have to find him fast.

Only I didn't get a chance to follow through, because as soon as I hit the town limits, several blocks from Tom's store and my house, I heard a loud bang. The right side of the truck was lower than the left side.

"Flat tire," Patti said just as I'd figured it out for myself. She jumped out, whipped a ski mask over her head, and ran down Main sticking to the shadows.

As if things couldn't get worse, they did.

Johnny Jay's police vehicle pulled up behind my truck.

Forty

Interfering in a police investigation is a chargeable offense.

So is withholding evidence.

Tampering with evidence isn't good, either.

Which reminded me of the shovel I'd thrown in the back of my truck.

This just goes to show how a completely innocent human being gets in deeper and deeper, and pretty soon they're buried in lies and deception right up to their necks.

In small-town politics, our elected officials leave plenty of wiggle room to move around. They take some laws as gospel, ignore a whole bunch, and even make a few up as they go along. Johnny Jay is a by-the-book type of guy, though, even if he wrote his own code book.

Anyway, here's what happened.

Right after Johnny Jay pulled up behind me, he and I started going back and forth with barbs like we always do.

Then he got a call about a burglary in progress behind

Tom Stocke's antique store. Tom, who had been home watching television, had tackled the masked burglar, planted several right hooks that disabled his opponent Patti (of course, he didn't know it was Patti yet), and called the cops.

Since I was in the vicinity, Johnny Jay just assumed I was involved. Go figure.

So, here I sat in the interrogation room, pleading my case. Spilling my guts, almost everything I could remember, starting with suspicions of local involvement and finishing with my hope to save Tom's money from the hands of a criminal known as Bob Petrie who might also have committed murder. I left out a few minor details. Like how many places I'd visited without invitations. And Noel's possible role in all this. I wanted to talk that over with Stanley first.

Patti was in another interrogation room waiting her turn.

"How about we make a deal," I said to Johnny Jay. "Patti and I promise we won't interfere anymore. You drop the charges."

That produced a laugh from the police chief.

I wasn't through yet, deciding to take an offensive position. "I should charge you with endangering my life," I said. "Expecting private citizens like me to do your job for you."

That was a long shot, but I was desperate.

"Sally Maylor checked out your allegations," Johnny said. "She gives you more credibility than I do, but that'll change someday soon. Bob Petrie and his family are at an antique fair something-or-other, two hours from here. They're all together and vouching for each other."

My best bet at this point was to make amends, play it low-key, even apologize for what was mostly Patti's misguided delusions. I opened my mouth, but Johnny beat me to the punch with another outrageous accusation.

"You called in another false emergency," he said next. "Didn't you?"

"What false emergency?"

"Sure, let's pretend. Somebody, like maybe you, reported a hostage situation in the house next to yours. The C.I.T. team was engaged. That's serious stuff, Fischer."

So that was why Hunter and the rest of the Critical Incident Team had been dispatched. I wondered who'd made the call. "I did not make that call, but I'm telling you, Patti *was* being held against her will in the basement."

"So you did make the call." He wrote something in a notebook.

"No, I didn't. I don't even have a phone anymore. I accidentally ran over it with my truck."

"Uh-huh."

In the end, I spent all night in jail. The crimes Johnny Jay was trying to pin on me were reporting a hostage situation that didn't exist (completely circumstantial) and stealing a shovel (maybe provable).

"Stealing a shovel?" I yelled. "That's beyond stupid."

"Aggie Petrie said you stole it."

"The nerve!"

I guess I should've been happy that I wasn't charged with tampering or interfering or withholding like I thought I might, since those were much more serious. Still, someday it would be nice for Johnny to believe me. Just for once.

Sally came by my jail cell at one point and gave me a blanket. "Will you check over at Stanley Peck's?" I pleaded with her. "Make sure Noel is safe?"

She came back later and said, "Stanley chewed me out for waking them up. Noel's fine."

Patti didn't get off quite as lightly as I did. Tom Stocke decided not to press charges after he heard she'd been attempting to save his life, but she still had a serious concealed-weapons charge to face after a brisk pat down at the station exposed her darker side.

Forty-one

We came out of the police station at dawn, blinking like moles, smelling like buffalos, and with slightly deflated egos. I didn't have a single thing to say to Patti Dwyre. And I wasn't going to let her intimidate me or bully me into any more stupid situations. I refused to feel sorry for her even when I saw her black eyes. Tom really knew how to plant his fists.

Sally drove us back home. She made a few attempts at small talk, but I wasn't in the mood. "Another storm is brewing," she said. "I can smell it in the air."

When we got out of the car, Patti said to me, "I think I might be partially responsible for all this."

I didn't even know how to respond to that understatement so I marched off.

My honeybees hadn't even missed me. That's one of the beauties of my favorite little gatherers. They are independent little things. Unlike Dinky, who has to be cared for every single second. Thank goodness for Grams.

A few foragers landed on me as I stood surveying my beeyard, calming myself, focusing on the important things in my life. Until recently, I saw the world just as the honeybees did, a mosaic of colors—blue, green, violet, orange, yellow. But not red. Bees can see ultraviolet, but red just looks like gray to them. Today, I felt my world was in shades of gray, too.

I needed to be like a bee and get back to basics, to simply sustain. These little girls only cared about flowers and honey. And making sure their hive was safe.

But my own hive didn't feel so safe. It felt threatened.

Somebody was watching and waiting and I wasn't at all sure that certain "somebody" wasn't watching me. For sure, Patti had a scary shadow. What if I was next?

And what about Bob's alibi? If he really had been at an antiques fair this whole time, where did that leave us? Nowhere, that's where.

The air around me was thick with moisture. I felt sweat running down the center of my back and guessed the temperature must be over ninety, with something like 100 percent humidity.

After showering, changing, and eating my standard toast and honey butter breakfast downed with plenty of coffee, I went down the street and opened the store. The day began like all the others.

Stu came in for his morning paper and didn't say a word about my night in jail. Had I slid through that one without any of the locals finding out? Was I saved from having to endure furtive glances and knowing smirks and secret whispers?

Milly brought in samples of her newsletter recipes for critique. This was my favorite part of composing the monthly newsletter. Milly's nutty rhubarb muffins were to die for—moist and delicious. And she'd used hickory nuts, though she said that walnuts were an acceptable substitute.

"A real winner," I decided. "Too bad none of the other

staff members are here to experience the next newsletter recipe."

"I made plenty. I'll leave some in the back. Then I'm heading home before the weather turns ugly. Wait until you try these."

Milly opened a plastic container. We peered in.

"Blueberry scones!" I said.

"With honey glaze," Milly added.

I downed a whole one at record speed and licked my fingers clean. I almost felt human again after a long, painful night away from my own bed with no sleep.

A little later, Carrie Ann called to say that she'd be in late, and that she couldn't find Holly to ask her to work for her. She didn't mention exactly how late before disconnecting. Holly, I suspected, was under the covers with her husband, sleeping off a romantic evening. She hadn't bothered asking off from work or finding anyone to replace her, though. Standard operating procedure.

Mom came in. By her sweet disposition, it was a sure bet she didn't know about Patti's escapade at Tom's yet. Or about me having been in jail. "According to Emily, your scarf hasn't surfaced yet," she said. "She feels really bad about it. It'll show up eventually."

I highly doubted that.

"Tornado weather," she said. "Be on the lookout. Tom and I are driving into Milwaukee for the afternoon. We're going to the zoo. If the weather doesn't hold, we'll end up at the art museum." With that, Mom bounced out.

Stanley came in. "How's Noel?" I asked.

"Why is everybody so concerned about my grandson?" he said. "Sally Maylor woke us up last night just checking on him."

"We like to look out for our young people," I said.

"His head is lost in space with all that chemical stuff, but his body is just fine. He left early again."

Mid-morning, Hunter called, but I was busy with customers

and couldn't talk. When I had a spare minute, I called him back.

"You don't have to say a word," Hunter said. "I know everything."

"Is that so," I said, wondering what he knew and what he didn't. My heart sped up just hearing his voice.

"Johnny Jay asked me to listen to the recording."

"Recording?" Why did I have such a sense of dread? Please don't tell me Johnny Jay had recorded last night's interrogation and delivered it to my boyfriend. "I never gave him permission to record anything. Isn't that privileged information?"

Hunter, good guy that he is, didn't mention that his position made him eligible for all that privileged stuff, but still . . . "He offered the recording as an explanation for the team's wasted effort last night," Hunter said. "I know you denied making the call to him about a hostage situation, but did you?"

Not good, not good at all. "I thought if anybody believed me, it would be you."

"I had to ask." Hunter didn't sound happy with me. "We need to talk."

I had a perfect excuse for dodging him. "I'm alone at the store. I can't leave."

"Promise me you'll stay right where you are," he said. "And stay out of trouble."

"Okay," I said, feeling like a child about to be scolded. I hated that feeling. Hunter and I had a lot of respect for each other and usually didn't waste our precious time together nagging or criticizing, so what was the deal with his attitude?

I put it out of my mind.

Thunder rumbled in the distance, making me wonder how Grams was doing with Dinky, since the little dog was terrified of storms. I'd hoped to keep that particular problem from my grandmother until she was in too deep to back out. What would happen now?

A little while later, Eugene Petrie came into the store for the second time ever. I considered hiding under the counter, but he'd already spotted me.

"I thought you were out of town," I said, plastering on a big friendly smile.

I didn't get one in return. "I'm sure you did," he said. "I'm here for two reasons."

I gulped. How had he picked a time to show up when nobody was in the store? Had he been outside, watching? "Okay," I said, dropping the smile.

"First, I'm warning you. Stay away from my family."

"That's easy," I said, refusing to whimper until later, after he left. "I'll do that."

His face was about two inches from mine. It wasn't pretty. Long nose hairs hanging out of his nostrils, pores like volcano craters, broken blood vessels, breath that could stop a whole hive of bees in midflight.

"Two," he said. "I want my shovel back."

"I gave it to Johnny Jay," I lied, just like I'd lied to the police chief and told him I'd returned it to the Petries' backyard shed. Since Eugene was asking, he hadn't gone around to the back of the building and found it in my truck. Otherwise he would have taken it and we wouldn't be having this conversation. Although, I had no idea why I wasn't giving the thing back.

Eugene wasn't pleased with my answer. "I don't know what you're up to, but it stops now. Or else." That was a direct threat, no doubt about it.

How dare Eugene! Coming into my store and threatening me. "You know where I found your shovel?" I said, narrowing my eyes, too.

"My shed," he snarled.

"No. In the house next to mine. The same place Ford's body was found."

Eugene smirked. "You're trying to set me up, aren't you? You and Patti Dwyre."

I could have said, *No, I'm not trying to get you, I'm after your son,* but that wouldn't be too smart.

"Unless you're going to shop," I said to him, "I suggest you leave."

I'd misjudged Eugene Petrie. All this time, thinking he was a better person than the nasty woman he was married to, but he wasn't one bit nicer.

Eugene swung his head around as if he were looking for something, like he maybe had another reason for being inside my store. His eyes landed on my honey display. "I need honey sticks," he snarled.

"Any special kind?" I asked, thinking the faster I got the jerk out of my store, the better.

"Root beer," he answered.

I almost keeled over.

Forty-two

Root beer honey sticks!

Noel Peck's favorites.

"We're all out," I managed to stammer. Which was true. Noel had wiped me out of every single one. Then the blurty, blabby part of me took over, taking control of my impulsive side, so I said, "Could I interest you in . . . oh, I don't know . . . a little fertilizer? Hydrogen peroxide, matches?" What else went into explosives? I tried to think of more ingredients.

While I was considering my next sassy response, Eugene headed for the door. He acted as if he hadn't heard me. He didn't say one single word more, which was creepier than if he had. At the door, he turned back. Judging by the expression on his face, I was doomed.

Me and my big mouth.

Why did I always have to have the last word? Thanks to my wayward impulses, I'd just let him know I knew what he was up to.

Jeez. Now what?

Part of me argued that lots of people like root beer. Why shouldn't Eugene be one of them? It could be purely coincidental. After all, who didn't like root beer? And the way he'd acted? That could be explained away, too. He'd been living with a professional sneerer his whole life.

The other part of me, the side that wasn't rooting for root beer, ran to the front door, threw the bolt into the locked position, tore through the store gathering my things, slipped out the back door, and blew out of the parking lot in my truck. The sky had darkened with black clouds, but I didn't turn on my headlights. The air was scary still.

This might be my only chance to find out if Noel was actually in trouble or just looking for trouble. I really couldn't see a twelve-year-old intentionally committing a crime of this magnitude, even if he was a fanatic about explosives. Which made me think he'd been fooled somehow, or threatened, or . . . something.

I didn't see Eugene Petrie nearby, so I took a chance and guessed that he would head north toward his house in Colgate. I headed that way, and picking up speed, pretty soon I spotted him ahead of me, driving the white van. I'd guessed right about the direction he'd take, thank God. If I stayed back a little, he wouldn't get suspicious. And while I did that, I'd call for backup. I'd call Hunter, tell him to get his gun and Ben and join me, and I'd explain all of it while he was on his way.

Only my cell phone wasn't in my pocket.

Then I remembered what Patti had done to it, and I was ticked off all over again. After this, we were through as so-called friends. Because of her, we might be attending a funeral soon—mine, or some innocent bystander caught in a blast, or, if I got my hands on her before my own demise, a funeral for P.P. Patti.

Ahead, Eugene rounded a bend in the road, vanishing from sight. My heart almost stopped working. I really didn't care about Tom's money or what happened to it any-more, but these people were ruthless. They'd killed once; they would kill again. And if Noel was involved, no way would they let Stanley's grandson live to tell the truth.

Even though I'd been using the *they* word, I hoped that Bob and the other Petries really were still out of town, because I really, really hoped to deal with only one of them. One was more than enough.

Several times, I thought I saw movement in my rear-view mirror, but each time on closer inspection, nobody was following me. My nerves were almost shot. Now I was seeing things.

Eugene's white van came back into view again. My hands were sweaty on the steering wheel and my mind refused to operate at full bore, which was a really bad time for it to shut down. But it had never been asked to handle a situation quite like this before.

Right when I was convinced that Eugene was going to his house, he abruptly slowed down and turned left. I slipped back a little to give him more space. Then I turned in, too.

He made another right into a driveway, one with a for-sale sign at the end of it. I stopped along the side of the road on the far side of the driveway and studied my options.

If I could find a phone, I could call Hunter. He would come. He wouldn't like it, but he'd show up. My boyfriend would give me as many chances as I needed to get it right. Wouldn't he?

The what-ifs started going through my half-numb mind.

I should have brought Stanley Peck along. He had knowledge of weapons, knew how to use them, and had a personal stake in the outcome. Sometimes I'm totally dense. I wanted to chastise myself more, but right now I needed to figure out exactly what was going on inside that house. Without something concrete, I had nothing.

Which meant sneaking up and scoping it out, while

staying furtive and in the shadows. I certainly wasn't going to announce myself.

I couldn't see the house from the road because of all the trees and bushes, maples and honeysuckles dominating the landscape. They would conceal me from view. Besides, Eugene didn't have any reason to be suspicious that I'd followed him. This should be easy. Sneak along the house, peek in a few windows, get my evidence, *then* go and find a phone and call Stanley and Hunter.

With a bit of luck, I'd even get a glimpse of Noel, alive and well.

A car passed by and the driver waved at me, something we tend to do in this area. If you're on my road, you must be my neighbor. Neighborly is one of our most striking traits. And if you aren't my neighbor, I'll still consider you a potential neighbor who might buy that house you're sitting in front of.

That's how we think, so I waved back. So much for being sneaky.

Once the car was gone, I got out of the truck, and stole along the edge of the driveway until the house came into view. Then I darted among the trees, feeling more than slightly silly. This was a job for Patti Dwyre, not me. Something about peeking around tree trunks didn't fit into the image I had of myself.

The sky was growing darker by the minute and thunder rumbled in the distance. The only positive thing about that was the extra cover the fading light gave me.

I could see the van. The back door was wide open, but I couldn't see inside. I didn't hear any rummaging around nearby, so Eugene had to be in the house, either getting ready to put something in the back of his van, or he'd just taken something out.

Either way, he'd come back out and shut the van door any minute.

I ran over to the vehicle in a hunched-down position and crawled into the back.

Right into the middle of enough proof to take down the head of any terrorist group. I recognized all kinds of chemical containers. I didn't know how to make explosives, but I was pretty sure you'd use some of this stuff. Especially that thingamajig that looked like the panel from the inside of a computer.

I had my proof. How easy was that? Piece-of-blueberry-pie easy.

I'd just tell Hunter this van was loaded with explosive material and he and his C.I.T. team would be on it like American tanks rolling through the Middle East.

Before I could retreat, a door slammed from the direction of the house. I slithered into the front seat, lying flat between the bucket seats, looking for something to cover my really exposed body. Footsteps on the driveway. I made like an ostrich and buried my head. It was the most I could do with a moment's notice.

While my head was buried in the sand, somebody grabbed my ankles. I felt myself sliding backward. There's not a lot a woman can do when a strong man has her in that position. I couldn't kick or karate chop or do anything other than dig my fingers into the van's smooth metal floor. That didn't work at all.

I felt ropes winding around my lower legs. I tried to wrench away and that's when I got a glance at Eugene. He was busy trussing.

And he was really good at it.

Now I knew why Patti hadn't been able to get away either time. Or why she hadn't seen her attacker. He had the element of surprise with her. I'd heard him coming and I still hadn't stood a chance.

I remembered that Eugene Petrie had been in the military. He must have been the sadistic GI who tied up the enemies. And waterboarded them. When he'd threatened Patti and me with that when he caught us in his garden, he hadn't been kidding.

Now Eugene grabbed one of my hands and wrenched it behind my back. I fought as hard as I could, considering my already compromised position, desperately looking for something to use as a weapon. Neither of us said anything while we struggled, but we were both breathing hard, focused on winning.

I lost.

He slapped a piece of duct tape over my mouth and left me there. I rolled around and managed to fall out of the back of the van. Which really hurt.

Eugene came out of the front door and held it open. Right behind him was Noel Peck. Not tied up or anything.

"What are you doing to Story?" he asked Eugene.

"I caught her snooping in the back of the van. She'll have to come along. Help me put her back in."

I tried to warn Noel, tell him to run, but all I managed was gibberish.

"Are you okay?" Noel ask me, which of course I couldn't answer, then to Eugene, "This wasn't part of the deal."

"It's her fault. What could I do?"

"Let her go."

"I will just as soon as you take care of your end of the bargain. And remember, one false move and I turn in your grandfather for murdering Ford Stocke."

"After I do what you want, you'll go away? Right?" Now Noel sounded like a twelve-year-old. Young, inexperienced, and wanting to trust.

Stanley had killed Ford Stocke? No way—but it was apparent that Noel believed it. This was worse than I thought. Eugene wasn't wearing a mask to conceal his identity, which wasn't a good sign. How did that saying go? Dead men tell no tales? Or in this case, add in boys and women.

They hefted me back into the van. Eugene anchored the ropes somehow so I couldn't do a repeat, and they got in the front seat.

"Shouldn't we wait until dark?" Noel said.

"Nobody will suspect a thing in broad daylight. We'll drive in the back alley. Everybody will think we're a service truck. And I verified that the owner is gone for a few hours. This is perfect."

Then I remembered what Mom said, about going into Milwaukee with Tom. The coast was clear for a robbery.

I hadn't seen or heard any other Petrie family members. That implied that Eugene was working alone today. I wondered where Bob, the telescope thief, was at the moment and how he fit into all this.

I also struggled with the ropes binding me without any success and thought about broad-daylight burglaries. When I lived in Milwaukee, they happened more than nighttime robberies. People were at work during the day. And neighbors didn't know each other that well. So even if a moving truck pulled up and hauled away every last piece of furniture, the neighbors probably wouldn't even get suspicious.

I couldn't see that working as well out here. Although going in through the back alley was a smart move. He might actually pull it off. Especially with a storm coming. The residents of Moraine would be hunkered down, preparing for bad weather.

After what seemed like forever, the van turned sharply, the road beneath it roughened, and the vehicle came to a stop.

Forty-three

The sound of thunder was much nearer now. The town's tornado siren went off, extra loud and extra long, announcing a tornado warning, meaning a funnel had been spotted. Eugene couldn't have planned it any better. The streets would be deserted.

The back door of the van swung out and Eugene's ugly mug peered in at me.

"Get what you need, kid," he ordered Noel, pulling on a pair of gloves.

Noel looked like he wanted to cut and run. Eugene noticed and brought him back with a reality check. "Your grandfather? Remember him? You want to start visiting him in prison?"

Noel crawled in next to me and gathered up the thing with all the wires and a few containers I couldn't identify. I tried to talk to him with my eyes. *Run for it*, they said. Forget the threats. They don't mean a thing. Plus, I was 99.9 percent sure Eugene was bluffing. He didn't have anything on Stanley Peck.

But Noel, just like any twelve-year-old, wasn't listening to my eye-talk. He believed he had no choice, that his grandfather's freedom depended on his performance.

"I should wear gloves, too," Noel pointed out.

"Not necessary," Eugene said, confirming my suspicion about witnesses and their future health.

Then Eugene closed up the back of the van, quietly this time, no slamming, and I was left alone with my thoughts. Which weren't pleasant. Nightmarish really. Sweat ran down my face, my heart was murmuring, and hope was vanishing.

While I was considering death and dying, the front driver's door opened. I strained to see what Eugene was up to now but couldn't get myself positioned right. Was he going to kill me even before the explosion? I struggled hard to get loose, expecting a bullet in the brain at any second.

Heard him coming through from the front.

Saw his feet.

Wait a minute.

Those shoes looked strangely familiar.

I glanced up to see Patti Dwyre standing over me with the sharpest knife I've ever seen. It gleamed right along with her crazy black eyes.

For a few frozen seconds I thought she was in on it with Eugene. That's how far my ability to reason had slipped. But instead of plunging the knife into my chest, she bent down and ripped off the duct tape across my mouth. I stifled a shriek of pain.

"Now you know how it feels," she said, with a grin. Like this was all a big joke and it was payback time.

I licked my chafed lips.

Then she went to work on my ropes.

"Where did you come from?" I said, never so happy to see anybody in my life, even if it was Patti. I take that back. *Especially* because it was her.

"I was in the back of your truck."

Then I remembered those flashes of motion I'd seen while I was tailing Eugene. "I *thought* I saw something in the rearview mirror."

"That was me," she said with pride. "When the van pulled out, I followed in your truck. You shouldn't leave keys in the ignition, you know."

With a few flicks of Patti's knife, I was free and rubbing my aching arms.

"We have to go for help," I said, my voice low. "Right this minute. He's going to leave Noel down there to blow up, too."

"No time. We're going in."

"Where's your phone?" I asked.

"Battery's dead."

Great. Just great. "I don't know if he's armed," I said. "I didn't see a gun, though."

"Here," Patti handed me a can of wasp spray, one of her favorite defense weapons. "I have a few other things, too, including that shovel from the back of your truck. We're going to take him down, but we have to expect him to put up a good fight first."

"Okay," I said, not feeling okay at all. I'd been in sting operations with Patti in the past and they didn't exactly go off without a hitch. "We better wrap it up quickly, or we'll all blow sky-high."

We whipped together a plan that I could only describe as a Plan D or Plan F, not exactly brilliant. The cellar door leading to Tom's basement was padlocked, just like the utility door below that concealed his safe.

Patti took her position.

Thunder rumbled and the air went deadly still.

I went around to the apartment door and quietly let myself in.

Forty-four

The basement door was wide open. I heard clinking and muttering coming from below.

Outside, I knew Patti had the shovel over her shoulder in attack mode. I had the can of poison. Not exactly a fair fight considering Eugene had explosives, a captive kid who knew how to use them, and Lord only knew what else. From my position at the top of the stairs, I attempted to regulate my breathing, so I wouldn't hyperventilate, pass out, and fall down the stairs.

Patti started banging on the cellar door with the shovel, making a bunch of racket. "Give it up, Eugene Petrie," she hollered. "You're surrounded."

Through the windows, I saw lightning slice through the air. The earth rumbled with thunder. On a regular day, somebody would have come running to see what the ruckus was about. Right now, they were all in their own basements, hiding from the approaching storm.

Patti repeated the banging and called again for Eugene
to give up.

I slunk back from the stairs, concealing myself from
view when I heard footsteps coming up. As soon as I confirmed it was Eugene, not Noel, I sprayed the wasp poison
in his surprised face. Patti was behind me in a flash and
before I knew what was happening, she'd swung the shovel.
It connected with Eugene's head.

He fell backward down the steps.

"You don't mess around," I said, afraid to look at the
damage.

Patti was already in the basement, stepping over her victim. I pounded down, too.

The utility door was open. I could see part of the safe.
Something ominous was attached to it.

When I ran into the room, Noel was sitting on the floor
next to the safe. He was gagged with tape and his right
hand was attached to a pipe running along the wall.

I saw that Eugene hadn't used ropes this time, which
was unfortunate for us since Patti had a razor-sharp knife.
The guy's MO said rope. It should be rope. This was chains
and a sturdy lock. I felt myself slipping into panic mode.
"Where's the key?" I said to Noel, trying to stay calm.

"No key," Noel said when I pulled off the tape. His face
was the color of chalk. "It's a combination."

I turned and stared over where Patti was making sure
Eugene was done causing trouble. Based on his condition,
he wouldn't be telling us the combination numbers anytime soon.

If we got out in one piece, I was going to rip Patti into a
bunch of very tiny pieces for braining Eugene like that. If
she had left him in a conscious state . . .

"How long do we have?" I asked.

Noel glanced at the safe. "Ninety-one seconds," he said.
"Can we stop it?"

"Maybe. If you knew what you were doing."

"I'll try," Patti said, and I had to give her a teaspoon of credit for not bolting up the stairs and leaving us to our fate.

I was already over by Tom's tool bench looking for something useful. I'd spent enough time at Grams's house and in her barn when she had a working farm, so I knew my tools.

By now, the storm had hit full force. The wind howled and rain slammed against the root cellar door.

I had no idea how much damage the blast was going to do, but I couldn't ask. Because Noel was talking to Patti, instructing her, his voice the only calm thing in the room. Tucked in a corner behind the bench, I found a chain saw, but I'd only end up removing Noel's entire hand with that. And a hacksaw, which would take way too much time. Then I spotted tin snips, grabbed them, and went to work on the chain, willing my hands not to shake.

"I'm not going to make it," Patti said, sounding almost as panicked as I felt.

"How much time?" I said.

"Forty seconds," Noel said.

I threw down the tin snips. "I need your help, Patti."

She didn't hesitate, just got up and followed me over to the wall next to the tool bench where Tom had stacked sheets of plywood.

Between the two of us, we hauled one of the sheets over.

"Twenty-nine," Noel said, watching the thing attached to the safe.

We wedged the plywood between Noel and the safe.

"Nineteen . . . eighteen . . ."

And scrambled onto the other side next to Noel.

"Ten . . . nine . . . eight. . . ."

We huddled together.

Just then, at the count of five, the cellar door blew in, and the world turned upside down. Wind howled into the basement, whipping objects into the air, and battering at the utility room wall.

I've never been great at physics, but there's something about wind shear—its speed, direction, and magnitude— and the way it met up with the force of the explosion that apparently saved my life.

While I sprawled on the basement floor, I counted my blessings in hundred dollar bills that rained down on me. Before I passed out, or maybe after, Hunter's handsome face gazed down on me. I thought I had died and gone to heaven.

Forty-five

I woke to familiar voices surrounding me, and an enormous tongue slurping my face.

"She's awake," I heard Grams say. "Good job, Ben. Let's get a picture. Everyone crowd together."

I opened one eye. The room was fuzzy. And all white.

"You're in the hospital," Hunter said. He was holding my hand, "You have a concussion."

I looked around at my visitors—Ben, Carrie Ann holding Dinky, Mom, Grams taking pictures, Holly, even Stanley was beaming at me. And Tom Stocke, too.

"Noel?" I managed to croak.

And there he was, right in front of me, notebook and all, several bandages on his head and face.

"I got the better end of the deal," he said to me. "You should see you."

A nurse came in and said, "No animals in here. This is a hospital."

"Ben's a service dog," Hunter explained. Carrie Ann hid Dinky under her arm.

The nurse didn't like it, but she left, taking Noel away with a promise of ice cream from the cafeteria.

"How long have I been out?" I asked.

"Awhile," Mom dodged.

"I've been managing the store for you," Carrie Ann said.

Now that I had more time to assess my body, it didn't feel so good. "What happened to me?"

"You were caught right in the center of the tornado," Hunter said.

Oh right, I'd been in Tom's basement. The last thing I'd remembered seeing was . . . "Eugene? Did he make it?"

"He's dead. A tree branch crashed through the cellar door and crushed him."

A moment of silence ensued while I absorbed that awful news, thinking about the impact it would have on the Petrie family. There could have been even more grieving families if Eugene had had his way. While I was surrounded by friends and family, Hunter filled in some of the blanks.

"Bob Petrie didn't play a big part in the overall plan," he said. "He was really just a gopher for Eugene, but he knew what was happening every step of the way. Once we arrested him, he gave us the whole thing."

"Aggie must have been right in the middle, too," I said. "The mastermind, I bet."

Hunter shook his head. "Bob, Aggie, and her daughter-in-law really were out of town at that antiques show. Aggie says she didn't know a thing about it, and Bob confirms her story. She's spouting off about filing a lawsuit over her husband's suspicious death."

Holly piped up with a little psychoanalysis. "She's overly aggressive, that's for sure. And aggressive behavior breeds aggressive behavior within a species. That's why the whole family is like that."

Everybody looked at her. She noticed. "I've been reading," she said.

I made a mental note to recommend a career path for my sister. She'd make a great family counselor.

Hunter continued, "Bob told Eugene about his time in jail with Ford, and it turned out that Ford and Eugene knew each other from their days in the service. Did you know that Ford was a munitions expert back then? That was where they got the whole idea to blow up Tom's safe, once the Petries told Ford that his brother was a lottery winner, and Ford said Tom always used to keep his savings in his house rather than a bank. Eugene's the one who connected with Ford and planned the whole scheme."

"The plan was to steal my winnings," Tom said. "And split the money three ways. Bob claims he didn't want anything to do with it, but he didn't have a choice. Then Eugene started getting greedy."

"So he killed your brother," I said.

"But not before he found himself another weapons expert," Tom added. "Remember when Noel lit off those cherry bombs by Aggie's booth?

I smiled, remembering. It hurt to smile.

"Eugene decided Noel could handle breaking into the safe, and that way he didn't have to split anything with Ford. That's when he decided to rid himself of his partner."

"But why did he move Ford's body?" I asked. "Why didn't he leave him in the cemetery?"

Hunter answered that one. "Eugene needed to buy as much time as possible. If Lori hadn't gone into the house, Ford's body might not have been found until after the safe had been cracked. The last thing he wanted was a lot of police activity in the area beforehand. Of course, that's exactly what he got. He couldn't have anticipated Lori showing up and complicating his plans."

"I must have interrupted him right in the act of moving Ford," I said, a shiver passing through me at how close I'd come to a confrontation with him under a full moon. I didn't want to think about what might have happened.

Another nurse came in at that point and shooed everyone out. Except Hunter, who used his badge to get a few more minutes.

"Did he strangle Ford with one of Alicia's scarves?" I had to know as soon as everyone else filed out.

"Why would you think that?" Hunter said, looking surprised. "No, we found a length of rope in the back of his van. It's a match with the brown fibers found on Ford."

So a scarf hadn't been involved at all. Not mine, or any other.

"And Noel?"

"Was being bullied. Eugene claimed he had evidence that would convict Stanley. Noel didn't see any way out. He felt he had to cooperate. Actually, Noel was trying to lead you and Patti to Eugene the whole time."

"What?"

"He was the one who left the trail of hickory nuts."

I tried to sit up, but the effort wasn't worth it. I plopped back down flat. "What did hickory nuts have to do with anything? They only led me in the wrong direction."

"Remember that tattoo you saw on Bob's arm? Well, he and Eugene had matching hickory nut tattoos. Apparently back in the marines Eugene was known as 'Old Hickory,' just like Andrew Jackson, because he was so tough. And Bob got one to match his dad."

"So Noel had been trying to lead us to Eugene, not Bob. And the false hostage report at Clay's house?"

"Noel again, trying to protect Patti. Eugene was using the house as his base. Patti was a serious threat to his operation."

Wait a minute. What about P.P. Patti? I'd forgotten all about her. Everything came rushing back—the wasp spray, Patti hitting Eugene with the shovel, watching him fall down the steps, trying to save Noel, the tornado and explosion. "Oh my gosh," I said. "What happened to Patti?"

"I'm over here," I heard from the far side of the room.

That's when I noticed a curtain drawn between the voice and me. When Hunter pulled it aside, I saw Patti lying in the next bed. She looked like she'd just woken up. She had big bandages wrapped around her head and her eyes were more purple than black.

"My head hurts," she whined. "I keep asking for more painkillers and they won't give them to me. And I had splinters all over in the palms of my hands from that stupid shovel. They pulled each one out individually, and boy did that hurt."

Hunter was trying to contain himself. But when he saw the expression on my face, he burst out laughing.

"And how does a person get any rest in this place," P.P. Patti went on. "The only good part of this whole arrangement is that"—she gave me a huge grin—"we're roommates!"

I sunk back in the hospital bed and grimaced.

Forty-six

Hunter brought me home from the hospital. We sat in my backyard with Ben at our feet. Having almost lost my life proved good for our relationship. My man even took time off from work to take care of me.

Now, as we sat gazing at each other across my patio table, he said, "I think it's time to take a step forward."

I needed clarification. "Like?"

"Like, maybe it's time we moved in together."

Wow! Really? On the inside I was bouncing up and down. On the outside, I smiled serenely and said, "My place or yours?"

He smiled back. "It doesn't matter as long as we're together. We'll talk more in a few days when you've recovered fully. I don't want to take advantage of you."

And with that, he did.

It felt good to get back into the daily routine, back to my busy but normal life. My honeybees buzzed happily along in my absence, unaware of my close call with death. Stanley Peck had made sure they were cared for while I was in the hospital. Noel had even helped out in the bee-yard before he'd had to head home to get ready for school to start. Stanley told me he and his grandson had had a serious conversation about keeping the whole safe-blowing escapade from Noel's mother, for fear she'd never let him come within a hundred miles of Moraine or his grandfather again.

A few locals expressed relief for the peace and quiet Noel left behind.

The store also ran smoothly without me for the few days I was out, thanks in large part to Carrie Ann, who put aside her online game playing to actually help manage the business. Maybe I *would* consider giving her a promotion.

I was back behind the cash register a few days later, though, when Mom came into The Wild Clover. She was holding hands with Tom and grinning.

"You need to put your money in a bank," I advised my mother's boyfriend. "We'll all feel safer."

"I already have," he assured me.

Grams was right behind them, with Dinky straining at the end of a leash. "I've decided to keep Dinky with me," she said. "I've grown so fond of her over these last few days. Even though she's still peeing where she shouldn't. Hunter promised to help me train her."

What wonderful news!

"Let's get a family photograph," Grams suggested, hauling out her point-and-shoot.

Holly came out of the storage room just in time to get into the picture. Milly took it for us.

Through the front window, I saw Lori Spandle and DeeDee Becker. Lori peered in, then rushed inside. "That dog isn't allowed in an establishment that caters to food products," she said with an airy sniff, indicating Dinky. "I'm filing a report."

Just then, DeeDee moved closer to the window, where I could see her better. She was wearing a scarf around her neck. It was an animal print. A bead or two in the fringe glistened and sparkled in the sun.

I heard Mom say, "Lori Spandle . . ." but that's all I caught. Because I was out the door, intent on the klepto who'd stolen my scarf from the library.

DeeDee saw me, recognized the look on my face as her death knell, and took off running.

Like the bulldog I could be (a family trait from my mother's side of the family), I was right behind her.

The Wild Clover
🐝 August Newsletter 🐝

Notes from the beeyard:

- As goldenrods and asters begin to bloom, honeybees will be busier than ever collecting nectar.

- Bees need water to drink and to dilute thick honey. If it hasn't rained, help them out with an outdoor water supply (bucket or bird bath).

- Late August and September are perfect times to visit a beekeeper, and if you're lucky, he or she will let you sample comb honey right from the hive.

Here are a few simple honey concoctions:

- Honey sticks—stir into a cup of hot tea.

- Drizzle honey over a wedge of salty cheese for a delicious combination.

- Add a little honey to your bath water for a soothing, silky soak.

Nutty Rhubarb Muffins

1 cup brown sugar + ½ cup
½ cup honey
1 cup buttermilk
⅔ cup vegetable oil
2 eggs

2 teaspoons vanilla
3 ½ cups all purpose flour
½ cup oatmeal
1 teaspoon baking soda
½ teaspoon salt
2 cups rhubarb, diced
½ cup hickory nuts or walnuts
1 teaspoon cinnamon

Preheat oven to 375 degrees.

Mix together 1 cup brown sugar, honey, buttermilk, oil, eggs, and vanilla.

Mix together flour, oatmeal, baking soda, and salt.

Combine all and mix well.

Add rhubarb.

Grease muffin cups, scoop in batter.

Mix together the rest of the brown sugar, nuts, and cinnamon. Sprinkle on muffins.

Bake for 20 minutes.

Makes 2 dozen.

Blueberry Scones with Honey Glaze

SCONES
2 cups flour
⅓ cup sugar
1 tablespoon baking powder
¼ teaspoon salt
6 tablespoons butter, cut into pieces
½ teaspoon cinnamon
¼ teaspoon nutmeg
1 large egg, beaten
½ cup whipping cream
1 cup fresh blueberries
Raw sugar or cinnamon sugar (optional)

GLAZE

1 cup powdered sugar
1 tablespoon orange juice
3 teaspoons honey, or to taste

Preheat oven to 400 degrees.

Mix glaze ingredients and set aside.

In a medium bowl, mix in flour, sugar, baking powder, cinnamon, nutmeg, and salt. Add pieces of butter. Cut the butter into the dry ingredients with a pastry blender, or two knives, until the butter is pea-size.

Combine egg with whipping cream. Add to the dry mixture. Stir until just mixed. Fold in blueberries.

Turn out dough onto a lightly floured surface. Knead ten times until dough is nearly smooth. Roll dough into an 8-inch circle. Cut it into 8 to 12 wedges. Sprinkle with raw sugar or cinnamon sugar.

Place scones one inch apart on an ungreased cookie sheet. Bake 12 to 15 minutes until golden brown.

Drizzle with glaze.

Notes from the garden:

• Leave ripe tomatoes on the vine for an extra week to capture their fullest flavor.

• First flowers from cucumbers and other vine crops are all male and don't produce fruit.

• Fertilization begins with the second set of blooms, which are males and females.

Grilled Corn
with Ancho Honey Butter

Corn on the cob
1 ancho chile—minced if fresh, seeded and torn in pieces if dried

1 stick unsalted butter, softened
3 garlic cloves
¼ cup cilantro
1 tablespoon fresh lime juice
1 tablespoon honey
1 ½ teaspoons kosher salt
pepper

If using dried chile, soak in warm water for 30 minutes, then drain.

In food processor, chop cilantro and garlic. Add chile, lime juice, honey, salt.

Add butter and blend until smooth.

Shuck ears, brush with ancho butter, season with salt and pepper, grill until brown 10 to 12 minutes.

–OR–

Toss unshucked ears on grill (silk and all), and cook over high heat until husks are charred 10 to 15 minutes, then serve with ancho butter.

Peach and Ginger-Honey Smoothie

1 peach, pit removed and sliced
½ cup milk of your choice
½ cup peach yogurt
1 tablespoon honey
1 teaspoon grated fresh ginger root
6 ice cubes

Blend and enjoy.

About the Author

Hannah Reed lives on a high ridge in southern Wisconsin in a community much like the one she writes about. She is busy writing the next book in the Queen Bee Mysteries. Visit Hannah and explore Story's world at www.queenbeemystery.com.

Cozy up with Berkley Prime Crime

SUSAN WITTIG ALBERT
Don't miss the national bestselling series featuring herbalist China Bayles.

LAURA CHILDS
The Tea Shop Mysteries are the toast of Charleston, South Carolina.

KATE KINGSBURY
The Pennyfoot Hotel Mystery series is a teatime delight.

For the armchair detective in you.

penguin.com

M6G0708

Searching for the perfect mystery?

Looking for a place to get the latest clues
and connect with fellow fans?

"Like" The Crime Scene on Facebook!

- Participate in author chats
- Enter book giveaways
- Learn about the latest releases
- Get book recommendations
- Send mystery-themed gifts
  to friends and more!

facebook.com/TheCrimeSceneBooks

Obsidian

M884G0511